THE GIRL BEHIND THE GLASS

EMILIO IASIELLO

Tumbleweed Books
Tumble through the pages of our books

THE GIRL BEHIND THE GLASS
EMILLIO IASIELLO

Tumbleweed Books
Tumble through the pages of our books

https://tumbleweedbooks.ca
Tumbleweed Books Books is an imprint of DAOwen Publications

Copyright © Emilio Iasiello

All rights reserved

The Girl Behind the Glass/ Emillio Iasiello
Edited by Douglas Owen and Miles Cruise

This is a work of fiction. Names, characters, places, and incidents either are the product of the author's imagination or are used fictitiously, and any resemblance to actual persons, living or dead, businesses, companies, events, or locales is entirely coincidental.

Cover art by MMT Productions

ISBN 978-1-928094-63-0
EISBN 978-1-928094-64-7

10 9 8 7 6 5 4 3 2 1

To my family who makes writing worth it,

and to my friends that make stories worth telling.

You know who you are.

"In between the punctuating agonies, life is such a gentle habit."

-Charles Bukowski

1

TUESDAY

I stand outside of SoBe smoking a cigarette, listening to some fat chick's caterwauling pour through the patio speakers.

It's a poor rendition of Alanis Morrissette. The chick's not so much bad as she is overly passionate about her singing. And as any serious karaoke singer knows, passion and an old 100 Hz microphone are a bad combination. Passion makes you think you're singing better than you actually are; that you're pitch-perfect, an exact replica of the original version. What it really does is make you scream into the mic, causing nails-dragging-down-the-blackboard feedback. It causes your voice to crack like an acne-marked teen.

Passion works in front of a sold-out crowd at the Verizon Center, but it ain't shit in a hole-in-the-wall bar with a bad sound system.

SoBe is my favorite bar. I've been coming here through its myriad iterations and re-brandings. First as a seafood restaurant (hence the name, SoBe), then to a pizza joint (oddly still named SoBe), and finally to a karaoke bar (SoBe). In its current form, SoBe has eschewed any sort of a culinary identity. There is no pretending to be anything other than what it is, and in that self-realization, the owner does not feel compelled to offer good food as much as alcohol-absorbing food. Sparse and predictable, the menu provides bar food mainstays such as undersized Buffalo wings, greasy cheese sticks, and gray, overcooked hamburgers instead of high quality seafood or innovative artisanal flatbreads. You don't eat at SoBe; you drink and sing.

Despite the forfeiture of its culinary vision, the aesthetics have remained largely unchanged throughout its evolution; a single entryway divides SoBe into two components: on the right is the small bar area, and on the left is a now defunct dining area littered with cheap tables and chairs that face a small makeshift stage where the karaoke happens. With the exception of the blue and green hued walls reminiscent of the ocean, you'd never know this broken bar once served the best Mahi Mahi in Washington, D.C. There are only a handful of us who remember. The rest don't even give the name a second glance thinking the sign above the entrance must be a private joke they weren't let in on.

SoBe's bar area is only large enough to seat nine people comfortably, which is why I find it so comforting. Since most of the regulars take up positions as early as four p.m. most days, it prohibits a bunch of strangers, and more importantly, "Philistines" (a term created by the Captain – more on him later – to refer to Millennials, or the young, narcissistic, and financially reckless) from rubbing elbows with you.

Before the owner closed "SoBe I" for its first reimagining, he engraved the names of his most valued customers on plaques on the backs of the bar stools. This was his way of thanking us for dropping hundreds of dollars in his till every weekend. Regardless, when word got out about his intent to do that, the lesser-stature regulars lobbied for their names' commemoration in brass. There were some heated drunken discussions, and more than a few times when these junior members were asked to take a walk to cool off. It was understandable. After all, there were only nine high-backed bar stools and to be among the chosen gave you a sense of legitimacy and validation. Even if you didn't own the bar yourself, you felt a notch above the twenty-something's who crowded the bar looking to order and pay for their drinks instead of opening a tab like a normal drinker does.

Back in the day, Bart and me logged serious hours in those seats and got our names forever emblazoned on two of the nine stools for all to see. Now we could literally tell someone to get off our stools because they were really our stools. But "forever" didn't last as long as we thought it would, because somewhere between "SoBe Redux" and the current manifestation, the owner deep-sixed all the stools. I don't know how Bart felt about it, but in retrospect, I thought Billy the owner should have given all nine of us a chance to keep them. It was less about nostalgia and more for the fact it was mine through the investment of time and money into a struggling establishment during the lean years.

ARLINGTON IS a part of its eponymous county located in Northern Virginia on the south bank of the Potomac River. It's right across from D.C., and if you live near or around the banks of the Potomac, you can see many of the national monuments poking up past the limited skyline. Arlington County was originally part of Fairfax County when Virginia was still a colony. Sometime around 1790 or so, Arlington County was given to Washington, D.C. as part of Congress' effort to establish a national capital along the Potomac River. Then in 1801, the Organic Act formally placed the District of Columbia under control of the Congress, including lands that had been ceded to it by Maryland and Virginia. Those living in ceded territory were no longer considered residents of the state that had given them to D.C. Eventually, Arlington was officially returned to Virginia in 1846 after county residents petitioned the U.S. Congress and the Virginia legislature.

I've called this city home six years longer than expected.

Coming out of college, I tried to stick around New England but relocated when offered a job. I had two choices: stay up North and work in a supermarket or take my chances at the law firm.

Professionally, I chose poorly.

One and done. That's what I promised myself. After a year, I'd be somewhere else, doing something else, being something else.

Well, here I am.

Traffic zips by on Clarendon Boulevard, a main artery that ties the "Corridor" – a stretch of road that unites neighborhood-centric North

Arlington – together. The closest of these neighborhoods to D.C. is Rosslyn, followed by Courthouse, Clarendon, Virginia Square, and Ballston. Clarendon has come a long way since my move. It's an immensely popular area now, although it wasn't just twenty years earlier when it was highly fragmented in diverse ethnic hamlets populated with an interspersion of small strip mall shops and used car lots.

Five years ago, a group of Guatemalans beat up a friend of mine in a parking lot a half block away from where I stand. The Clarendon neighborhood had one of the largest Latin American populations at the time. However, investment brought development which brought in an upwardly mobile populace that commanded higher incomes. They infiltrated and rooted, pushing the poor to the other side of State Route 50, the demarcation between North and South Arlington, Virginia's nod to its Civil War roots, but with economics and not politics as the divisive factor.

———

THE CAPTAIN MEETS ME OUTSIDE. His name is Don, but we call him the Captain because he dresses like a pirate. Not in full regalia, mind you, just a black ostrich plumed hat and a swashbuckler's dirty white waistcoat. The moniker is a reference to everyone's favorite spiced rum seafarer. His salt-and-pepper goatee and long hair only solidify the image. I'm not sure who gave him the nickname first, but it stuck, and he doesn't seem to mind it.

Don runs the karaoke machine. I'm not one hundred percent positive but I think that's his only job. I imagine it's a tough way to make a buck. Hustling jobs all over the Metro D.C. area from Frederick, Maryland to Fredericksburg, Virginia. All karaoke all the time. He doesn't make much; he always has a tip jar out on his deejay stand looking for handouts.

He lights a Kool menthol and through the window stares at the woman on stage. The fat chick holds the mic with both hands, her face frozen in an expression of pain and suffering. Jilted love should not be sung by people who have never experienced it.

"She sucks." He blows smoke out his nostrils.

I turn to the window. Alanis' crew sits right in front, rocking their thick bodies to and fro to the beat. I can't tell if they're really into it or just trying to show support for their friend. They'll have their turn soon enough and as any karaoke singer knows, nothing is as cold as standing on stage and not getting any karaoke love after you finish singing.

"I don't want to find out," I say. It takes the Captain a second to get the joke and he starts cracking up.

"She's not that bad," he says. "More cushion for the pushing, so to speak."

"That kind of love needs commitment and imagination," I say. "I'm too old and not drunk enough."

"Drinking solo? Where's the crew tonight?"

He's referring to my group of friends that usually drink together. Sometimes we meet up after work in the city for happy hour bliss before making our way back home to sing songs and drink shots. Tonight, people had other things to do: work happy hours, a blind date, tickets to some concert. Me, I had nothing going on, so I just came straight here.

"Beats me," I say. "I think Bart is still at steak Thursday. G-Love and Georgie? I don't know. Kurt rarely makes it out on Thursdays. Haven't talked to Jessica or Wendy."

"Steak Thursday." The Captain shakes his head. He checks his watch to make sure he can jump back inside in time to seamlessly transition from 90s angst to grunge, or metal, or pop, or whatever is the next song in the queue.

"How does that man not clog his colon?"

Steak Thursday is Bart's self-indulgence after a long week of managing the estate planning of individuals with net worth starting at 100 million dollars. He always tries to get me to come with him on these lavish early afternoon junkets, but I usually can't disappear from my desk for two-hour lunches. The one time I went I never made it back into work, passing out in the back of a cab before I could tell the driver the firm's address. He ended up shaking me awake and dumping me at a run-down park in North West D.C. where homeless people sat around drinking 40-ounce beers.

Bart starts at noon at an upscale steakhouse for martinis and raw oysters, followed by a bottle or two of wine and steaks (of course), and ending with a few glasses of very good scotch. He does that every week, prompting the Captain's colon question with good reason.

Once I asked Bart why he chose Thursday instead of Friday to go on his hedonistic gluttony binges.

"Well," he told me in an extended Bayou drawl. "That there's the point. Friday is always going to be Friday. You could have the shittiest day, and it's going to end and you're going to get good and drunk no matter what. Thursday you need something a little bit extra special to tide you over to the next day."

Made sense in a "no shit" kind of way.

Bart (from Barthelme, a very Louisianan name) is a big guy, pushing near three bills, and my best friend. He's also the most successful guy in our group of outcasts, earning double six figures easy. When it comes to making sure the affluent have enough tax shelters to keep their offspring at the top of the food chain, Bart has few peers. Last year his end-of-year bonus was more than my annual salary.

We weren't always friends. The first time our paths crossed, we sat on opposite ends of the bar. Sometimes we'd be the only two inside, everyone else having flocked to the waterfront to watch the boats parade by and the people who partied on them. They'd crowd around the outside bars, willingly accepting the fountain tax – the increased price point for the privilege of drinking and being seen with other beautiful people in the heart of Georgetown. Warm beers poured into plastic cups was acceptable for those more focused on the spectacle than substance. For these social climbing aspirants, looking important was far more desirable than actually being important.

Not us. When Saturday came, we found ourselves in Days, perched in our usual spots, not speaking, not even looking at each other. We'd just sit and drink, trying to jockey for influence over the young bartender, Carrie, with bad jokes and lame innuendos. Tired of running back and forth to replenish our competing empty glasses,

Carrie finally forced us to sit together, bought us each a bourbon, and told us to make nice. Six hours and countless shots later, we made nice and have been inseparable since.

I shrug. "It's his thing. He likes his steak. He eats a lot of it."

The Captain smiles. It's no surprise he lives in a group house somewhere in South Arlington with a bunch of like-minded misplaced hippies and free spirits, smoking bongs or whatever, just doing what comes naturally. He told me once they had crazy parties and then showed me the pictures to prove it. I swear it was straight out of a David Lynch movie. There were naked people parading around, some wearing costume animal mascot heads. This one woman sat against the wall, legs spread, wearing clown makeup and little else. Her big red shoes looked like canoes. She sat there with a distant gaze in her eye. I was terrified, repulsed, and turned on at the same time. He was going for that reaction. Running a karaoke business, I imagine you have to be a little bit desperate, a little bit crazy, and a hell of a lot weird.

He takes a quick drag and flicks the butt end over end, the lit part disappearing over a potted plant.

"You're up in ten," he says, running back inside.

Through the window, her appreciative entourage welcomes Alanis with a group hug. They give each other big sloppy arm embraces, burying their noses in each other's hairspray, and patting each other on the back with meaty hands. The prettiest one is crying so I imagine the song was a homage to a relationship that had finally run dry. When I see an order of nachos hit the table, I can't help but smile; comfort food always softens ruined love.

TONY JITTERS ACROSS THE PATIO, making a beeline for me. He's already had a few drinks judging from his hyperactivity and the unmistakable sheen of red in his eyes. Tony's drink of choice is anything you put in front of him. If he prefers a type of alcohol, I don't know about it. This is a guy who will drink anything, and I mean anything. Two Saturdays ago, Tony manned the last seat of the bar with no less than four

EMILIO IASIELLO

different beverages: a Budweiser longneck, a Red Bull and vodka, two
fingers of bourbon in a tumbler, and a shot of chocolate cake. One by
one, he drank them down over a span of twenty minutes. He might
have an Italian last name, but his appearance is all Irish from his tall
lanky frame to the short auburn hair cropped closely to his head.

"You got one of those for me?" Tony gestures to the cigarette in my
hand.

I fish out Rothman's, blue package, out of my shirt pocket. Excited,
Tony snatches one and takes the lighter I hand to him.

"You love these things," he says, having trouble getting the
flame lit.

"If I'm going to smoke, I'm going to smoke what I like."

"Yeah but what are these? Eight bucks at that cigar store down the
block?"

"Ten."

"You're fucking nuts." He looks around checking out the scene
inside. "Where is everyone?"

"It's early."

"So why aren't you at the Tavern? That chick Tiffany's over there
and she's looking F-I-N-E, fine."

Tony means their newest hire. Tiffany's a pretty buxom brunette
with a southern accent and bright eyes. She's outgoing and friendly,
which is a change from their last bartender, who would get on her cell
phone the moment she served you a drink. It doesn't hurt that
Tiffany's body is top notch. The Tavern has drawn larger crowds than
expected the last three Fridays in a row, no doubt to the new talent. She
should ask for a raise.

I shake my head. "I don't do sausage fests."

"You and me both, brother. You and me both," Tony says, drifting
to the window.

I hated Tony when I first met him. He always came across as a
person who had to know everyone, to be at the center of attention,
who always had something to say. He was the type of guy who always
one-bettered you. You met the lead singer of Def Leppard at a casino?
He drank with Michael Jordan in the V.I.P. room. Shit like that.

But Tony has a good streak in him, one that he keeps cleverly concealed beneath the hardened exterior of someone who is always in pursuit of a good time. For this I give him a pass. If for nothing else, he makes me laugh. That counts for something these days.

"All right, catch you in a bit," he says, tossing his unfinished smoke aside, which makes me cringe. He enters and heads immediately over to the bar where one of his peripheral friends sits with a comely blonde.

Three Philistines make their way into the courtyard. Any hope of them turning right and going into Calypso's, the bar across from SoBe, is quickly dashed.

Luck is not on my side.

Tonight's infiltration commences.

They come post-work, wearing blue suits with their ID badges tucked neatly into their shirt pockets, their not-so-subtle way of "hiding" the fact that they work for the government.

The only people who wear lanyards with badges on them in the first place are government employees or government contractors working in government spaces. It's not elite as much as boring and predictable.

Truth to tell, I don't feel much like being here. The more SoBe is overrun by the younger generation, the more I want to burn the place down. Sort of my own version of Left Eye Lopes (rest in peace) torching her boyfriend's mansion when she suspected him of cheating on her. If I can't have it, then no one should.

The reality is if I'm not here, I don't have anywhere else to go.

And that's a thought I just can't abide by.

The Captain sticks his head out the front door.

"You're up," he says.

I suck my cigarette down to the filter and hold it in my lungs. The exhale is low and slow, the smoke trailing out the corner of my mouth as I open the door and head inside.

2

Springsteen, baby. The Boss. He's always my opening number, especially if there are Philistines already at the tables. But I don't do *Born to Run* – that's too on the nose, even if it's consistently ranked as among the top five rock songs of all time and just a great fucking tune overall.

Tonight, I'm looking for a statement.

I want jagged stones, not polished rock.

To separate myself from the Philistines, I have to blast a chasm between us.

After I do Springsteen, one of those chumps will probably come up and do *Born to Run* thinking I blew my chance.

Fools.

My job is to educate the narrow minded and soulless what good music really is.

And I like my job.

Badlands.

Very underrated.

I start off strong. Once the music starts, heads turn, and people smile. They recognize the song even if they can't remember where they have heard it. But they know they like it.

That's a good sign.

I slip into the song, quickly finding my comfort level. This isn't my first go-around. Singing Springsteen is all about connecting with the message. His songs are about tension, about somebody struggling, trying to break out of where they're at or trying to find another place, a better place than the one they're in.

You sing it because you know the pain behind it.

That's the biggest reason why the wannabe Alanis fell short.

You can't fake guts.

It also doesn't hurt that Springsteen's voice, while distinct, isn't exactly on pitch.

Searching the room for familiar faces, I take a breather before the next verse. For a regular, I don't know many people in the bar tonight, which is a bit disconcerting given how frequently I'm in here. Sure, I recognize a few people like Tony, and the guy he's talking to at the bar, but they aren't in my crew. If no one's here after the song, I'll probably sit with them and buy them a round, but I'd rather have a friendly face to pass the time with.

The beauty about SoBe is that it's still just a word of mouth place known only by those people who like to spend their time in bars. It doesn't advertise. There are no drink specials. There are no video games. It isn't a sports bar. It doesn't have a hundred TVs mounted on the walls. It isn't a glitzy club. It doesn't have dancing. And it sure isn't a trendy throwback speakeasy, the kind of place Philistine Millennials typically frequent when they pretend they are F. Scott and Zelda.

No. SoBe is just a place where people claim bar space and drink into the wee hours of the morning. Mechanics, tool and die workers, a fucking company VP. It doesn't matter what you do or who you are as long you know when to speak, when to listen, and when to buy a round or two. The beauty about SoBe is its unwritten protocol. For those who belong, it's a unifying undercurrent. It's instinctual. You know because you just know. For everyone else, it's not that they can't understand, it's just that they never will.

Maggie works the bar. She comes from around back with a box of alcohol and starts arranging the bottles according to type along the back wall. When she hears Springsteen, she immediately looks toward the stage and gives me a curt wave.

Recognition is one of the best things about SoBe.

I nod back. Maggie is the best bartender around. She has short black hair and even blacker eyes. Her natural beauty is accented with a little bit of eye shadow, and nothing else. Some of the other bartenders layer it on. I'm talking bold reds and greens, lip gloss so shiny it looks like they ate a bucket of greasy chicken, and cleavage so deep you can get lost in it if you're not careful. Sure, they get their tips, don't get me wrong. But generally, they don't have much upstairs, using their looks as the lure to keep the big fish coming. Maggie prefers to converse. And by focusing on the simple exchange of human discourse, she commands more attention than the other two night bartenders combined.

If I'm going to be honest, aside from karaoke, Maggie's the other reason I keep coming back to this place.

It's rare to find a good-looking bartender who shows a genuine interest in how you're doing or what's new in your world. For the regulars, Maggie is a booze angel who delivers more than just our alcohol. She has a personality, knows how to crack a joke, and if you push her in the wrong way, spits venom with the best of them.

If it isn't obvious already, I have a crush on her.

But that's a fairytale that doesn't happen too often. It's an extraordinary moment when a bartender will date a bar regular. It's not without precedent, but those cases are exceptional, and if history is any guide, those crossovers usually end quickly and in disaster.

Thing is, it's difficult dating service industry people unless you're in the same industry or keep similar hours. Otherwise, the timing is all off. For most, your weekends are their busiest nights. Their days off usually start your work week. Their existence borders on vampirism.

I once went with a bunch of bartenders after their shift ended at two a.m. We went to one of their houses and partied until seven in the morning. They drank hard and they drank fast. Glasses were an afterthought. Bottles of vodka and Wild Turkey passed around with a frivolous nonchalance while someone spun vinyl on an old record player. I split when the marijuana and coke came out. The cab cost me fifty bucks to bring me back home. It was almost 9 a.m. by the time I reached my apartment.

Maggie is something special though. She leans against the bar as I finish my song.

Half of me wants to find out if I have a chance with someone like Maggie. Like wondering how many rounds you can last with the heavyweight champ or how far can you make it on a game show.

But there's the other half.

And that half is usually littered with the remains of those who didn't like the results of taking a chance only to find themselves ruined in the process.

MAGGIE HAS a healthy glass of Maker's Mark neat waiting for me.

"Nice one" She slides me over the glass when I make it to the bar. "Most anyone else would have sung *Born to Run*, but then you aren't like anyone else."

I raise it up to her in a makeshift toast. "I'll take that as a compliment."

"It was meant as one."

"Thanks. Happy Thursday."

"Happy Thursday to you too. How did the week treat you?"

"Like it caught me in bed with its wife." She furrows her brow for a moment before catching the joke. It's from an old sitcom called *Cheers*, but I don't feel like explaining a sitcom that she likely has never seen.

She lets out a lovely lilting laugh. "Ouch. That bad?"

"Let's see... My week started by getting chewed out by the senior associate on my case because I had knocked six months' worth of unbound depositions on the floor during a Nerf basketball game."

"Did you win?"

"Lost by two. Then I got put on a hot tasker by this asshole senior paralegal to produce two complete sets of exhibits – five hundred each mind you – and FedEx them out to California by Wednesday morning. And then on Wednesday night, my blind date bails on me."

Maggie's eyebrows perk up. "A date? Do tell."

"A colleague's sister was in town and he had to work late," I confess. "He wanted me to take her out, but she found a better offer."

Maggie nods thoughtfully. "That is a bad week. Let me help take the sting away." She tops off my bourbon in a conciliatory gesture.

"Serves me right for lacking the fortitude and general ambition to find a new job."

"You don't like what you do?"

"I'm a paralegal."

"Oh. Yeah, you need to find a new job."

"Thing is, I'm jealous of the people I work with. They make me want to vomit but at least they know what they know they want to be lawyers. I haven't the slightest idea what I want to be when I grow up, and time is ticking..."

"You write. Can't you get a job doing that?"

"Starting off I won't make enough to pay my rent. Doesn't matter if it's journalism, speechwriting, or advertising. And that's if I can get a job doing that."

"Ah." She scans the bar to see who needs drinks. "One sec."

Maggie takes off to wait on two couples at one end of the bar. They look in their mid-twenties, and so Maggie checks their IDs. She's not a pushover like some of the others. At the beginning of summer, Billy got hit with a sizeable fine when one bartender served her underage friends from Northern Virginia Community College. She missed the undercover ABC (Alcoholic Beverage Control) officer there watching it all go down. Let's just say, that was the last drink Brittany from Tennessee poured at SoBe. Last I heard she was bartending at Shooter O'Connell's in Centerville, a testament to Billy's juice to excommunicate those that disrespected his establishment.

"Hey man, what's up?" Tony's friend slaps me on the back as he passes by heading to the bathroom.

"How're you doing?"

I make a mental note to ask Tony what his friend's name is. He's always following Tony around like toilet paper stuck to the bottom of a shoe. And even though we've drank together a thousand times before, I can never remember his name. This has more to do with him being a completely forgettable person, which isn't a bad thing if you're trying to stay anonymous. However, in this trying-to-pick up-girls climate, it's definitely a significant drawback.

Once his competition extricates himself from the immediate area, Tony takes little time in sitting down across from the blonde and commences his courtship.

So much for friendship.

Tony is a man of little conscience or little consequence, depending on your point of view. He cajoles her into taking a shot, and whispers something in her ear. If she's with his friend, you can't tell from their body language.

The blonde leans in close to him, her knee brushing up against his. I wonder what would happen if they both had girlfriends or wives.

Tony's crew has always been this way. The four of them – Tony, Big Mike, that guy whose name I can't remember, and Shawn something-or-other – all go out together and compete for the same women, often trying to move in and steal them away from each other. The volume of booze they consume prohibits their nights from ending in flat-out fist fights with each other. The cliché is almost funny if it wasn't so damn unoriginal.

The blonde grabs a pen off the bar and writes something down on the back of a matchbook and hands it to Tony who pockets it quickly. I catch Maggie's attention and she rolls her eyes at the sight. Typical Tony.

"Sorry I'm late, you been here long?"

I turn to find G-Love standing at my side. He slides onto the barstool next to me checking his phone for messages. G-Love is mid-thirties like me. He has a Mr. Clean bald head and is dressed neatly in a checkered button-down shirt and faded jeans. He's very meticulous about the way he dresses. His shirts, even his Polos, are pressed to perfection. G-Love does it himself ever since the dry cleaner in his building fucked up one of his French-cuffed shirts. He's self-sufficient that way.

G-Love's a government employee at the IRS, and true to the image of boring bureaucrats, rarely over-indulges in spirits even on the weekends. His preferred vice is stargazing—the celestial kind, not gawking at named politicians. If the viewing conditions are right, G-

Love has been known to disappear from whatever bar we're in to get home in time to look up at the stars. He hooks his camera to a two thousand-dollar Orion Skyquest telescope. Every so often he brings some into the bar and shows us impressive shots of galaxies, nebulas, and star clusters.

"Where's the Big Guy," G-Love says, after Maggie sets him up with a CC and ginger.

"Where do you think?"

"Ah, right. Steak Thursday. What's the over-under on his being hammered when he gets here?"

"Vegas won't set those odds. They try to actually make money."

He laughs. G-Love is a good guy, a man of few words.

A late addition to our crew, we used to see G-Love on Saturdays during the college football season. He'd hang on the periphery of where we sat, a table typically reserved for Billy the owner but loaned out to us during sports games as a thank you for our frequent patronage and off-the-charts tipping. Like the story about the Little Prince and the fox, G-Love gradually got closer and closer, until we recognized him as a friendly. Two weeks later, he was sitting right along with us, the latest member of our group of social dissidents that fit no pre-set established societal order.

We are generally a welcoming lot. We might not grant you entry with open arms at first meeting, but once you pass the ocular pat-down and an unspoken probationary period during which you don't piss anyone off, we usually let you in.

Our mantra should be: *We provide social homes for those who have none.*

G-Love catches me watching Maggie talk to some patrons at the end of the bar. It's a familiar habit that comes too naturally for me, something I consistently remind myself to break or else risk being labeled a stalker.

He groans. "When are you going to ask her out already?"

"Yeah. I ask her out. She smiles and makes up some excuse why she can't. And I got to find a new bar to drink at. No thanks."

"Fortune favors the bold."

"Bourbon favors the bold. And I'm bold enough to order another."

I finish my drink and set the glass down a bit harder on the bar than I wanted. It makes a loud "chink" noise that solicits an off-putting comment from one of the Philistines on the other side of G-Love. I give them my best dead-eye, "don't fuck with me" look and they turn back to their own conversation. Sometimes I wish I was a bit larger and more intimidating but sometimes the gods give you what you deserve and laugh.

Maggie hurries over and refills my glass.

"You could have just flagged me down," she says, half-kidding and half-serious.

"Sorry about that. I misjudged the distance."

She purses her lips enough for me to know that trying to figure someone out can assume many forms. "You've only been here an hour. You're not that drunk yet."

"I'm not drunk at all. That could be my problem..."

She turns to G-Love. "You singing tonight?" she asks.

"No, not tonight."

She flashes me a quick wink. "You say that every night, and then by eleven you're up there with Bart absolutely destroying Elton John's *Levon*. You sound like two cats fucking."

She replaces the napkin under G-Love's glass before she can ask the next logical question.

"Steak Thursday," me and G-Love say almost in unison.

"I bet you could yank a small cow out of that guy's colon," she says, shaking her head and walking to take care of a small Philistine herd.

Poor Bart, I think. Everyone's concerned about his insides.

On stage, two young kids, Hill interns by my guess, are butchering JayZ and Linkin Park's *Big Pimpin'*. The one singing JayZ's part is too serious about the song and it shows. I mean, he's not young and black, nor are his pants hanging below his ass. He's as cracker as can be, a fact further punctuated by the gray suit slacks and white oxford shirt he's wearing. The smaller one is his doppelganger, only about four inches smaller. He's not much better with the lyrics. It's like he's never heard the song before.

The JayZ imposter struts around the small stage and I can't help

EMILIO IASIELLO

but think I'm getting an inside look at a Philistine mating ritual. He grabs his crotch, hunching his body over as if he's "cripping" or whatever those contortions signify. His focus is on one of the two women in front. They too are likely interns based on their professional length skirts and conservative blouses.

They smile at the two buffoons, giddy with puppy love.

If I could projectile vomit, I'd soak them both down.

"I'm gonna smoke, wanna come?" I ask G-Love.

He shakes his head, focusing on his phone. I want to ask him who he's texting or what he's looking at, but I don't really care. He's still scrolling through his messages when I exit the bar.

3

Outside I watch this hot Korean girl make out with a Philistine. They're oblivious to where they are or who is around them. They don't care, immersed in each other.

That's what you call can't-keep-you-hands-off-each-other passion.

It's also a gross public display of affection.

The first girl I dated after I moved down to D.C. liked to get busy whenever the mood hit. Spontaneous and fiery. In tune with the rhythm of her body and willing to obey every note. She was good like that.

Her name was Diane, half-Korean, half-American. The best-looking girl I ever dated. I was going to grad school at the time, taking master's classes on how to be a writer. She was an older student finishing up her undergraduate degree. We met over cigarettes in the courtyard in between classes. It was the start of the spring semester and she and her younger sister called me over when they noticed me smoking against a wall near the library.

They said they liked my hair. It was a strange thing to say to someone you just met but who complained when two attractive sisters commented positively on the way you looked? We talked for a while and then I headed to my playwriting class. And then lo and behold, who was there? Diane. I thought if this wasn't fate, then fate was a lie made up by failed poets and artists.

We got drinks after class. That weekend, I took her out for dinner. For two years we dated until, like all things, newness and excitement ground down to routine and boredom.

In the end, I suspected she was cheating on me. I wasn't even angry about it. Things ran their courses and there was nothing you could do about it. She moved out to the Midwest where this guy was and got married soon after. They ended up moving back to the area a year later with a kid in tow.

Two years later, I haven't run into her yet, although we exchange infrequent emails now and then. Sometimes Arlington is just big enough to avoid unpleasant chance encounters.

Even now I'm not even upset she went away to be with that guy. You just can't get upset with a girlfriend's infidelity if she ends up cheating on you with her own Mr. Right.

That's just bad karma if you do.

I LIGHT a cigarette and watch the groups of people shuffle along the far sidewalk, pausing to take in a CVS window display. The owners of the newly opened drug store have posted a series of large black and white prints of Arlington circa 1860s in an appreciative nod to the area's history. Reproduced photographs depict scenes of stern men and women in various situations. Two men stand in a muddy road outside a store. A group of women stand on the second-floor porch of what I can only imagine is a whorehouse. Another photo features grim faced soldiers leaning against cannons.

Virginia's culture, in case you didn't know, is rooted in its past. Similar to Boston and Philadelphia, the fact that people tread over the very same ground that original colonists once did is not lost on Arlingtonians.

An important player in the establishing of the United States, Virginia was surprisingly not a prominent participant during the Revolutionary War. Many Virginians remained loyal to the British

Crown despite small county-formed militias that ultimately formed the "Virginia Line," the Virginian component of the colony-cobbled together Continental Army. Most Virginians serving in the Army were ultimately captured during General Benjamin Lincoln's surrender to the British in 1780 at Charleston, South Carolina. Yet despite a rather average showing during the Revolution, some of the fledgling country's most influential leaders and founding fathers were of Virginia stock, including George Washington (first U.S. President), Thomas Jefferson (third U.S. President), James Madison (fourth U.S. President), and Patrick Henry (orator).

It wasn't until the Civil War that Virginia asserted itself as a state leader among the rebellious group that threatened the union of the nascent country. Although Virginia wasn't the first state to secede the Union, it was the chosen location for the Confederacy's capital. Most of the battles fought between North and South during this period occurred in Virginia, including the first major engagement at Bull Run as well as the final surrender of Robert E. Lee to Ulysses S. Grant in 1865. Arlington had a unique role during the Civil War, as it represented the southernmost part of the North as well as the northernmost part of the South. This may have been a leading impetus for why there were no actual battles fought in Arlington between the two sides.

In many ways, Arlington was a microcosm of the larger issue that was the Civil War: it was technically part of a seceded state whose most notable military leader was a resident, yet home to a third of the defensive forts established to protect the nation's capital from invasion, as well as home to "Freedman's Village," a social effort whose objective was to prepare slaves for their futures as free men. Even the names of the two major armies – the Union's Army of the Potomac and the Confederate's Army of Northern Virginia – seemed to take their identities from the Arlington/D.C. area.

Arlington was a social mishmash of people, a condition that still perpetuates today. End of history lesson.

ONE OF THINGS I like best about SoBe is if you don't know where it is, you'll miss it. It's set far back from the street in a courtyard next to a building housing some hush-hush Defense Department offices. The front door is nondescript; the windows bereft of any flashing neon. The small sign featuring the bar's name doesn't even light up.

It's the best kept secret.

At least, it was.

No one knows how the Philistines found it. No doubt, a straggler must have tagged along with an already vetted member of the establishment. I picture him running back to his baseball-cap wearing brethren like a skinny-jean-clad Columbus bearing the news: a new place. No lines. Good looking bartenders. Cheap drinks.

To be able to travel back in time and put two in the back of that guy's head…

Philistines are the new generation that has adopted an attitude of self-entitlement based simply on their age in conjunction with the people around them. Between the ages of 23-28, they represent the new young professional set, educated but lazy, ambitious but lacking the ethic to drive them to the very upper echelons they believe is their birthright. What's more, they make no apologies for it.

Male Philistines are self-mimicking, always wearing the same types of things: suits post-work, but on the weekends, clothes that easily transition into a clubbing environment. They rely on color rather than style to differentiate themselves from one another. If they wear baseball caps, they are twisted around on their heads. Their grooming habits are similar as well. Their haircuts are of the same mode; close cropped, sometimes spikey. Their sideburns typically run a bit long on the sides.

Female Philistines' hair runs the same length, naturally straight or ironed-into-submission straight. Makeup is always subtle. If they are at a post-work function or happy hour, you can identify them by their Armani or St. John's suits. As civilians, their skirts are short and always form-fitting. Baseball caps and jerseys are strictly reserved for game day. Any time else their clothes have to be tight enough to show body contour; enough skin to be provocative but not slutty.

They come in groups showing up at least one night a weekend. No one knows why. SoBe is not the type of place that *The Washingtonian* sends paparazzi to capture young Washington in all of its splendor.

And yet they are here just the same, filling SoBe with their have-to-be-heard voices, buying their overly sweet craft shots. They have single-handedly brought Pabst Blue Ribbon back to popularity, not because they enjoy drinking the beer, but because they want to display their hipness by drinking something so far beneath their social status that they think it makes them cool. Believe me, if my grandfather and his brothers would have some choice words to share with the Philistines about the merits of a blue-collar beer that extended far beyond showmanship.

One thing's for certain: their numbers increasingly swell like an invasive species of plants in a fragile ecosystem. They nibble at the space around them until the territory is forced to retreat in order to accommodate the infection.

I'm not going to lie. Some of my crew started to panic. We held an informal meeting at Days one afternoon. Wendy, the law librarian and one of Bart's original friends, threatened to boycott SoBe. Jessica and Kurt, the latest additions to the group thought it was just a phase that would end once the newness wore off. Philistines were like dogs, Kurt said. They had no memory but the present. Jessica said they'd be gone when the next new bar came along.

That seems right. All storms have to pass, right? Hold tight, and any storm can be weathered. That's what they tell you. Scales always balance in the end.

Only the end isn't here. Just the beginning.

And they are fucking up my favorite bar.

Worse, they are fucking up my karaoke.

Karaoke isn't driving them away. Their song slips litter the Captain's podium like out-of-cycle cicadas. So much for being the next best thing to birth control.

On first meeting me, people don't think I sing karaoke. They assume I view it like bowling, something you do once in a blue moon, because going to the well too often tarnishes the fun of it. And true, standing up in front of strangers signing someone else's song seems ridiculous. There's no denying that. Listening to a bunch of nobodies massacring crowd favorites is an odd way to spend a Saturday night. Listen sometime to drunk frat boys singing *Sweet Caroline* and you'll know what I'm talking about.

. But still, there's something to it.

There's a fine line you have to walk. You have to invest something into it. You can't take it too seriously, but you can't just blow it off either. If you're too serious, people label you an *American Idol* wannabe, and if you're just a jackass up there, people want to know why you are wasting their time and filling up space on the roster.

That's one of reasons the Captain hates the Philistines. Because at the end of the day, this is his profession. Make fun of it if you want, he does this because he likes it.

We should all be so lucky to find jobs like that.

IT'S ALMOST 11 PM. G-Love converses with a colleague of his at the IRS. I can only imagine what they're talking about. Tax talk is like golf talk; it's a type of dialogue that only occurs between people who are bona fide members within its ranks. The fraternity of codes and penalties is as exclusive as it is boring, and the uninitiated typically don't cling to the periphery of this chatter – at least, not for any length of time.

I think about taking off when my ex comes in with her entourage of friends. She looks great, which disappoints me, and makes me feel a bit self-conscious about my own appearance. Like everyone else she's coming off an over-extended happy hour at a previous destination. If she was headed downtown, she'd have stopped off and changed into more accentuating clothes. Now, she's just dolled up enough to make a point, but not all the way that she'll be hit on by every guy who has had more than four drinks in him. Even she has standards.

She almost makes it a point to ignore me on her way in, but then suddenly turns around in a sweeping motion. The grandeur of the gesture is overplayed and awkward, as if it's been rehearsed to exhaustion in the private confines of her apartment just in case a moment such as this presented itself. Her friends stand behind her like they're a gang ready to rumble the moment she gives the word.

"Hey Rach," I say, looking over her expertly tailored skirt suit. "New suit? Where'd you get that? Marshall's?"

She flips her auburn hair with the side of her hand and lets out a grunt of disgust. With her, I always know which buttons to punch.

"Oh, Michael. Didn't see you there."

I'm the only one standing outside. She fans her hand to dispel the lingering smoke.

"I thought you quit."

"I quit for you," I remind her. "Now that we're not a thing, I figure I'd go back to an old friend."

Her friends shoot me nasty looks. There's a gray area about who broke up with whom, and such lingering uncertainty puts good looking women at a disadvantage in the larger social scene. No one can claim victory, and while everyone saves face, no one assumes the upper hand. This is exceptionally difficult for women seeking to adjust their position in the coop's pecking order as any exposed weakness is subject to attack and ridicule. Hens can't control the rest of coop if they can't control their own situations, a fact of which Rachel is well aware.

I learned this the hard way, thanks to a series of unsuccessful strings of dating, and experiencing firsthand how my exes preserved their status by constantly tearing down mine behind my back. It was a strategic play really; instead of engaging the adversary directly, they preferred to implement soft-power tactics to erode whatever influence I might have had. Then over time, my credibility over the events that transpired would ultimately be called into question because the truth became whatever had been created and disseminated and retold through a vast propaganda machine of hearsay, gossip, and social media.

We first met when Rachel was just a rank-and-file paralegal at the firm. A first-rate bitch, we flat-out hated each other. Like others that equated success with a corporate litigation stature, Rachel ran with those paralegals bucking for a chance to become full-time attorneys. Thing is, unlike those misguided actors seeking to join a profession that profited off people's sufferings, she was fixed on not actually attending law school to get to her destination. An MRS degree could easily achieve the same result, as long as she carefully chose a future star to whom she could attach her future. When Rachel left the law firm, she had a serious husband-to-be, and well on her path to becoming a trophy wife for an up-and-coming litigator living in a well-to-do suburb.

But the best way to make God laugh is to announce your plans.

On her last day, a bunch of paralegals took her out for happy hour. What started out as a couple of goodbye drinks turned into a dizzying haze of beer pitchers, shots, and way too many cigarettes. I don't know how it happened, but I found myself alone with her at a Chinese restaurant at two o'clock in the morning. We were having a nightcap and making fun of one of the partners, when she grabbed my leg and told me that she wanted to fuck me.

I had to ask her to repeat herself. Mistakes happen when you drink, I told her, and I didn't think I heard what she had said.

So, she said it again so I would not misinterpret her. And then as if to add clarity she stressed – not once, but *twice* – that nothing was off limits.

We went back to my place shortly thereafter. Our mutual loathing had turned into full blown passion. I woke the next morning to a thunderstorm and Rachel laying naked in my arms.

God had a Biblical sense of humor.

Aside from physical engagement, we had little in common, and like most fragile things held for too long, everything quickly collapsed and broke into a million pieces. The same reasons we had always come into conflict at the firm resurfaced with regularity. We were fighting or fucking with little in between.

The month before the end of the relationship I'd quit smoking, as she was getting in shape and didn't want me to drag her down with my vices. Apparently, she forgot that the only difference between her vices and mine were brand names. But I wanted to put my best foot forward. If she wanted to better herself, there was no reason why I couldn't also give it a shot as well.

Those first few days were rough; withdrawal was never easy, and quitting cold turkey sent me into fits. You smelled the lingering traces of tobacco everywhere – your room, your clothes, hell, even your fingertips. Everywhere was a reminder of what used to be, and it drove me crazy. One thing was certain–I was a son-of-a-bitch to be around then.

In the end, we didn't make it. We had a long talk at her place in D.C. She even bought me a bottle of good bourbon for the summit. We hashed over every minute we were together, laughing and crying as we recalled specific incidents. Mostly, we drank. We drank *a lot*. In the end, I left.

Neither one of us knew who actually "ended it". One moment I was there, the next I was at the Crowbar near Foggy Bottom winning a Pearl Jam ticket in a trivia contest. Rachel and I saw each other one more time after for the final exchange of goods left at each other's respective apartments, but there was not much to say when everything had already been said.

She moved onto the State Department where, as far as I know, she's still a program officer, whatever the hell that is. The new director, an old friend of the family, brought her in. Must be nice to have those types of connections with enough juice to open doors with the clout of their last names. My mom's a travel agent, so, yeah.

"Well, anyway… Later." She walks inside SoBe, her posse close on her heels like baby ducks to their mother. They head to one of the few vacant seats at a table filled with large men in t-shirts too small.

I wish I could care more about our break-up, but the truth of the matter is I don't.

It's difficult to feel much of anything when it comes to people right now and that worries me.

My problem is that I just don't know how to un-feel it.

———

ON STAGE I'm getting prepared for my next go-to song – The Knack's *Good Girls Don't.*

Judging from the median age of the faces that stare at me, it's doubtful if any of them has heard of this song, or if they have, it's probably because an older sibling has played it at one time or another. That or they watch too much VH1 *Where are They Now?*

It's a good karaoke song. It's short, has a good beat you can really get into, and it flawlessly rhymes – all key components when you're up on stage and you're trying to win over an unfriendly audience.

Besides, the song's about trying to get laid in high school, and who can't relate to that?

Some of my favorite songs are from the late '70s because they seem to focus on the themes of transformation and self-wakening. Take Meat Loaf's *Bat Out of Hell* for example. That album is an entire rock opera dedicated to recapturing the best moments of adolescence: the rebelliousness, the athletic heroism, the sexual enlightenment. *Paradise by the Dashboard Light* is quintessential karaoke, but it's a duet that requires equal parts passion, lust, and disdain from both male and female vocals. You don't half-ass that song.

The Captain starts my song. The harmonica intro kicks in, an unobvious choice for a rock-and-roll song.

The first line of *Good Girls Don't* identifies the crush as the speaker's ultimate fantasy. It gets me thinking about all the girls I lusted after in high school but never got to kiss. Or feel up for that matter.

Britt Miller my freshman year. My first real crush.

Suzanne Sheridan my sophomore year. First time I ever saw dark hair and blue eyes together.

My first real experience dating occurred junior year. Laila was a freshman and a gymnast. It was a first for both of us; not sex mind you, but having a significant other. But my lack of experience and her awkwardness were too many hurdles to overcome to evolve together. We only lasted seven weeks.

Senior year was split between Andrea Lewis, the manager on the soccer team, and Alexandra Flynn whose raven hair, dark eye look has set the beauty bar against which other women have been compared to throughout the course of my adult life.

Except for Laila, I never kissed any of the other women, was never even close to doing so. For two of them, we shared a class or two, but that was all. My one romantic gesture was carving a heart in the desk of one of the girl's before class started. It was large and deep and said "I love Alexandra" in big bold letters, a reckless proclamation. I never forgot how her eyes lit up when she saw it, the flush of her cheeks deepening as she looked around the room, wondering.

My affinity for this type of music is a nostalgic optimism of what things might have been like in high school were I better looking, richer, more athletic, or any combination thereof. I certainly can imagine myself in this boy's predicament of trying to make a move on a high school girl on her parent's couch. In my case, it just never really happened.

Large groups of men and women intermingle by the bar, flirting, starting the ever- important process of trying to get phone numbers. It's a clumsy engagement but it is one that has withstood the test of time. Each subsequent generation adds their own unique spin to the equation, whether it's dropping corny pick-up lines, sending drinks over as a means of introduction, or exchanging business cards as is the case of what's happening now.

The Philistine mating ritual is underway, and I wonder if a song dedicated to trying to get into a girl's pants has played a part in it.

4

The front door opens, and the Big Guy stumbles inside. He moves like a bear that's been shot up with enough tranquilizers to make him sloppy but not enough to put him down. His suit is disheveled, tie awry, and his normally neatly coiffed hair is poofy.

He's drunk.

Bart looks around the bar. His eyes are wild and even from my vantage point on stage they are glassy and red. He turns when he hears me on stage.

"I love you, man!" he bellows, rescuing the Bud Lite bottle from the bar where Maggie set it up for him.

Five years ago, I cringed to have anyone scream at me like that. Public embarrassment was a powerful intimidator, especially for a person who had tried to keep his post-college presence beneath the social radar. But a lot of growing up happened in five years, and more importantly, a lot of "who gives a shit" attitude started to develop. It must have something to do with the first wisps of gray that spawned at the temples though I could not empirically correlate the two.

Bart weaves down toward the stage, occasionally knocking into people. Some of the women are victims of his spilled But Lite, their reactions registering the requisite displeasure via wide eyes and shaking heads. He doesn't give a shit. These pissants are nuisances to Bart. He's a big guy and the tables are almost on top of each other. One of the Philistines looks as if he's going to make a comment, but a friend pulls him back from that misstep. He leans in close, imparting advice to his chivalrous friend, who rethinks his course of action.

Most of the young Turks know Bart either by sight or by reputation, and until they can collectively outspend what he drops over the course of a week, they concede who their better is. Short of Bart killing someone on the premises, the Philistines know they will lose the fight with management.

Chalk one up for the good guys.

And that's the thing these kids don't get.

As long as we keep showing up at SoBe, we are going to be treated like kings.

We kept this bar going through the dark ages, when they were still drinking Jungle Juice at fraternity parties. Bart and I cut our teeth here and for this the bouncers will always have our backs, even if we're too drunk to function properly. SoBe policy is all unruly or incoherent patrons are immediately shown the door and denied re-entry. If they've opened the tab, they can pick up their card the next morning, with a 20 percent surcharge on it, of course. For us, the bouncers help us flag down cabs and give the drivers directions to our apartments if we're too fucked up to speak.

Membership has its privileges, even if the club isn't official.

I finish strong and the crowd offers up some light but legitimate applause. Rachel and her table don't acknowledge me, too busy rifling through the song books looking for Brittany or Christina, or maybe even Pink. I step down from the stage and Bart immediately embraces me in a bear hug. He's been drinking so long that his sweat has blended in with his cologne making him smell like Polo jockey.

"How are you doing, brother?" I gasp, hoping to hell he doesn't crack a rib with his over-enthusiastic salutation.

"Steak Thursday," he giggles, like it is a big secret where he's been.

"I know. Ribeyes and scotch. Two great tastes that taste great together."

"Damn right! Had Big Bad Ben join me."

Bad Ben is an associate of the crew. He's five years older than me but can match anyone drink for drink and didn't make fun if you can't keep up the pace.

Once a full-fledged member when he lived in Arlington, he got married and moved to the District. Bad Ben made an appearance every blue moon, or when his better half doled out a hall pass.

Bart wraps an arm around my shoulder and gives me a shake. "You know, you should try and see if you can take off half-day some Thursday so we can run it back again."

"I'll see what I can do. I'm not exactly on anyone's hit parade at the firm. You see G-Love?"

"He's talking to that weirdo with the curly Q-tip hair," Bart slurs. "How about we do a shot?"

My liver whimpers.

"Pass. I should have a clear head at least one Friday a month."

"You file papers. It's not like you're defusing bombs."

Apparently, he forgets how he treats the paralegals under him. Last year at his firm's Christmas party, I talked with his secretary who told me the paralegals played their own version of Russian Roulette to see who had to take Bart's assignments when they were processed down the chain of command. He was a stickler for his insistence on prompt, excellent work, and was rumored to have had significant input in the firing of three paralegals.

It's funny being best friends on opposite ends of the legal food chain.

"Okay," I relent. "One shot. One. Just one."

Bart presses the meaty arm over my shoulder to guide me to the bar. Along the way, some dude gives me props for my Knack song. He's not a Philistine so I take the compliment as it's offered.

Bart makes space for us between two sets of couples.

"Shots, Maggie! Two Blantons."

Maggie cracks a smile when she sees my reaction to the camaraderie.

"No Blantons, tonight. How about Woodford?"

He looks at me for a sign of approval and I nod "yes." Bart's a scotch guy by habit but knows I can't drink that peaty stuff. If we're doing shots, he settles for bourbon, and lets me pick my poison. He's good that way.

Maggie pours two extremely generous shots in tumblers rather than the small shot glasses customers usually receive. This elicits some envious looks from the young'uns down at the far end of the bar.

"You trying to get me drunk?" I ask her, holding up the tumbler to the light.

"Maybe," she says with a half-smile.

"Then how will I ever get home?"

Before she can answer, Bart slaps me on the back hard.

"Quit your flirting and start your drinking!"

Maggie smiles and shrugs. Another time.

I raise the glass and touch its base on the top of the bar in a barfly's toast before knocking the whole thing back. I don't even feel the burn anymore, a tell-tale sign that I'm consuming more liquor than intended. Why am I such a slave to my passions?

"Gotta pee!" Bart yells happily, weaving his way toward the restroom.

I motion for Maggie for another round.

"I thought it was just one." She pours the shot.

"Well it's one more."

I'm hoping it comes off witty and makes her smile. It doesn't. She frowns.

"You should go home, Mike."

I should be offended, but the sincerity of that statement catches me off guard. She's merely stating a fact I know is one hundred percent correct. I also know that's not going to happen. Her soft dark eyes are bereft of judgment, and for the life of me, I struggle for something meaningful to say.

"But then I'll have to be with myself."

It comes out awkward and desperate. Maggie just nods her head.

The stilted moment thankfully ends when Bart barrels over and grabs me by my shirt, dragging me to the stage.

"Def Leppard," he growls.

Maggie glances every so often at the two of us. I can't tell if she thinks I'm a lost cause and therefore not someone to date, or just plain lost.

It occurs to me to let the music speak, to use it when I can't use my own voice. The Captain has already turned off Bart's mike without him knowing, so I'm essentially singing solo. Even Bart's regular tipping can't influence Captain's decision to censor butchered singing.

The song's *Photograph*. Another 80s classic of unrequited love, bittersweet and melancholy with a metal's edge. I mentally prepare myself for the part of the verse that is speaking to her. When it comes, I nail it so that even Joe Elliott would be proud.

But Maggie's not paying attention, already helping another customer. She shows no sign of listening to me.

As the song ends, I turn to hand my microphone back to the Captain who just stares through those dirty broken glasses of his, stroking that long-peppered beard, wishing he was anywhere but here among the misplaced and soulless.

I PINBALL off the wrought iron stair railings and through the front door of my apartment building. Fortunately, my door is the first one on the left after the entrance. I close my eyes and lean my head against the door for balance as I fumble for my keys. It takes three tries to find the one that opens the lock. When I open my eyes, a note stares me in the face – a FedEx slip. I dig out the pen from my shirt pocket and scribble my signature for them to leave it for me. No one's ever around to sign for FedEx slips so why they even bother escapes me. You never can sync up times. FedEx is like the new cable company – always showing up when you're not at home, always a pain in the ass to reschedule.

Instinct, or the fact that this place is less than 300 square feet of living space, allows me to navigate to my bed – a broken-down futon that doubles as a couch if you fold it up right.

I should probably eat something to start soaking up the alcohol, but the bed just feels too good to get up from.

My body craves sleep, but my mind starts racing as soon as my head finds the pillow. Did I make a fool of myself? Did I tip enough? Am I ever going to get laid again?

The LED glow of the digital clock taunts me with "2:00". The blood-red light burns into my retinas, a just punishment for my promise to be home no later than eleven.

In five hours it's back to work. The firm has a work camp quality about it, with distinct sections of grueling labor – quality control, photocopying, filing, cite-checking – each tormenting in its own way, each delivering increasing amounts of suffering.

Sure, there are times when I've seriously considered shooting myself. Who hasn't at one time or another? But shooting requires a gun purchase which just seems such a hassle as there isn't a gun shop in thirty miles of where I live, and I'm too lazy to find it. I can buy a small caliber rifle at a sporting goods store but figuring out how to shoot yourself with a .22 just seems silly. Hanging yourself is too drastic, plus there's the added stigma that someone may misinterpret the suicide as an auto-erotic asphyxia mishap (rest in peace, Michel Hutchence). Overdosing seems too unreliable. There isn't a high enough building in the area from which to jump.

You know you're in hell when you can't even off yourself, because that's punishment in its purest form: forced to live an existence that torments both your soul and consciousness where escape is always just out of reach. If you don't believe me, ask Sisyphus if he's made it up the hill yet.

I must live above myself, which shouldn't be too difficult since I haven't necessarily set the bar too high. But you can't play saint when you haven't put in the time.

My head starts to go into the alcohol spins.

Damn my vices.

IN MY DREAM, I'm at the ocean. The last few nights for some reason my dreams incorporate the ocean. It's my subconscious telling me I need a vacation, or at the very least, to be away from people. Find a refuge from the annoyances of others. In this dream, I'm at a small town nestled against the ocean—the Atlantic presumably, as I've never stepped foot in the Pacific.

In dreams, you don't question too much, because really, what can you do? You just accept things for what they are. A guy's chasing you with a machete? So be it. You can swim in the sky? Fabulous. You're playing croquet with Jim Morrison? Who am I to argue?

I'm sitting at a bar right on the water. It's nearly empty. My kind of spot. There aren't many people around, which is a plus. I sense them but none come into my view, which is a win in my book.

My best friend Austin is with me.

It's confusing, I know, but bear with me. Bart's my best friend. But to clarify, Austin was my *first* best friend when he worked at the law firm. When he moved away, Bart assumed the pole position.

Anyway, Austin's telling me he's leaving, which is not a surprise because he's been in Los Angeles a little over a year now. His face is serious but I'm too busy looking at the water. There's something reassuring about watching the waves unfurl onto the beach. You know it's coming but you still watch it come in anyway. I think this is what psychologists would call "therapeutic."

The bartender is Catherine, a fairly new paralegal at the law firm. She asks me if I want to see her bra. I nod my head and she removes her top.

Like I said, I don't ask questions when it comes to things happening in dreams. I go along for the ride.

Austin doesn't pay her any mind. Instead, he asks me if I wrote my part of the story. I tell him I haven't. He says we have to finish it. Time is running out.

"What time?" I ask him.

He ignores my question. "Just finish it," he says.

Catherine just stands there. He hasn't mentioned her or even looked in her direction. This is odd since they overlapped a month or so between the time he left and she on-boarded.

Plus, she's wearing only a bra and panties (I looked).

Next thing I know Austin is walking toward the water.

"Where are you going?" I ask. He doesn't turn back but just keeps walking. First up to his ankles. Then his knees. Then his waist. Then his chest.

That's weird, even for a dream, in my opinion.

I scramble to the water's edge to call him back.

"Austin!" I shout, but the word comes out in the loud, deep moan of a steam whistle. Every time I open my mouth to call him back, painful and sorrowful bursts bleat out across the water.

His face slips under the surface and the last tuft of his hair is washed over by a wave.

And then there's silence.

Only the quiet rush of small waves breaking on the beach.

Catherine stands next to me with a drink in her hand.

Where did he go? But she doesn't respond. She only offers me the glass.

Because it's a dream, I do the only thing I can.

I take it.

5

FRIDAY

Friday morning hits me with the force of a freight train, the "simulated horn" clock alarm bleating in my ears.

I bolt up from bed with both hands holding my head trying to stop my skull from splitting apart. For the hundredth time, I remind myself to change the alarm setting.

Christ, now this is a hangover.

The pain stabs like a migraine over my eyes; even the volumes of lumens from my lamp inflict agony. I lie back on the bed and try to focus. Aspirin. Ibuprofen. I don't care. I need it. And I need it now.

The bathroom's medicine cabinet is a tease away even in this oversized shoebox I call my apartment. I try to plan a route, but it hurts too much to manage such complex thoughts.

Do or die. Just go for it.

I inch my way off the hard mattress in slow, purposeful movements, and fall to the floor with a dull thud. The wood is cool against my cheek and I'm thankful for how it feels on my skin, although there are remnants of pizza crust now stuck to my arm.

Vacuuming will have to wait.

The bathroom taunts me from across the room. It's like a desert away, the open door shimmering like a mirage that can never be grasped. My head throbs with every beat of my pulse, tolling like a cathedral bell. There's not enough aspirin in the world to take away this pain but I have to try or else subject myself to the indignity of a life rendered helpless by indulgence.

I gauge the distance to the closet/bathroom, and after a deep breath, drag myself in that direction.

My mom would be so proud if she could see me now.

While this shows promise, crawling on the filthy floor is not a good sign that the day has started off well, and will undoubtedly end up worse.

One elbow-crawl at a time. Hand outstretched, I grip a table leg, and pull my body forward. Then the next hand. Then the first. Christ, how many drinks did I have last night? Five? Six?

I try to count backward but that only serves to spike the pain. A real man would force himself to throw up and get these fucking toxins out of his body, but the truth is, I'm a girl when it comes to vomiting. I'd literally rather feel like shit than force myself to expel the depths of my stomach or taste its acridity in my mouth for like the next seven hours.

Fifteen minutes later, I'm hugging the toilet bowl, lifting myself up very slowly to my knees. Beneath the medicine cabinet, the small white bottle beckons like a promise of good things to come. I grab the sink and inch my way over. Some whimpering and two curses later, the bottle is in my hand.

Bingo.

And then it hits me.

The childproof top.

Careful prep is critical. Lining up the arrows on the cap so that the points face each other perfectly is a cruel joke devised by sadistic human beings. Trying to do that with a skull-pounding hangover is like trying to defuse a bomb wearing mittens. I only have one shot to before resigning myself to spending these critical recovery hours on the bathroom floor.

My fingers tremble as they catch the lip of the cap. I squeeze the bottle with my left hand directing the efforts of my right to pop the cap. After a silent count of three, the top pops off but the victory is short lived.

The bottle's empty.

It takes me a minute or so to realize the strange dry-wheezing sound I hear is my own laughter. Murphy's Law said nothing about hangovers.

My consolation prize is a few handfuls of warm water from the sink before closing my eyes.

The thing about sleep is that it comes one way or another, and you will gladly accept it whether you're in a feathered bed at The Willard or on the cold tile of a grimy bathroom.

I'M LATE. The Metro is an imperfect beast shuttling a mix of people to their various jobs throughout the Washington, D.C. area. My train car gradually fills with commuters at every stop. An array of men's and women's suits climb aboard. Perfume and pungent cologne permeate the tight confines. Everyone seems to have more important careers than me. Even a guy dressed up in an unstained blue maintenance jumpsuit emblazoned with the nameplate "Harold" looks heraldic with pressed creases and unstained work boots.

It reminds me of some graffiti I read in the bathroom at Union Station. Someone wrote that he saw a pigeon on the subway car he was on and it got off at the financial district. He was like, great, even a bird makes more money than me!

I hate my job.

This is nothing new, I know.

Everyone who makes less than six figures seems to have a pent-up aversion to their occupations. The Philistines want a fast track to higher positions based on their widely held belief they should; older workers want to be acknowledged for their experience and time in position. There should be a happy medium some place, but it seems most companies don't get it right. Or don't want to. Or don't have to.

It costs too much, and besides, replacing bodies in seats is as easy as changing underwear.

I've worked at the law firm about a year longer than I should. It was my first real job out of college at a time when recent college graduates couldn't land any jobs. My application to work at a Nantucket bed and breakfast washing and folding linens got deep-sixed in favor of a graduate from Wesleyan. Can you believe that shit? A recession forced college graduates to compete to wash piss-stained sheets. So much for *summa cum laude*. At that point I was happy to get out of the supermarket and worked a white-collar position. An English lit degree and trimming lettuce heads did not seem a match made in heaven.

At first being a paralegal was a pretty easy job. My responsibilities largely consisted of copying things for attorneys, going on document productions all over the United States, and putting together exhibits for trial. The most intense activity a paralegal might engage in during the day is pouring through documents with a yellow highlighter and marking those containing text that registered on a "responsible word" list. The base salary for all starting paralegals was twenty grand, but no one made that base. Overtime was a never-ending gravy train. That first year I cleared 50 thousand easy.

But the job gets stale fast, especially when you see your peers go off to bigger and better things. Ex-girlfriends included.

My best friend Austin, the guy from the dream, knew when to get out. We started at the firm about the same time, but he recognized the writing on the wall. Once that decision was made, he packed up his shit and moved to Los Angeles, without so much as a blink of an eye.

A balls-out-move like that deserves massive props. Not knowing anyone there, no family, no friends, he just gets up and splits. Buys himself a used car and piles his crap in and drives out to the land of dreams. Now he's a crime reporter for one of the local papers. One moment he's blue-backing filings for California courts, the next, he's reporting on the decisions made by them.

Not exactly a rags-to-riches story in the purest sense but a model of some modicum of success, nonetheless.

The dream reminded me of the short story that we're working on. Originally his idea, it's a creative collaboration experiment of sorts. We each take turns writing sections. Like two musicians riffing off one another, the object is to see where the narrative takes us, if the author leads the story or vice versa. I mean, it works for jazz, why not a short story?

To be honest, I was skeptical at first. In my opinion, good creative work wasn't the product of two minds. Too many chefs, one soup, that kind of thing. But he pushed back, didn't see it to be a problem in our case. We were serious writers, he said. And left it at that. I didn't understand what he meant but he was always funny that way, saying things that kind of made sense but not really. After he had been in Los Angeles after a couple of weeks, he sent me the first installment.

He started it off. *"The girl behind the glass reads Henry Miller..."*

I would find out later that was in homage to the hotel he went to once he got to Los Angeles. It was a club in a trendy hotel on Sunset that featured an attractive twenty-something woman who slept, ate, and stayed in a large glass one-room efficiency behind the hotel bar. She worked a daytime job, he found out later, but four days a week she had to be behind the glass from eight in the evening until six in the morning the next day. The room was complete with a bed, desk, chair, and a bathroom with a privacy screen. For this she was paid a set amount, plus free-living accommodations.

Austin said it was totally surreal, totally what he expected Los Angeles to be: an exhibitionistic thrill ride that pushed the boundaries of any normal sensibility.

But what got him he said, was the girl. Not for the voyeuristic thrill, mind you, but what she did while behind the transparent glass encasement.

She read. And not just the trades, or a magazine, or Facebook on her phone.

But Henry Miller's *Tropic of Cancer*.

Austin's favorite book.

It was fate, he said. There was a story here, somewhere. It was up to us to figure it out.

So, he started it and I continued. Each taking over where the other left off. The writing was raw like a picked-over scab. Not perfect, even sloppy in areas, but honest.

Almost ten months since we started, this innovative expurgation remained unfinished. We started off with that good energy of starting something new, with an excitement that came with impending discovery. We sent our contributions to each other almost as quickly as we received them. But then shit got in the way. Life. Work. Girls. Whatever. And things got pushed to the side, reprioritized, and ultimately forgotten.

The story focused on a guy, the anti-hero, who found himself in this trendy bar full of glamorous people.

He didn't belong there, but L.A. was inescapable for those who inhabited it. Even those who tried to lose themselves in the underbelly of the city invariably found themselves in places where the glare of sunlight was too strong for their eyes.

Complicating matters was L.A.'s transient nature. It was a congestion of transplants, the hopeful and the damned, that tried to discover themselves and their places in a city that rewards the image of the person rather than the substance inside him. When these misguided souls reached their personal epiphanies, an indelible mark was burned on them. Some embraced this mark. Others reluctantly accepted it. And still others, the dire minority, rebelled against it.

The anti-hero lived in the reality of the last category, rebelling against an established system fraught with perils and challenges. There was a reason why there were so many fractured bones of would-be heroes littering the halls of the labyrinth. The Minotaur was not so easily bested. I knew that's why Austin put him at the center of this libertine sanctuary, ready to send a hearty fuck-you to these soulless heathens.

At least, that's what I thought when we started. Now where we are with the story is beyond me. I know I sent it back to Austin because, well, I don't have it. My guess is that he's scrapped it jumping on something better that's come along. I mean, let's be honest. First-time writers don't always finish what they start. Hell, even Fitzgerald had an entire notebook filled with such "first starts" – a collection of musings, snippets of dialogues, unfinished descriptions, interesting scenarios that simply had no legs or steam to be completed.

I've been meaning to call him, but the business of living seems to get in the way. His and mine.

Or my drinking.

The last time I spoke to him was about five months ago. He seemed upbeat at the time, like for the first time in his life he was having fun. If you knew Austin, this was pretty out of character for him. He rarely exhibited positive energy – an oddly compelling trait. Our friendship was largely based on the general apathy we felt about life in general, and the disdain about the people around us specifically.

During one phone call, he told me I had to come out there. There were no ugly people, he said. All the girls were nice to you because they had to be; they didn't know you and didn't know who you might know. Once they knew you, he said, all bets were off. But for at least a little while, you got to experience how nice they could be, even if it was all an act.

It was strange listening to him talk about anything but the news with so much excitement. He sounded… well, he sounded very L.A. Or how a recent transplant sounded like when he first encountered the flawless faces and sculpted bodies of virtually everyone working in that town with an eye toward the big or small screens. He talked a mile a minute, barely taking the time to breathe before he dropped a dozen names in under forty minutes. Places like the Frolic Room, the Dresden, even the Lava Lounge. He used first names like "Brad" and "J-Lo" when referencing the celebrities he saw down by the Santa Monica pier. Some people I heard of, most I hadn't. He even said he got a personal trainer to help him get back in shape.

It was very un-Austin.

Finally, he told me he got a lead for a reporter position at a local paper but for the time being was earning his bones working for a wire service covering cases at the county courthouse. For the first time since he picked up the phone, he dropped the L.A. lingo from the conversation, and it was good to hear the old Austin again. I caught him up on the law firm gossip, and for a brief moment, we closed the distance between us just a bit.

Truth is, I'd love to follow him out there. Crash on his floor until I find my footing. But the fact of the matter is I'm a coward, lacking the courage or the conviction of jumping into the unknown, uncertain of where or how I'm going to land. Stability in hell is still stability, and in a country with an unemployment rate hovering consistently above 7.3

percent, I should be fucking happy I have a job, even a debasing one that overpays me.

But I'm not.

Pride tells me to walk from the law firm. Skate into my boss's office butt naked with a clap hat on my head and drop my resignation letter on her desk. Roll out the door nice and slow so she gets a good shot of my ass on the way out with a "FUCK YOU" written in lipstick on my cheeks.

But VISA doesn't take checks written on grandstand theatrics. Marching out on principles works in movies made prior to 1980. In this economic climate it's just stupid, and I can't afford to be stupid at this juncture in my life.

MY DREAM last night was weird. I don't usually dream of friends, and when I do, they don't just storm right into the ocean like they're heading to China on a walk-about.

My dreams are better dreams, sexy dreams when I can manage them. When I can't, dreams of better times in my life. Like playing soccer in college, or Cape Cod week after senior year.

Dreams are funny things. We want them to be so much more than they end up being. To have more value and meaning than they do. They aren't our unconscious thoughts but the products of thoughts already running around in our heads. They are very much focused on our present conditions not what the future may be or hold. We don't dream the numbers for winning lottery tickets; we dream numbers we are all too aware of or know.

Lately I've been dreaming of simpler goals. That's the thing. Like getting a real apartment. Not a car. Not new clothes. Just a little tax shelter I can call my own. My slice of the modern-day equivalent of the American dream. A house is nice but fuck it. Who can afford one? I want a one-bedroom condo with enough space I don't have to smell the toilet when I go into my closet for a jacket.

I dream of working a job that's worthy of someone of my talents, whatever those may be. Free of humiliation, and alphabetizing, and weekends spent in conference rooms creating endless stacks of paper in triplicate. I'm still working on that one.

Lastly, I dream of something – anything – better than this. "This" can be my present reality; it can be the day-old milk I think I can drink down without getting sick. It can be a pretty girl who doesn't ask what you do, who you know, what level of clearance you have, or how long it's going to take you to get up to the next rung on the ladder.

The founding fathers dreamed of creating something lasting and purposeful in a new country by drafting new laws that promoted new possibilities. Martin Luther King, Jr. dreamed of a country of equality and fairness for everyone and not a privileged few.

At its core, D.C. is a city built on dreams.

Dreams are cheap in this town.

6

Bowrey & Lymon occupies a modest office building two blocks from the White House. You would think a corporate litigation firm would be showier and project more wealth and stature – glass and steel frames and all of that crap. But it's just plain Jane, as nondescript as the other thirty buildings nestled closely to the power teat of 1600 Pennsylvania Avenue.

Bowrey is small by corporate firm standards, but still gives some of the heavy hitters in town a run for their money. The fact they are successful is testimony to the fact this country has way too many billion-dollar companies eager to avoid potentially costly trials that might chip away at partners' bonuses.

The firm recruits attorneys from the most impressive schools, but corporate litigation firms are worse than professional sports. It will take the cream of the crop, ride them until they break, and if the aspirants don't make junior partner in five years, the firm will unceremoniously kick them to the curb. Thanks for playing, here's your parting check.

That's the thing about law firms – they churn out ambitious attorneys like potato chips. If one can't live up to his potential, fuck him. There're twenty more to take his place. Maybe they will be hungrier. Maybe they can increase profit revenue.

If not, there's always the next summer's associates to woo from Stanford or Harvard or Yale.

I share an office with two other paralegals in our file room. My desk is tucked in between the last row and the back wall while theirs are closer to the front door and in direct line of fire of any associate looking for labor. When the senior paralegal on our case took off for law school, I claimed his desk on seniority. It's a smaller space but it portends the illusion of privacy. Five metal rows of red file folders provide enough coverage to dissuade anyone but the most persistent of attorneys from venturing in farther.

Offices like mine are few and far between and offer the only respite to the paralegal "ghetto," a wing on the third floor where most of the firm's other sixty paralegals wait for assignments like day laborers looking for a twenty dollar an hour job. Unsurprisingly, the ghetto is the most run-down floor of the building. It doesn't matter if it looks like war-torn Kabul, the clients are never brought there. They only see the mahogany desks and large floor-to-ceiling-window offices of the senior partners with their flattering views of the Washington Monument and the Old Executive Office Building. I wonder how they would feel if they knew that the work backbone of their cases lived in slum-like conditions and their state-of-mind is directly connected to how they handle the paperwork.

Paralegals fervently wait for the phone to ring. Time is money, and if it can't be billed it comes out of the firm's overhead. Paralegals who bill an inordinate amount of time to the firm are paralegals soon looking for other opportunities. Those not assigned full-time cases scramble for assignments, especially when the end of the month looms near. Everyone has a nut to make.

However, there are those occasions when there is just not enough work to go around. These large sections of time are prime for idle chit-chat, when paralegals stand in the hallway outside their office doors engaging in a game of verbal one-upmanship. You play intramural football? I started at Lehigh. You're thinking of going to Hawaii for vacation? Once my trust fund kicks in, I'm headed to Phuket. On particularly slow days, spontaneous games of floor hockey or Nerf basketball break out to the delight of the young attractive paralegals who evaluate prospective mates like pre-Revolution Paris society. Puffed-up chests and coy smiles fuel contests to the delight of everyone involved.

Austin and I relentlessly made fun of them. How could you not? Despite their family names or any past glories they may have enjoyed, they seemed to overlook the simple fact we were all in the same boat as paralegals. We fed from the same shit-trough, wading through the same shit-work. The difference was they seemed to tolerate the taste whereas Austin and I refused to train our palates for it.

Not sharing the same aspirations of the banal, Austin and I enjoyed the luxury of doing everything in our power to point out the connections between the ends of their noses and the beginnings of the assholes of the firm's partners. We played practical jokes on some of the more annoying paralegals and ridiculed their low LSAT scores. Austin took the LSATs for a gag and with the exception of two paralegals who had taken the LSATs three times, did better than everyone else wanting to go to law school. He posted his scores on the front of his cubicle in a glorious "fuck you" gesture that elicited disgusted commentary and hard stares.

With no one to pal around with, now I usually keep my head down, counting the hours until the weekend when I take the stage and pretend I'm someone, anyone, else.

———————

I BARELY SET my coffee down on my desk when Catherine cranes her head around the corner.

"You're here early. I didn't expect you until later."

Catherine is mid-twenties, blonde, has a kicking body, and is also obviously sarcastic. But she is attorney-minded, her one drawback. Other than that, she's pretty cool and wants for whatever reason to sleep with me, I think. Normally, I would let the legal snafu slide in favor of actually bumping nasties, but she's currently dating an incredibly large black man named Julius who, based on her weekend stories, likes nothing better than to twist human pretzels out of any guy ogling his girl.

For a split second I contemplate telling her she was in my dream but decide against it.

"You know me. Early bird, worm, you know how it goes."

"That's what I love about you, Mike." She makes herself at home on the seat in front of my desk. "You were born with the gift of laughter and a sense that the world is mad. Didn't see you at happy hour last night."

"You know, I was going to go, but my Millard Fillmore fan club met then. What are you going to do?"

She smiles. The fact that she gets my humor scores points.

"You know, not everyone who wants to be a lawyer is a douchebag. I'm not a douchebag."

"You're different."

"Really? How so?"

"You have hope. And an ass that doesn't deserve to be confined to woolen gray maudlin skirts."

She stands and checks out her posterior. Her tight white skirt does nothing to conceal the tight thong panty lines that thongs are supposed to eliminate.

"I don't know," she says. "I haven't been to the gym in a couple of days."

"You got nothing to worry about." I enjoy the view perhaps a bit too long.

"You're sweet. I'm not. You should spank me sometime."

"Julius might take exception to that."

"Who's going to tell him?"

Before I can answer she's out of my space. She's like a perfumed angel – one moment there, the next she's disappeared in a cloud of Chanel.

I immediately think of the Lana del Ray song whose title I can't remember. Something about an angel looking to get fucked hard or something like that.

If she's the angel, I wonder what that makes me?

And then it occurs to me that maybe I'm the angel.

I work this philosophical conundrum over in my head for a bit then look at the clock on the wall.

It's ten o'clock.

I deflate. This day is not even going to try to go by fast.

AN ANGRILY WORDED note taped to my computer monitor from one of the partner's insists that I expeditiously put the Steele files in order. This entails clearing the shelves, and rearranging coded files, truly the most boring of tasks. Apparently, last night the newest associate on our case asked Jeff, the other paralegal on the team, for a copy of the *Motion in Limine.* When Jeff couldn't find it, a whole big thing erupted.

Paralegal lapses like this enable partners to "remind" the teams the legal environment's natural hierarchy: partner shits on senior associate who shits on junior associate who shits all over the paralegal staff. Repeat often and as many times as necessary.

They forget or choose to ignore the fact paralegals don't casually sift through court documents out of interest or boredom, meaning someone (see junior associate), has just enough interest to read the document and just enough carelessness to lose it.

"Fucking Auchmanek," Jeff says, referring to the impetus of this major waste of time.

Jeff, Catherine, and I pull down every red file folder off the walls, ensuring that the correct documentation is in each, before assembling them in reverse chronological order, and replacing them back on the shelves. I have 30 thousand dollars in student loans and I'm leveraging the same skill set I learned in the third grade.

"You'd think this was his living room the way he makes himself at home in here," Jeff grumbles.

"What can you do? He's Nesbitt's bitch-boy," Catherine replies, bending over to pull some files off the bottom shelf. She has a tendency never to bend at the knees, a habit I've quickly taken note of. She glances back to see if I'm looking and busts me as usual.

Jeff is a second-year paralegal who has already taken the LSATs twice. Like everyone else who thinks that good things happen in threes, he's hoping that next month's test will be the charm. After investing a thousand bucks on one of those review courses, his score only went up marginally from the initial outing, prompting this rededicated, reinvigorated effort. Every so often I hear Catherine quiz him during lunch. He has a tendency to repeat every question she asks like he was preparing to go on a quiz show. This could infinitely raise my opinion of him or at least make him more interesting. Sadly, his repetitions are a product of trying to "visualize" the question, a practice rooted in insecurity, and makes him look pathetic instead of intelligent.

Sometimes when I'm hungover like I am now, I fantasize about cramming that Kaplan's test book down his motherfucking throat. Other times, I write down potential songs I want to sing for karaoke. It's usually fifty-fifty. For now, it's the song list that preoccupies my mind. I look at Jeff and think of Pat Benatar's *Hit Me With Your Best Shot*, and make a mental note.

"You know he's in here every weekend trying to suck up to the boss. He probably wanted to look important and took thirty files, spread them around on his desk, and lost some of the paperwork in the process," Jeff says.

"Spoken like the world's next legal asshole." I'm immediately sorry for saying it. Jeff may not be my cup of tea, but his douchey-ness is just a product of who he is and not borne out of purposeful intent. Too little sleep and a sick stomach tend to ignite the fuse of my short temper. I constantly remind myself not to take the low hanging fruit, especially after imbibing a nearly endless supply of Blanton's from the night before.

"Here he goes again. You going to cite what's wrong with the legal profession for us again, Mike? It's always a treat when you do. What was it last time? Lawyers are paid to be cynical. Oh, how about, 90 percent of lawyers are bad, and the other 10 percent should be shot?" Jeff says.

"Haven't been proven wrong on that yet," I snipe back.

"Easy, Jeff. He had a rough night," Catherine says.

"Why do you always defend him? He says things about you too."

"Give it a rest, fucktard. She knows where I stand on all of this."

"Why don't you tell us what job you think is worthy, Mike?" he presses. "Come on, I'd be illuminated on what you think is a worthy profession."

"Jeff–"

"No, Catherine. I'm tired of his shit. He keeps putting everything down. I want to know what he's willing to put up for the same type of scrutiny. What do you say, Mike? Care to enlighten us? You going to wax poetic for us money grubbers?"

Catherine doesn't back me this time. She's looking for me to respond, to give a retort. And as much as I want to, I can't. He's right. I do put down everything. But maybe that's because there just isn't anything to raise up. I rub my temples and shake my head.

"Go fuck a duck." It's a weak come-back but the only one that comes to mind. I walk out of the room and head down the hall.

"Fuck a duck, really?" Jeff says and starts to laugh. "What the hell's that supposed to mean? Yeah, you're going to be a great writer."

Not my best work at all.

I LUNCH AT MY DESK, which consists of two cups of black coffee and a pack of peanut M&Ms. Fortunately, Auchmanek called Jeff into his office to do some cite checking on a brief he's filing. No matter the situation, Jeff is Auchmanek's go-to guy despite my senior tenure. Jeff's the equivalent of his legal concubine; someone who exists solely for the whims and pleasures of his master. Instead of sex, it's the legal give-and-take grunt work that makes a relationship like theirs symbiotic: late-night deposition preps, and rush-filings, and the special copying jobs that need to be farmed out of house because Auchmanek wants them just so.

If I cared, I'd be upset, but this is their world not mine. The suck-up can polish Auchmanek's knob as well as his shoes.

Jeff is always dressed in a dark suit with a shirt pressed so tightly and starched that it reminds me of a knight's armor. In this way, he's dressing for his next job, showing he's responsible and professional. A member of the club, so to speak. Me, I usually wear khakis, an unironed shirt, and the same stained blue tie I've had since high school. The firm's official dress code for paralegals is jacket and tie, not suit and tie. I'm one of the few who accepts and champions the common standard. Most of the rest don their Sunday best, mistakenly thinking earrings on a pig makes the pig more attractive.

Silly paralegals.

I'm about to go out for a smoke when I hear the file room door close. Moments later, Catherine comes in carrying two shopping bags. As usual, she comes around the stacks and makes herself at home in my office space. She's that type of person, always just assumes permission is granted rather than ask for it.

"One thing I love about this area is how close we are to stores." She sets the bags down on my desk, nearly knocking over one of my many half-drunken cups of coffee. Her hand reaches for my cigarettes on the desk. "Can I have one?"

"I was just headed out."

"Screw that, let's just light up here." When she sees me about to protest, she pipes up, "It's not like you haven't before."

A small desk fan and some air freshener provide the necessary odor concealment. I light a cigarette and hand it to her, then light myself one. A social smoker, she coughs at first but quickly finds her smoking rhythm.

"Sorry about earlier," she says.

"It doesn't matter. And for the record, I don't say things about you. Not like that anyway."

"You should have punched him."

"Yeah, only he'd be the type to press charges instead of taking his beating like a man." That's the other thing that I hate about lawyers. They're the type to get into a fistfight then sue you if they lost. Most people can respect someone for taking a beating because it shows he fought back in the first place.

"Good point," she says. "So, what's on tap for tonight?"

"I don't know. I've lost imagination for the weekends. I'll probably do the usual. Drinking. Karaoke."

"You really like that, don't you?"

"Drinking or karaoke?"

"Karaoke. Your appetite for spirits has already been long established." She looks at me as she slowly exhales smoke from her mouth and inhales it through her nose.

"I like when you talk dignified."

"I'm a slut in the bedroom but a fucking princess out of it," she says.

"Evidently."

"So, what's the deal? You want to be a singer or are you just a closet exhibitionist?"

"Well, I'm definitely not a singer. I won't be cutting any demos anytime soon. I don't know, to be honest. I used to think it was fun. Now, I think it's just the way I cope."

"Cope with what?"

"Terrorism. Unemployment. Ebola…"

"Be serious for once."

"I know it's hard to believe, but I don't really have my act together. I'm drifting and I'm not sure if I'm headed in the right direction, or if there is a right direction for me. Nothing is really pushing me anywhere else. When I sing, I exist in the moment of the song. I didn't write it and I don't sing it as good as the originals, but for that moment, it's like I can do no wrong. It doesn't hurt that it's in my favorite bar, the kind of place Kerouac would drink. Where angels would go and slum it for a while if they could."

"Good band name. Slumming Angels."

"Noted. So, what's your story? What big plans do you have this fine Friday evening?"

"It's Julius' birthday. So, I'm surprising him by cooking him his favorite dinner – steak and roasted potatoes."

"You cook?" I don't know why I'm so surprised. Everyone cooks at least one dish well. Or if not, they should.

"I *can* cook," she says with mock indignity. "I didn't say I can cook *well*. Besides, his real present comes after dinner."

"What did you get him?"

Mischief flashes in her eyes. She digs into one of her bags and retrieves a white satin garter belt and thong.

Happy-fucking-birthday, Julius, you son-of-a-bitch.

"Jesus…"

"This way when he says, 'assume the position' I can lean over the couch and he has complete access."

She looks at my reaction although I'm doing my damned best to take it all in stride like it's no big deal. It obviously doesn't work because she laughs.

"You never have a girlfriend treat you like that, Mike?" she asks.

"Most have treated me the way a baby treats a diaper and just as messy."

She purses her lips ignoring my comment or just not thinking it's funny.

"Although I have to say, I'm a better lay than I am a girlfriend."

"Is that a fact?"

"Fact check yourself sometime."

Catherine slowly puts out her cigarette and blows the smoke ever so lightly into my face. She's the kind of girl who doesn't mince words mostly because she doesn't have the patience for them. Her credo is simple: say what you mean, mean what you say, ask for what you want. She drops the butt into one of the coffee cups and grabs her bags.

"Wait a few moments before you come out in the main room." She glances down at my lap. "You're tenting."

7

Back when Austin was here, I dated Kaitlyn, another paralegal, for the briefest of times. She was a cute blonde with short hair and a big wide smile that showed large, almost oversized front teeth. Regardless, I thought she was the cutest paralegal at the time. In the beginning, we really hit it off. After one paralegal happy hour, we separated from the group and ended up having dinner at a French joint in Georgetown. It was pretty romantic for a makeshift first date. We ended up walking over the Key Bridge so she could catch the Blue Line Metro at the Rosslyn Station to get back to Crystal City. I thought it was the start of something special.

Austin wasn't for it and told me it would bite me in the ass if I didn't watch out. I asked him to explain.

"Scar doesn't rub against scar," he says to me one night after we got off work. He promises to have a beer with me even though he wants to get back to catch the various cable news nightly updates. I want to talk to someone about her, and since he was my only friend at the firm, like it or not, he is the chosen one.

"What the fuck are you talking about? You don't think she's great?"

"Nope. She's looking for an easy life, and you, my friend, ain't bringing that."

"You're crazy. She's not like the others," I say. "I've even heard her talk shit about the managing partner Nolan."

"Look," he says. "Paralegal relationships are doomed at the start. No two paralegals are ever in the same mind set. You're either both content with your lots, in which case you have both hit your peaks, which would be a sad state of affairs. Fortunately, this we know is an impossible match as in the history of this firm there has been no paralegal couple. Or one of you will become an attorney and one will remain a paralegal, which has no chance of success because there will be an imbalance in the hierarchy of things. Why do you think Blasingame on the sixth floor has been divorced twice?"

I nod. He raises a good point. It's like when a movie star marries a civilian. While on paper that sounds like a good match, in the end, it's a fundamental mix of water and oil. There are different priorities, different sensibilities, and different schedules. A movie star marrying a movie star also typically ends poorly, although that may be more of an indictment of the profession rather than the fundamental incompatibility of two people.

"Or finally, you both become attorneys, which we know at least one of you wants, and one of you doesn't. Defunct yet again."

"How can you be so sure I won't become an attorney?"

"Please," he says, waving me off. "And for what it's worth, she won't either."

"I don't know about that." I had seen her practice test books and LSAT review material on her desk at work. She seemed pretty serious to me.

"Kaitlyn likes the idea of being an attorney more so than being one. Easiest way toward that endgame is to marry one. She's in for the status not the work. She likes the money not the hours spent earning it."

He takes a deep pull of his beer, makes a face, then sets it aside. Drinking is not the way he has fun.

"The rest of that shit, the law school apps, the recommendations. It's all for show. It's the secreted nectar to lure the fly close to the trap, so to speak."

"The trap meaning her legs."

"Precisely. So, by looking hot, talking legalese, laughing at bad jokes, and enduring halitosis, when the time is right, her legs will open, the fly will enter, get stuck, and the trap will close. Roll credits."

"You're wrong," I say. "Trust me."

Turned out, he was right. Kaitlyn's still at the firm.

She has had three relationships with attorneys, the latest rumored to be heading down the engagement path. The first two were flings with senior associates who knew their way expertly around the paralegal pool. Surprisingly, fraternizing with paralegals, while frowned upon, was not off limits per firm policy.

At least Kaitlyn's current go around is with a junior whose insecurity is something that she can take advantage of. Poor guy. A long series of attorney rejections and false promises have been fermenting for so long that when she does finally explode, it's going to be all over him.

Kaitlyn and I hardly speak when we pass each other in the halls although I will make a certain clucking sound to remind her, I remember the sounds she makes when her special itch is scratched properly.

I LAY my head on the desk trying to recall if Maggie is working tonight or if she'll be out and about. Where bartenders go for a good time when they are civilians is something that has always fascinated me. Theirs is an almost aristocratic social club, a Skull and Bones for those who spend most of their time slinging drinks and talking to drunks. Getting to accompany them anywhere is a step-up in patron status; not quite romantically involved but certainly not just an anonymous paying customer. There is prestige in the association, a validation of your bona fides that makes other bartenders take you seriously and makes your face one worth remembering.

Catherine comes in without notice and slaps her hand on my desk.

"Get your things," she says. "You're coming with me."

"Where are we going?"

"You can keep asking but you're not going to get an answer."

"What about Julius?"

"He wants to celebrate on Saturday night. A friend of his got some tickets to a battle of the rap bands down at the 1030 Club. So, I'm free as a bird, and that means you're not. You can come willingly, or I can make you."

She smiles broadly. Her eyes glisten in invitation under the shifting brightness of the fluorescent lights.

I wonder if the innuendo is intentional or not.

It's a little after five o'clock. I thank God silently for getting me through this day without shooting myself or someone else. That's a small moral victory, but a victory, nonetheless.

"Fine," I say. "But I'm not getting drunk."

"Of course not."

"I'm serious, Catherine. I don't deserve to feel that good."

"And why is that?"

I don't have an answer. But lately punishment via deprivation of vice seems the only acceptable consequence for my overall lack of ambition and sour disposition. Self-flagellation may work for Opus Dei, but I've never been overtly religious. Although I can't admittedly put a finger on a specific incident that needs correcting, I figure someone like me who is as sarcastic, self-centered, drunk all the time problem maker has done something that deserves the surrendering of pleasure on some commensurate level.

Catherine capitalizes on my hesitancy and jingles her keys.

"Get your things and meet me downstairs in ten minutes."

She leaves with a bounce in her step.

I wonder what she has in mind. Part of me wants to call it off and just slip out through the garage stairwell and get to my familiar stomping grounds at SoBe. A move like that shouldn't come as a surprise. Any of the paralegals think I take the easy way out, and they're not entirely wrong.

At that moment, I hear Auchmanek enter the file room.

"Anyone give me a hand on a California filing I have to get out today STAT?"

I grab my jacket and walk out. He looks at me in disbelief, as if how dare I leave until he does.

"Jeff's in the can. Your boy says he's got nothing going on tonight, so he'd be happy to stay if anything came up."

Auchmanek gets the not-so-subtle dig.

"Jeff's reliable, something you could be a little more of," he says.

"Yeah but he's Reliable and Catherine's Ambitious, I'm that third dwarf every good team needs – Indifferent."

"Keep it up, wise guy, and you're going to be looking for a new job," he says.

"But then who will you get to put all of those exhibits together in numerical order?"

"You know, I asked around about you. You came in here pretty bright. You did some good things. And then you started to slide. And you haven't stopped. If you had half of Jeff's drive, you'd make –"

"Senior paralegal? Brrr... Shivers my spine. It's just too much to think of right now."

"I was going to say attorney."

"Please, not the 'A' word. Anything but that."

I walk past him and out the door. Jeff nearly clips me coming out of the bathroom.

"Big Poppa's looking for you," I inform him.

"What? But I have a date tonight!"

"So, grow a pair and tell him to fuck off."

"I can't do that. He's my boss."

"You got that right."

I leave Jeff with his mouth open to gather flies in the hallway. Take that bitch, I think to myself, and the quiet dig makes me smile.

I'm back.

CATHERINE'S white Honda convertible pulls up alongside the curb. She wears Gucci sunglasses and has removed her jacket to reveal her almost sheer black sleeveless blouse. A contemporary Audrey Hepburn, her arms are toned and perpetually tan.

"Get in," Catherine says.

I toss the cigarette and climb into the passenger's seat.

"Here," she says, subtly sliding over a Miller Lite tall boy. "Keep it low. I don't want to invite D.C.'s finest to the party."

"It's an artillery shell. There's no subtlety in it."

"You're smart. Think of something."

I do what I'm told and am thankful for the cold fermentation. Each sip washes the day's indecency away.

"Where're we going?" I kill half the can in two swallows.

"Check out Inferno's happy hour then see where the night takes us," she says.

I don't get out to upper North West D.C. much but as long as I don't have to drive in the Friday afternoon jailbreak from the office, I'm game for anything. It's a slow progress and at last count, there are at least four more tall boys with my name on them if I so choose.

Catherine drives aggressively, slicing through D.C. traffic with the confidence of one who knows she will never get into an accident. I don't know if this is a nod to her good eye-hand coordination, or a private deal she's made with the powers-that-be. Either way, the wind feels good on my face when she accelerates. I put on my own non-designer sunglasses to reduce the glare and subtly stare at the way her skirt is hiked-up mid-thigh. She doesn't need talk to pass the time, and finds a Leonard Cohen song on the radio.

"Good Song," I say. *"Everybody Knows."*

"Now how'd I know you like that?"

"Not the type of music I think you'd listen to."

"What? You think it's all rap, all the time?"

"No, I mean, I was just saying..." I try to dig myself out of the hole my mouth just put me into.

"Relax, Mike," she says. "I'm kidding." And then she says, almost as an afterthought, "I do like rap, too."

INFERNO WAS SUPPOSED to be the hippest bar/nightclub in the city. The owner intended to design the four-story building into a rendition of Dante's Inferno, with each floor representing one of the (abridged) rings of hell. You walked into the center of hell, which featured a large bar decked-out in dark oranges and reds. Then as you ascended the steps, the décor lightened to intimate an emergence out of hell, into purgatory, and finally heaven.

Well, as anyone in the restaurant business understands, things rarely go as planned. Zoning issues emerge where none are previously. Investors who promise millions suddenly disappear when bills show up needing remittance. Co-owners bow out unexpectedly. You get the idea. So, what happens is that Inferno ends up turning into a trendy dive bar instead of a must-see nightclub. During the week the upper floors are closed, corralling a steady albeit light stream of drinkers to the hell level. On weekends, the upper floors become dance floors, or else they are reserved for private parties. It's safe to say whoever finally ponied up for this space to get it off the ground will be in the red for the conceivable future.

The happy hour crowd has not arrived yet, so we claim prime real estate at the bar. Catherine wisely chooses space on the far end eliminating anyone from setting up on either end of us. The bartender bolts right over and asks what we're having. I'm liking this decision already.

"Bourbon," I say to a twenty-something-ish girl. She has a prominent nose ring and multi-colored hair. Her exposed midriff reveals another piercing in her belly button.

"Cosmo," Catherine says, crossing her legs carefully as to avoid an inadvertent panty flash to the older gentlemen who, judging from their PEPCO service shirts, look like they just got off work from the local power company.

My instinct is to light a cigarette as I wait for my drink. I hate the fact you can't smoke in bars anymore. Restaurants make sense, people are eating. I get that. But a bar is a place where you are supposed to resort to the seedy activities of life.

People thought New York wouldn't fall but it did, leading to a cascading effect down the east coast. Many of us thought Virginia would sidestep the pressure. After all, the Old Dominion was still considered a tobacco state, and even if Americans didn't want to smoke, U.S. companies still produced cigarettes for the rest of the world. So much for a cash crop. Virginia didn't even make a last stand, capitulating like a penitent monk.

Our drinks arrive and I knock back half of mine in one sip. I don't usually like patronizing new bars because I don't know the bartenders. When you don't know them, they don't generously pour, and it takes a serious investment to get their pours where you want them to be. If it's a one-and-out place like this, it's typically not worth the effort unless you know you'll be here again and it's in your interest to cultivate a bartender-patron relationship with generous tips. Judging from the glass in my hand, punk rock chick makes an initial play for a good relationship, and accordingly, will be rewarded handsomely for the initiative.

"It's good to get out of your element once in a while," Catherine says seeing my reaction to the general vibe of my surroundings. There's a growing mix of artists, musicians, hipsters, and like the PEPCO guys, some older, more blue-collar clientele. She sets her glass down on the bar.

"And what's my element exactly?"

"Dive bars. Karaoke. You're like Bukowski only that Bukowski would have kicked your ass for singing at a bar."

"Touché."

"That may be why you're so down," she diagnoses. "You're going through a mid-life crisis without having the benefit of being in your forties."

"Sounds like a rare affliction."

"Not as rare as you think."

"Thanks. I just feel like I should be doing something more. Look at me, for Chrissakes. I work at a law firm of all things. Yes, it's a job, but it's not the one I envisioned for myself."

"I work at a law firm," she says. There's a sting of hurt in her voice.

"You want to be a lawyer. It's different."

"It's money. Law school is expensive, you know."

"I just look at Austin and part of me is really jealous of what he did. He got out. I'm still here."

"You can move too. No one's got a gun to your head."

"I can but I won't. I'm a pussy that way."

"Don't fool yourself. When you're ready you will. You just need your *raison d'etre*. You just haven't found it yet. And leaving for the sake of leaving is not reason enough for you. I wouldn't sweat it too much. Your days are numbered at the firm."

"You got that straight – one way or another."

"On your terms, not theirs. They won't fire you."

"That's what I'm afraid of."

Catherine laughs. We order another round. I give punk rock girl a knowing look – she can expect her tip. She comes back with the healthy pour I expect. It's always a pleasure working with professionals. Relationship sealed.

"So, what's the deal with Austin anyway? I was here like a month before he bolted. I've heard a lot about a guy few people have a kind word for, present company excepted. He left quite an impression on some of the others."

"I think he was more hated than I will ever be."

"Your jealousy shows. Was he just antisocial or was it something else?"

"He just didn't like fake people. He didn't like bullshit. That's why he liked writing and

journalism so much. You have to write the truth. At least, that's what he always said."

"I wouldn't call fiction the truth," she says. "Or some news articles for that matter."

"Not the story, but what's behind it. Characters' names can change. Locations can change. But situations? The human condition? That's got to be real and honest."

Catherine takes a sip of her Cosmo.

"Okay," she says. "I can see that."

"Law firms – corporate litigation law firms especially – are the antithesis of that. They are the Grand Puba of fake. There's no truth in them because they make the truth as they see fit to suit theirs and their clients' interests. I mean, look at the cash cows the firm represents – these are businesses that should be broken down, and whose CEOs should all go to jail. You haven't been to a trial yet but watch closely when you do. We engage the adversary and browbeat them into a favorable settlement, and we call it victory."

"That can be its own truth, can't it? How the system really works. The way it is, not the way it's supposed to be."

"Maybe. But it shouldn't be celebrated. No, Austin and I have particular disdain for most people in this city. Especially with our paralegal brethren at the firm."

"No kidding. When's the last time you went to a paralegal happy hour?"

"I'd rather have a case of the clap."

"Gross."

I kick back the rest of my drink. I'm feeling pretty good. The warmth has settled in my stomach and is radiating out and upward. I've almost forgotten about the day, about Auchmanek and Jeff and all the rest of the assholes who chip at my spirit a little each day.

"You were in my dream last night," I say.

She perks up. "Oh? Did you get laid?"

"No, I got a drink instead."

She shrugs. "Close enough."

"You really want to know what my problem is? I'm a miscast actor in play. These aren't my times. I would have been better served growing up in the 1950s with a pompadour and a pack of Luckies rolled up in my t-shirt sleeve."

"That's an image, not the truth," she says. She reaches over and pats my arm. "Drink up, DeNiro. The night's just started."

8

The house borders Maryland, a few million dollars' worth of ugly. The construction is self-serving: large and ostentatious without even trying to be purposeful. This resembles more of an architect's perception of greatness rather than what greatness really is, which is probably what the owner wanted in the first place. An overcompensated tribute to himself.

From what Catherine tells me, the house is owned by some junior partner of some international trade law firm on New York Avenue, the kind of operation that covers securities, litigation, antitrust, and government investigations. As big and sprawling as it is on the outside is as lavish and gaudy it is inside.

Room upon richly furnished room spills into one another creating the sensation of walking through an opulent maze. Several of them are very similar in design as if the owner did not know how to decorate yet another three hundred square feet of living space and so copied his own creation altering pattern hues instead of the actual chair or sofa. It doesn't really matter; the gloss and shine of the house coupled with the strategically placed ornaments such as the baby grand piano or snooker table draws the admiration of his guests as intended.

The most important room in a place like this and a time like this is the bar, naturally. Fortunately for the hundred or so guests pressed along the walls of the mansion, three rooms have bars so getting drinks isn't a problem. Bottles of top shelf liquor run rampant along their marble countertops: Belvedere vodka, Macallan Reflexion scotch, Nolet's reserve dry gin. Aside from the gross ostentation of it all, I have to say I'm pretty impressed with the alcoholic buffet and make a note to pinch a bottle or two of Elijah Craig 21 year bourbon on my way out of here.

Catherine talks to two attorneys who have yet to take their suit jackets off or loosen their ties. It's almost nine and they still feel the need to look as if they're ready to file a motion or try a case. They are so on-point it's almost sickening. The two parrot one another, doing the "Washington nod," a polite smile and slight adjustment of the head so they can take in the rest of the room to see if there's someone else they should be talking to rather than the person actually in front of them.

I can't believe I let Catherine take me here. She's probably trying to make a point or at least feels as if she's giving me a consolation prize of limitless booze and ridicule fodder we can banter about on Monday. I wander around the large spacious rooms, slipping anonymously through the wannabe power crowd. It's amazing how you can be truly alone in a room full of people. They make indiscriminate eye contact, and in that instant, they have conducted an equivalent of a visual assessment of your worth, either in gross sum or career advancement, before pressing on to someone else.

Washington can go suck a dick.

My thoughts turn to SoBe and Maggie and karaoke. At this hour, the bar is usually slammed with Maggie hustling drinks up and down the line like a champ. She must be wondering where I am and why she hasn't heard my weekly playlist. But I'm stuck in a house full of attorneys and those who want to be like them, or at least be around them. A throng of fake smiles and fake talk in a fake house in a fake neighborhood. This party begs for a guy with a guitar singing something by John Mayer.

I walk out to the patio for a cigarette. There are people out here smoking too. Two guys puff large round cigars that would be home in Castro's mouth. Thankfully, someone's had the foresight of leaving a bottle of Remy Martin XO on a nearby table and I help myself to it.

"You going to share that or are you intending on drinking it all yourself?"

I turn to see a long-haired brunette standing with her glass outstretched. She has a dark complexion – dark hair, dark eyes, dark skin tone – and I put her to be of South American origin. She has a slight smirk on her face and I'm not sure if she's trying to make an entrance or just really needs a drink. I fill her glass half-way.

"Thanks," she says. "I'm Veronica."

"Michael."

"Nice to meet you, Michael. So, should I play the name game with you?"

"I'd rather you didn't."

"An altruist. Either you're fresh to D.C. or you've been here long enough to wonder if you should stay longer or have already overstayed your time."

"Winner, winner, chicken dinner," I say.

She smiles and doesn't conceal the fact she is trying to surmise me up. I appreciate the fact she's doing this in an obvious manner because she seems, at least on the surface, to be actually interested.

"Okay, so you're definitely not an attorney. You lack that self-important air about you. The fact you're out here alone means you're not a lobbyist trying to line up your next meeting. My guess? Teacher."

I'm amused at this. The first job I tried to get out of college was an English teacher but was shot down because I lacked experience and any state-level certifications. Like that improved test scores in the classroom.

"Maybe. What subject?"

"English, definitely. Literature. Poetry. Maybe even a creative writing class or two. How'd I do?"

"Paralegal," I say.

The expression on her face tells me she's disappointed.

"Oh."

"Nice talking with you." I turn to head back inside.

"No. Wait. I didn't mean that like it sounded. It's just that I'm usually better at guessing than that."

"It's fine. I gotta get going anyway. No harm, no foul."

"I'm an attorney," she says.

"I figured. Can't swing a dead cat without hitting at least fifty in this house, right?"

"Your turn," she says. "Guess something about me. It's only fair play."

I look at her and sip my drink.

"I'd say you are South American, Argentinian, second generation. You have a faint accent but have done well to bury it as to avoid any potential office repercussion standing. You specialize in international law, drive a BMW because, well, you can. You either live in a high rise in North West, or have a large, overly priced place off Dupont. No pets because you have no time for them. How'd I do?"

Veronica remains poker-faced. If I'm right, she does a good job concealing it. She avoids answering and looks around.

"These people bore me. Want to go inside?" She beckons me toward the door with her drink.

I shrug.

"I think there's supposed to be an indoor pool. Let's find it."

She walks inside and turns back to see if I'm following.

I don't typically dig attorneys. Sooner or later the subject of money is going to rear its ugly head. Whether it is clothing brands, car makes, or annual salary. Someone always comes out looking like the smaller person.

She glances back and gives me a look as if to say, "Let's go!"

So, I do.

Right now, I couldn't give a shit if money does come up.

Hot is hot.

AFTER SOME WRONG left turns and inadvertently interrupting a fast and furious make out session in the game room, we finally find the indoor pool, which is basically a large lap pool encased in an all-glass weatherproofed sunroom. Veronica walks over to a wooden bench beside the pool and sits down. She pats the space next to her. I go over and sit next to her and can't help but feel like I'm in junior high school and rack my brain for something to say.

"I'm Brazilian, not Argentinian," she says. "And I don't do international law. I'm in trade. The rest of what you said is close enough. And for the record, I did have a cat, but it died. Not my fault, just old age."

"I'm sorry," I say.

"Don't be, she was old, cranky, and didn't like anyone including me."

The conversation slowly dissipates. She looks at me intently. The darkness of her eyes is warm and inviting. She looks like a woman who knows things or at least wants to know them.

She brings a hand to my cheek and caresses it.

"So, Michael, you going to let me get to first base?"

I turn to her. Her hands roughly cup my face and draw me onto her mouth. Her fingers are deceptively strong. Our tongues dart into each other's mouths and I can taste the familiarity of whiskey. My hands rub her back and I immediately am struck at the softness of her hand-finished wool suit jacket and even more so with the strength of her shoulder muscles underneath it. This woman must work out a lot.

As if reading my mind, Veronica shrugs out of the jacket. She pulls me in, crushing her store-bought breasts against my chest. They feel full and with just enough heft to show cleavage above her shirt line.

She's an expert at this dance. A woman accustomed to knowing what she wants and getting it. She fastens her mouth firmly against mine as her fingers undo the buttons on my oxford shirt. It falls to the ground in promise of things to come. She runs a finger down my chest to the top of my belt. Her hand finds my crotch and feels me harden beneath her touch. My zipper is down in three quick tugs. The unmistakable sound of metal teeth fills the quiet of the room.

It's been a long time since I've been in this position.

A long time.

I try to remember not to come too quickly. That's amateurish for a woman like this; it's not a compliment.

Her hand works its way in through my open zipper. She deftly finds my boxers' dick opening and grabs the already hard shaft.

Our breathing is rushed. It's like primal panting, rising and falling in anticipation of what's about to happen.

I try to keep my mind off what's happening. Top five lists? Favorite movies. Favorite karaoke songs. But every time I head down a path I go blank and get sidetracked by her hand working up and down like that. I try to list my top ten books. Then favorite books. Then any book.

My hand slips slowly under her suit skirt. I want to tease her. Drive her crazy. The skin on her thigh is smooth and soft and warm. My hand inches up, poised just below the hallowed ground.

Veronica breaks our kiss, breathing passionately. I think she has sucked all the moisture out of my mouth.

"I should tell you something before you go any further," she says. "I'm transgender."

The confusion on my face must be evident because she quickly follows up, explaining, "I'm getting bottom surgery next month."

THE DRIVE BACK IS CASUAL. Catherine and I both smoke the last two cigarettes in my pack. The night is unusually humid, the ominous foretelling of what portends to be another muggy D.C. summer. Catherine hits the CD disc changer. I really dig the fact that I hear Morrissey croon out of the speakers. Somehow the melancholy is the right sentiment to end a night like this.

I wonder how Julius likes this deviation of music. Not to stereotype but he's a hip-hop fanatic. He takes Catherine out to the types of clubs in North East D.C. that have smoke machines, laser lights, and dueling deejays. Not my scene, and based on what's been playing in her car, I'm thinking not entirely hers either. While she says she likes rap music, Catherine strikes me as a people pleaser, always trying to help or sacrifice something for the betterment of someone else. I wonder how she's going to cut it in the legal world. Even those attorneys who do family practice or children's services play shark to someone's bleeding sea lion.

She pulls up in front of my apartment building and leaves the engine running.

"You have fun tonight?" she asks. "Be honest."

Diplomacy is a prudent course of action. "I had something."

"I noticed. Five foot five inches, long brown hair, nice tits…"

"And a cock."

"Excuse me?"

"Let me rephrase that. Soon-to-be ex-cock. She's having it removed next month. So that's good."

It takes a few seconds before Catherine comprehends what I've said. When she does, she bursts out laughing. Maybe it's the booze or just how tired I am, but I like the sound of it. It's unforced, aggressive, and completely genuine.

She catches me looking at her differently and straightens up.

"Get some sleep. It's late."

"Why ruin a perfect night?"

I climb out of the car. She double taps the horn and drives off. The fourteen stairs to the front door seem a Herculean task. Might as well climb Everest in this condition. It would take the same amount of time, at least, in my mind.

Another night comes to a close with me coming home alone, and ultimately not coming at all.

Hello, weekend. Long time no see.

―――――――――――

THE DREAM AGAIN. By the ocean. Not the exact scenario as the previous night's dream, but similar. This time I'm at a bar called Skipper's Reef on a pier overlooking an inlet. Skipper's Reef is a place in Deale, Maryland. An East Coast bar with a West Coast friend. Catherine is not the bartender in this dream. A faceless inconsequential person hands me my drink.

Austin stands at the edge of the pier looking out over the water. From the distant look in his eyes, he's seeing something far off. But he's not observing anything in particular. No, this is a thinker's stare, an expression you get when you are so far inside your own thoughts that your body is just the thing that's keeping you together.

I get up off my stool and go over to him.

"What are you looking at?"

He says nothing and just points to something only he can see amidst the waves in the distance.

"I don't see anything."

"Look harder," he says.

I squint. The glare off the water is blinding.

"Nope. Got nothing."

"That's the thing. You can't look for it and see it. That's not the way it works, Mike. First you have to know it's out there, or at least sense it's out there. Then you can see it. Understand?"

"Not in the slightest. Want a drink?"

Austin's face gets serious.

"Mikey, you never call me."

"We don't have that type of relationship, Austin. You don't call me. I don't call you. We don't chit-chat. We don't go on trips together. We don't need to validate each other. We don't do that."

He nods, more out of obligation than of really understanding what I mean. We've always been friends without having to be dependent on one another for that friendship. That's one of the things that separates us from the rest of the paralegal droids, or anyone else for that matter. They have to go out with each other. They have to date each other. They have to go to law school with each other. Austin and I are cut from a different bolt of cloth. We are self-sufficient, coming together in mutual interest, not out of self-preservation or social necessity.

"It's not always easy going alone," he says finally.

"It never is, but that's what we like about life. We don't need anyone else. We are outsiders because we are happiest when we stand at the periphery, masked in anonymity, drawing strength from that obfuscation."

He says nothing.

"Look at our favorite writers. They wrote best and lived best when they avoided people," I add.

"You've never been alone, Mikey. Not once. Not really."

"I wouldn't say that. Yes and no."

"No and no."

He's right. I've never been put to that test. Austin has. But I seem to continuously sidestep that decision. I could have gone to L.A. right after college, but I didn't. It was my plan once, when all of the other job opportunities ultimately failed, moving to L.A. seemed like the only legitimate option. Instead, I chose the familiarity of D.C., because my brother had moved down a few years earlier and it was someone to help me out if I couldn't hack it. And when I did manage, I was going to work for a year or two then move with some dollars in my pocket. But I didn't. I stayed, like a damn doe preferring the comfort of the oncoming lights to the unknown darkness on the side of the road.

"You finish the story yet?"

"I sent it to you. You owe me my pages."

He stares at me.

"Sometimes you just get lonely," he repeats.

With that, he turns away from me and hops into the water. He treads water for a little bit before his head disappears below the surf line.

I stand there waiting for him to surface but he never does.

"Austin?"

The water rolls in. One wave after another.

Why don't I jump in after him?

"Austin?"

No one's around. No Austin. No Catherine. Just me. And that makes me sad.

I hate being bummed out in dreams. Life is depressing enough.

9

SATURDAY

An aggressive knock at the door pulls me out of my slumber. I find myself on the floor, the consequences of too much booze and restless dreams. The familiar throb in my head reminds me I overindulged once again. Story of my life recently. One of these days I'll remember to take some aspirin and drink a lot of water before passing out.

A quick glance at my watch tells me it's almost nine o'clock.

Shit. I have to do errands.

Another, more insistent knock. I get to my feet and steady myself before committing to the walk toward the door. It's times like this I really appreciate living in an efficiency the size of a walk-in closet. Less square living space means shorter distances to your destination, which is beneficial in most situations. When you're hungover like I am, even five extra steps can mean the difference of getting the door or sleeping it off until noon or one.

I open the door revealing the mailman holding a package and a clipboard. It takes me a moment to put him in context.

"Sign here," he instructs, pointing to a place on a form. He's all business, which is fine by me. I wouldn't know how to fight the urge to dry-heave and make small talk at the same time.

Pen in hand, I scribble something close to my name. He doesn't care that my signature is about as legible as a two-year old writing it. He just wants to finish his rounds and go drinking or smoke dope or whatever they do when they're not dropping off envelopes and flyers.

Aside from postman, paralegal, and peep show booth cleaner, there are very few jobs I'd like less. My cousin is a postal worker in Connecticut, and he's told me some fucked-up stories when he used to deliver mail. There are some real whackos out there. One guy met him every afternoon in a robe that was never closed. He'd try to engage my cousin in conversation with his franks and beans on display. One woman always insulted him. He never understood why but he'd deliver a package, or some bills, and she bitched him out, calling him the "N" word even though he was just a short, overweight Italian man with a bad moustache.

Every day you have to engage with someone, and people, as I've already mentioned, pretty much suck. When you factor the weirdos into the equation, it just makes you want to take your head off with a shotgun.

The postman thanks me and runs upstairs to deliver something else to one of the other fools in my building who think that paying seven hundred and fifty a month for a broken shoebox roach community apartment is still a good deal.

I shut the door and look at the package. It's about sixteen inches long, wrapped in a "Priority" white mailbox. The return label has the classic three-named moniker indicative of a law firm: Meeps, Wilcroft & Marks. The parcel has some heft to it too.

God, even on weekends I can't escape the long reach of paralegal hell. I don't recognize the firm, so fuck it. On the desk it goes for later consideration. It makes a dull thud.

I'm up now, so I figure I should do something. On the far side of the room is a laundry pile that seems to increasingly swell the longer it's not addressed. Sleep is a preferable alternative, and one that my body craves, but I've passed that grace period. Like it or not, a plastic basket spewing dirty clothes and lack of wearable underwear dictate my next course of action. Besides, being ambulatory outside is not a wise decision, especially with a glaring bright sun punishing me for the previous night's frivolity.

The mound obviously is too large for the basket, so I shovel shirts, pants, t-shirts, and underwear into a big blue laundry bag left over from my college days. "MOM, I'M HOME," it screams on the outside. Before heading downstairs with my quarters and detergent, I mix up a makeshift Bloody Mary of V8 juice and pepper vodka for the trip.

I'm not sure how old the vodka is since I never really mess with the stuff, but if my choice is nursing this hangover the old-fashioned way or having the hair of the dog reduce it down a more manageable proportion, then there really is no choice at all.

My BUILDING WAS BUILT in the late 1940s for returning World War II soldiers who needed a place to stay. The nearby fort had limited barracks space leaving these fortunate soldiers a chance to live on their own and escape military conventionality for a brief moment. What's now billed as three-level "garden style" apartments, are actually forty-eight one-roomers with the barest of amenities. The landlord does the absolute minimum to keep the place functioning. For every new tenant who moves in, he just covers the walls with a fresh coat of opaque white. I'm no expert, but this approach has no doubt reduced the living area over time.

The bathrooms are decked out in the era's classic small black and white checkered tile pattern. There's even an electric outlet in the overhead light above the bathroom sink, which is a testament to the landlord's desire to maintain the original fixtures for as long as possible. Nothing like having an electric cord dangle directly over the sink. I wonder how many GIs who made it out of the shit in Europe or Japan ended up frying themselves trying to shave with an electric razor.

The kitchens are tucked into a tiny alcove and feature a small four-burner gas stove and a slender refrigerator. There's no counter space of which to speak. Any elaborate cooking efforts such as cutting or mixing have to be done in the main room on my small all-purpose table.

The one plus is the radiator heat. There are four radiators throughout the efficiency. It can be 10 degrees below zero and a blizzard outside, but you can stay in shorts and a t-shirt when the heat kicks in. Unfortunately, in the summertime, air conditioning is relegated to a small window unit. As small as this place is, even at full-blast only half of the apartment ever gets noticeably cool.

The building's tenants range in age and background. A good median estimate puts most in their late twenties-to-early-thirties, single (that means while their significant others may stay over, they don't cohabitate here), and have a decent paying job earning at least 60K, and for one guy who is a government GS-15 downtown, 120. There are exceptions, of course, like the Vietnam Vet in one of the basement apartments, or the old man in the "A" wing who walks up and down the sidewalk for exercise. I've lived in the building going on four years and have seen an almost 100 percent turnover since I first moved into my wing. Fortunately, the previous renters in my section have been replaced by women, which provides me some eye candy in the summer when they sunbathe outside my window on what we refer to as "the beach".

The current woman living downstairs from me is a grad student at a university in D.C., and an apparent nymphomaniac. I hear her and her boyfriend go at it late at night and early in the morning four or five times a week. She calls out for God so loud I'm surprised a line of Christians don't line up outside her door for services. She's a good-looking girl so it's fun imagining her "O" face, especially when I run into her getting the mail.

The basement houses the washers and dryers – two each for the entire building. Trying to find a time to do laundry is a bit of a challenge. Any time during the week is generally an impossibility, with Sundays being the absolute worst time. Your only real shot is to pick the off-hours, early in the morning or late at night, when people usually have something better to do. Of course, when you realize that, you realize your life is not so fantastic if you're doing laundry when you should be sleeping or out in the bars with the rest of the world.

Sure enough, one washer and dryer are already in service. I quickly use one of the nearby tables to set my bag and detergent, claiming at least the next four cycles. Doing laundry in a building community is a lot like playing pool at a bar. Instead here you reserve your space with a laundry bag rather than a stack of quarters.

I take a big gulp of my drink before firing up a load of colors. The dryer next to it churns methodically. Who beat me to the punch at this hour? Someone has less of a life than me? Fuck it. I check the three entryways from the three wings to make sure all is quiet on the Western, Eastern, and Southern fronts and then pop the dryer open. The clothes stop spinning. A quick inspection reveals they are a woman's "delicates" – bras, panties, and *good* panties.

Jackpot.

I pick out a few of the thongs, inspecting their color and fabric.

Whoever invented the thong is a genius and my heretofore hero in life. Such a magnificent invention that comes in so many various shapes and styles. G-string, Whale-Tail. Cheeky. Satin. Silk. Lace. Sheer. Black. White. Midnight blue. Leopard skin. I place them all back except for the black Whale-Tail and restart the dryer. Such a piece de resistance deserves special acknowledgement, and only the sound of shuffling footsteps approaching rescues me from being caught in the act of smelling my ill-gotten gains.

I stash them in my pocket and sit on the table taking another sip of my morning pick-me-up. At that moment Jennifer, one of the originals on the "A" Wing of the building, enters with a handful of quarters.

"Hey there, stranger. What's going on?" Jennifer's about 27-28, with shoulder-length brown hair and an Ivory soap complexion. Her body is slender, with proportionate bust and hip dimensions, which are accented by the black yoga tights. I've known her on a first name basis for the past two years, which says something about the transient nature of this place, and the long probationary period associated with communal living before inhabitants actually acknowledge each other by their first names.

We've gone out for drinks a couple of times as friends and commiserated over the landlord's lack of attention to fixing things. She told me the guy upstairs from her had a leak that ran down to her kitchen light. The light fixture filled with water and came crashing down, missing her head by inches. It took the landlord two weeks to fix the mess and three more to rewire the circuitry. Jennifer was without electricity and had to resort to a combination of candles and flashlights at night. The attorney tenant advised her not to take the landlord to small claims court as Virginia was landlord-friendly, meaning she'd probably lose the claim and would have to find another cheap shithole to live in.

An artist by trade, Jennifer doesn't make any real money. Mostly, she paints lobby murals for offices or local government spaces on commission. I've seen some of her work – she favors the abstract and integrates lots of swirls of various contrasting bright colors. Whether she's talented or not doesn't matter when it comes to art. Subjectivity comes with its own challenges, mostly revolving around times of feast or famine. Because it's not steady work, I imagine she gets some help from her parents from time to time, though she has never offered or admitted to this.

The washer and dryer stop almost simultaneously. Jennifer goes over to the dryer and places her undergarments in a nearby plastic laundry basket and switches over her wet clothes to the dryer.

"This is my last load so it's all yours," she says.

"Thanks. Can't believe there wasn't a line when I came down."

"You just missed it. Seven thirty this morning, I had to wait behind the old lady in 208 and that Hill staffer in 206."

"Crazy," I say as I load up the whites. I see her separating her panties into piles on the folding table.

"What'd you do last night?" she asks as she sorts.

"The usual. Painted the town red, then it painted me black."

Jennifer laughs. "Pass out?"

"Hard not to. I went with a colleague from work to some rich guy's house in Maryland. He offered up expensive booze and I did my damned best drinking as much of it as I could. How about you?"

"Was downtown at a happy hour. I did this large wall piece for this consulting firm's lobby and the partners took me out as a 'thank you.' Consultants are worse than professional athletes. Did you ever meet one that didn't have an ego?"

I shake my head. "Who are you kidding? I do paralegal work at a corporate litigation hellhole. Consultants, staffers, lawyers, lobbyists… they're all a bunch of pricks."

"We were at Brannigan's. This guy who heads up the trade section hit on me the whole night. Used one corny line after another. 'Want to see my hard drive? It's not 3.5 and it sure isn't floppy.' Crap like that. At one point he actually put his hand on my ass for a squeeze."

"What a dick move. I hope you slapped him into next week."

"I told him if he did that again he could expect to lose three fingers. They aren't a subtle breed, are they?"

She bends over to pick up a shirt she dropped. Her ass is fine and apple-hard, two qualities that will garner the attention of the sexually frustrated. I think about what it must have felt like to squeeze it and get an immediate adrenaline rush through my groin. Then I remember her panties in my pocket, and I try to think about more serious things like terrorism and starving refugees to stop my swelling from becoming too noticeable.

Jennifer finishes folding her clothes, momentarily distracted by the piles in front of her. "Don't know what you're doing later, but a bunch of us will be at Days watching the game. Three-ish or so. Stop by if you're bored."

"Yeah, sure. Thanks."

She smiles at me and gathers the rest of her things together.

"Now, I have to go back and take inventory," she says.

"What's the matter?"

"Some perv keeps stealing my panties. I've lost three pairs this month."

My face flushes red but I try to keep it under control.

"Really? What's up with that?"

"Gotta love this building. Degenerate losers who have to jerk off into panties to get their jollies. Infuriating. Anyway, see you later, Mike."

"Yeah, see you."

Her ass cheeks move back and forth as she heads to the door. I lean against the washer and admire how it winks to me as it leaves.

The guy who invented yoga pants? He's number two on my hero list.

JENNIFER. Jennifer-Oh-Jenny. Ass. Panties. Ass. Panties. Ass…

My laundry sits on the floor. Meanwhile, I sit on the edge of my bed getting my rhythm going. The silkiness of the Whale-Tail provides its own sensuous lube. My mind tries to hold that image of Jennifer bending over, inserting my own spin on the scene: brushing up against her. Pulling her tights down. Entering her from behind.

I'm not proud of this but it's been a long time since I've had any action.

My pace quickens.

What would Jennifer say if she knew I had stolen her panties?

They are so soft.

Would she be mad or give me a pass?

Oh, there it is. That's the spot. Now faster.

I wonder if she'd watch me use them like this.

Reaching my peak, I immediately think of that Divinyls song.

Touch myself, indeed.

And then it all comes out. The tension. The frustration. The loneliness. It's powerful and my head spins from the intensity.

Goodbye hangover, hello…

Looking at the mess, I take a deep breath and realize I'm hungry. I grab some paper towels and mop up the stray splatter, then hit the showers and start my day.

MEEPS AND COMPANY are some law firm in California, and not one of the ones with whom my firm does business. I use a knife to open the tight wrapping and free the box from the packing tape. Inside is a gunmetal colored urn. Nothing ornate or fancy. Just an urn.

An urn. Like for ashes.

I'm about to open the urn when I see an envelope buried at the bottom of the box.

The letter therein is from Mr. Meeps.

We regret to inform you of the passing of James Austin. As part of his will, you have been designated with the responsibility of interning Mr. Austin's remains to a final resting spot of your choosing…

I stop reading.

What?

I re-read the note again and again and again. This can't be right. I read it fifty more times. This must be a joke. Austin put someone up to this. But I know that's wrong. This is not our type of humor. We're dark and crass but this is Stephen King-level shit.

A quick call to Austin's phone number in L.A. reveals that it's disconnected. How can that be? I talked to him like…

Four months ago.

Fuck.

I scramble around seeing if I have any contact information for any of his family. He mentioned a sister a while back–in Texas? Tennessee?

Of course, I don't have anything. Why would I? She's not my sister.

Fuck again.

I sit down and tap the caterpillar ash off my smoke and finish what's left of my Bloody Mary.

Austin's dead.

Where the hell have I been?

Fuck.

A second sickening realization replaces the first.

What the hell do I know about interning remains?

I can't think of anything I should do but call the number of the law firm and ask for Mr. Meeps. It's a long shot being Saturday, but one call and a walk-through a complicated voicemail directory, his secretary finally answers. Once I explain who I am and the reason for my call, she puts me on hold subjecting me to a Muzak version of Cyndi Lauper's *Girls Just Want to Have Fun*. This only makes me go back to thinking this must be a practical joke.

"Byron Meeps," a gravelly voice announces. This guy must be somewhere in his 70s.

"This is Mike Mitchell. I received a package from you today –"

"Yes, Mr. Mitchell, I'm glad you called. Did everything arrive alright? Do you have any questions?"

"Like at least a hundred, but the first one is to make sure you have the right person."

A pause on his end. "You are Mike Mitchell of Arlington, Virginia? Your place of employ is Bowrey and Lymon?"

"Yes, but that's not what I meant. Are you sure you have the right James Austin?"

"Yes, Mr. Mitchell. Mr. Austin's sister Deidre confirmed identification of the body on Wednesday."

Wednesday!

"So, wait – this just happened? Can you tell me how?"

"I'm sorry to say it was self-inflicted. Mr. Austin took his own life by drowning. He walked out into the Pacific Ocean. From what his sister said, he had never learned to swim. Whatever was troubling him must have been absolutely horrible to commit to an act like that."

Drowning.

The dreams. My body shivers involuntarily.

"Mr. Austin filed a will and testament with our offices a few months ago. Two people were addressed – Deidre and yourself. His mother is deceased, and his father was notably omitted."

"He hated his father."

"So, it would appear. Is there anything else I can help you with?"

"Yeah. What am I supposed to do with his ashes?"

"I can't answer that, Mr. Mitchell. That is something Mr. Austin thought you would best be positioned to execute. But if I may offer some advice? If you don't have an immediate plan, then I would recommend giving them to the family. Let them have some closure on this."

I hang up the phone. The one thing I know is Austin hated his family. His old man is a first-class prick who busted his balls since he was seven. He hated Deirdre for a long time, mostly because she didn't shield him from their father's abuse while they were growing up. That was one messed up house growing up and Austin carried the scars –

mental and physical – with him through life. Give them his ashes? I may be a bad friend, but I'm not a *fucking* bad friend.

A quick check reveals another envelope in the box. It's a regular white letter-sized envelope, but it's thick with paper.

I'm hoping this provides me some clues, maybe a note from Austin giving me an idea where he wants to be spread.

No such luck.

But inside is the story. Well, our unfinished story. Ten pages worth of different handwriting, different ink. It reminds of me of the way an insane person would write a confession or testimonial. Some sentences have been crossed out in heavy black. Other pages have notes written on the side. There are places where the pen has burrowed so deeply on the page that it feels like braille on the other side.

The experimental story.

"The girl behind the glass reads Henry Miller..."

Why did he send it now with his ashes?

It seems so out of place and yet so characteristically Austin. Even in death, he is unflinchingly committed to doing the unexpected. To making people sit back and question and wonder why, rather than spoon-feeding them the answer. His never-ending quest of eliciting a reaction.

Vintage Austin.

He pressed people without them ever realizing they were being pressed.

Like Andy Kaufman, just not as funny.

Fucking with everyone else is one thing, but this is me.

Spreading his ashes is a proverbial kick to my crotch. A controlled demolition at my expense. That S.O.B. is probably laughing at me right now.

Maybe I should give his sister the urn. Spin this right back on him and have the final say.

But even hungover I know that's just talk.

I'm not a great friend, but I'm not an asshole either. He'd rather have his ashes dumped in the garbage, or in back of a strip joint, then let his family have them. They would use them as justification to pretend they were good to him, to build up their own personal narratives of family history and settle in the comfort of those fabrications until they each kicked it themselves.

No, I'm not giving them up. No one deserves a family like that. But what the hell am I supposed to do with them?

As if on cue, my stomach makes a funny noise and I remember I haven't eaten in more than 12 hours. Another day of postponing errands.

"Beer time," I say to the urn. I stuff the envelope into my coat pocket. Before I head out, I glance once more at the urn.

It's so diminutive, just like Austin. Unpolished and plain. I wonder if he chose this model or it was the standard given to those seeking refuge in the next life.

Possibilities turn over in my mind until I finally settle on a course of action.

"Let's go get something to eat, then see if we can't find you a home," I say to the urn, tucking it in the crook of my arm like a football.

You shouldn't make big decisions like dumping someone for eternity on an empty stomach.

10

Not having a car is not such a bad thing in Arlington, especially if you stick to keeping to a neighborhood or two for all your social activities. I've only had two cars since living in this town. My first was a used 1992 Volkswagen Jetta. Mint green. Faulty ignition. Too much mileage. But it was the first car I could call my own. I drove it home from the lot and parked it on the street in front of the group house. First thing I did was give it a good wax until that Calypso color shined, making sure every nook and cranny got TLC with a shammy cloth. The whole process took me close to three goddamned hours. Afterward, a cold Miller High Life rewarded my efforts. However, that moment of pride was short-lived. To mitigate the fear of losing that pristine moment of perfection, I never waxed that car again, and even purposefully dented the front panel with a hammer. When my roommate asked me why, I told him that if someone dinged my car, it would be a non-event. The car was already dinged. By accepting that inevitability I had liberated myself from commitment.

The second car I bought was my other roommate's old car, a 1989 Dodge Shadow. Black Cherry. Like the first, it had a decent amount of mileage on it. It turned out to be a complete and total lemon. Granted, I drove that thing for a year and a half before things started breaking down one after another. I gave him four thousand dollars for the car and spent another four thousand in repair work over a twelve-month period. The last payment fixed the electrical system before I totaled the shit-box on my way to grad school. I wasn't so much mad that I had totaled the car as much as I was that I had just paid to have the fucking thing up-and-running two days earlier.

Since then, I held off on buying cars seeing I didn't have much luck with them. Shortly after the last totaling, I moved out of the group house and got the efficiency in which I currently reside. The goal was to find a cheap hole in the wall and sock away as much dough for a down payment. A car was a needless expense when you lived in a city built on public transportation. You had the purchase price, gas, insurance, repairs, a parking space to rent... too much money when you didn't have any tax shelter. The Metro worked fine and city buses for all intents and purposes did the job as long as you knew which one to get on, and more importantly, when to get off.

THE SUN HITS my eyes hard, prompting me to don my knock-off Ray-Bans. All around me are signs of construction – neon orange pylons, yellow tape, a Bobcat or two. Rhodes Street is in the middle of perpetual development. Most of the other buildings on this street are like mine – one room garden style apartments. But the last couple of years, developers have been buying them up, eager to transform the eyesores into high-class townhouses or luxury condominiums. They leveled three of the dwellings down the block and evolution is steadily pressing in this direction.

My landlord is a greedy prick and won't sell the building. He knows he stands to make more money steadily bleeding many people over a long period of time rather than just going for the big sale. Knowing him, he'll hold out until the very end, when this decaying testament to an older generation is surrounded by million-dollar homes. Rich people tend to not want to look out their windows and see a beer cans littering the street or smell the rank odor of cheap cigars and cigarettes wafting from next door. Sooner or later, capitalism will offer a price he can't refuse. Until then, he can keep getting his cheap thrills fucking over the rest of us.

I'm not sure where to eat. Walking up the hill is always a good way to get the appetite stirring. On days like this, fast food doesn't cut it. Something more substantive is in order to dissolve the acid in the pit of my stomach and give a foundation for the beer I want to drink with it. Near the top there's an Irish bar that fits my criteria. I generally don't do Irish bars as a night thing due to the kids who think it's cool to drink Guinness and sing tacky Irish songs with Mick Paddy McGonigle (not a real person), the folk "artist" du jour straight from the Emerald Isle. In my early twenties, sure, I was one of that crowd, but like any aging sports star will tell you, know when to leave the game. I don't believe in nostalgia and know enough not to try to physically recreate the good times of the past. If nothing else, *The Great Gatsby* taught me that much.

It's cool inside McDougal's, and I mean temperature not aesthetics. On the right side of the main room, the bar forms a long "L" with the elbow pointing to the entrance. Booths and tables are strategically positioned on the left, facing the area where the musicians perform. A small, chin-high divider separates the two rooms and stops spillover from encroaching on a dining patron's "authentic" Shepherd's Pie experience.

I make my way to the short end of the "L" and sit near the wall where I like to position myself to see the other bar patrons. It's always good to size up your competition, or in this case, have advanced warning if one of the bar patrons wants to come over and talk. Anyway, there are two off-the-boat Irish fellows at the far end. Judging from the grass and dirt stains on their rugby attire, they had an early morning match on the fields adjacent to the Mall in D.C. They laugh loudly and heartily, speaking so quickly their brogues make their talk unintelligible. The dark-haired, blue-eyed bartender from Dublin stands with them, laughing at whatever they have said that's so funny. Once I sit down with the urn, she hurries down to take my order.

"Start you a beverage?" she asks, the faint lilt of her own Irish brogue coming through.

"Guinness and a turkey club. Coleman's mustard on the side, please."

"Sure thing, darling." She whisks over to put in my order before drawing my Guinness. The correct pour of this beer separates the pros from the newbies. Ms. Dublin does it right, taking her time with the two-part pour. First, she selects a room temperature tulip-shaped 20-ounce glass. She holds it up to the spout (never to touch the beer itself, mind you) at 45-degrees, filling it up two-thirds before setting it aside to allow ample time for the surge to settle gracefully. The second part requires the bartender to hold the pint glass straight underneath the spout, and to open the tap up until a white creamy foam dome is created that rises just above the glass' rim.

I sip my water. Being the only other person at the bar, I've attracted the attention of the two micks at the far end. My head's not in the game for idle talk and I pray they don't come down to try and be friendly and share in some inane conversation. Polite fake talk is fine for cocktail parties but strictly on a volunteer basis in a bar. On my home turf, I like to pick and choose the bar patrons with whom I converse. On the road it's different, and I don't mind talking to strangers, largely because I genuinely enjoy lying to people who I'm never going to see again.

Case and point. Two years ago, I went to Philadelphia to visit a friend. When he got sick, I ended up killing time drinking CC and gingers at a small bar next to my hotel. It was the kind of place that used black lights and showed Kung Fu movies on the televisions to convey a sense of cool. Two couples next to me initiated a conversation when they saw I was there for the long haul. They were young, drinking gin and tonics, and speaking about the latest movies that were out. Both girls were blonde and could have been sisters. One guy had a beard, the other glasses. We exchanged a round before they settled into their Q and A that went something like this:

"Where are you from?" the blonde closest to me asks. She has beautiful pale blue eyes and a smile that reveals perfect white teeth.

"L.A.," I tell her.

"Never been," her boyfriend says. He wears round-rimmed glasses. "You see any celebrities or models?"

"One or two. They usually congregate in places where they can be seen but not too conspicuously. They liked to be looked at, not ogled."

"What brings you to Philly?" the other blonde says. She doesn't do as good a job dying her hair as her friend. Her roots are prevalent and dark.

"Wedding. A buddy of mine from college. They got hitched yesterday and I decided to stick it here for the weekend and see how you guys do it on the East Coast."

The first blonde leans in close.

"L.A.? What do you do in L.A.?"

Now the key to spinning a good yarn is to drop morsels off so the prey consumes them quickly and hurries for more. Her eyes are thirsty to hear more. It's obvious - they want to know about movie stars and gossip, but I decide to spin it another way.

"What do you think people do in L.A.? I work in film. I'm a writer."

My audience exchange eager looks. Their mouths literally clamp down on my baited hook and I have them.

"Like movies are my most favorite thing," the hot blonde says.

"Me too," Glasses chirps in.

The other guy nods as well. Who doesn't love movies? But in providing backstory, a true storyteller or liar, depending on your view, has to keep the facts straight. The lie can be magnificent as long as it is believable, and most of all, provable. Or un-provable depending on what the case might be.

"Write anything I'd have seen?" The hot blonde is so ready for more I can feed her bullshit through a garden hose. I play the card I know will get the biggest reaction, and best of all, whose integrity cannot come into question.

I pause to play with my drink.

"Doubtful. I write for a specific type medium."

"Oh, really? Tell us. We might have seen it, you never know."

"Okay, let's see. There's *Anal Intruder 4*. *Schindler's Fist 3*. *A Midsummer's Night Cream*..."

Confusion settles on each of their faces as I finish my drink.

Of course, the guys get it first.

"You write porn, dude?"

"Someone has to. That gorgeous dialogue doesn't happen by itself."

"Holy shit," the hot blonde says. "I didn't think they actually had scripts."

"They do. I know it doesn't seem like it, but I'll let you in on a trade secret. The lines don't sound half-so-bad if actors with real training say them."

I raise my hand to order another drink. The hot blonde's boyfriend stops me.

"This round is on me," Glasses says. He leans in closer. "Tell us more."

"What do you want to know?"

"Do you get to…you know… get to bang the chicks?"

This elicits a slap from the hot blonde.

"Truth? Yeah. But it's not like required and you obviously can't force them. If they like you, sure. They'll bang you. But do you really want to bang a porn star? They might have fucked someone right before you."

This initiates a brief debate on the merits and drawbacks of sloppy seconds.

Glasses presses forward. "Now, you don't have to say anything, but I have to ask… Did you? Have you?"

"Did I what?"

"Bang a porn star?"

I let the question hang in the air. The longer I leave it unanswered, the more these bored kids fill in the blanks with their own creative solutions.

"Look, I don't know if I'd call her a star, but yeah, the first three times I did. But you know what? It loses its allure like anything else. You ask anyone in the business, and they'll tell you. There is nothing as unsexy as being on a porn set."

"But you get to watch it being shot," the other guy says. He had kept quiet the whole time listening attentively like a ragged dog. It makes me wonder if he is getting any from his girl or is seeking inspiration for the night's bedroom festivities.

"If I want, I can. It's interesting in the beginning, but it gets to be a real big bore. It's as business as it comes, no pun intended. I mean, it's not like porn people look at porn to get aroused. You have the director lining up the shot. He's working with lighting and sound. The starlet is making sure her hair and makeup are just right. And the star? He's getting a handjob from the fluffer as he's reading the sports pages. So yeah, in the beginning, I used to be on all of the sets. You're a teenager, and you dream about a job like that. Now, I turn in my pages and go out and grab an In-and-Out Burger."

"No pun intended," the quiet guy says, eliciting a high-five from his friend and groans from the two girls.

The night goes on like that. I don't pay for another drink.

I tell them shit I make up on the spot. How I got into the business (I wrote 300-word "true" letters for cheap porn magazines. They liked my stuff and intros were made to some directors). How much money I make per script (A flat rate of a thousand bucks for thirty pages, industry standard). Is there a set amount of scripts I write a year (Now? Thirty to fifty. I have a side job script doctoring legitimate scripts for a studio that pays way much more).

It's all shit, but who's going to call me on it? It's not like any of these kids is an East Coast pornographer. I keep it mellow and I keep it believable and they eat it up spoonful after spoonful. That's the thing about lying –you either go over the top or keep it dialed in. Much of it depends on your target, but anything short of either approach will expose you for the fraud that you are.

That's the kind of B.S. I love doing on the road. It's harmless. Everyone wants to be told a story. You just have to make sure it's a good one that needs to be told. Your audience will be appreciative. You will buy very few rounds, trust me. And you give them something that they can tell their friends. They'll probably even sensationalize it more. So, it's no big deal. I have a cardinal rule about not lying in places where I'm easily recognized or known.

That's just bad policy.

THE BARTENDER SETS the Guinness in front of me.

"Order up in a minute, love," she says before heading back to the two Irish ruggers.

Guinness goes down easier than regular beer. It's rich, which makes it easier on my stomach. I take a tentative sip then tip the glass for more. The thick malt fills my mouth and goes down without a hitch. Halfway through my pint I start looking at the selection of whiskeys on the back counter. You gotta hand it to the Irish; when it comes to drinking the dark liquors, they are the champs of the world. Russians take the gold with the clear liquids, but the Irish, God bless them, know what they're doing.

The turkey club comes with a side of fries and a little container of Coleman's mustard. The bartender winks at me, setting the mustard down.

"The sweet that burns," she says. "Don't put too much on. It'll blow your sinuses to Kingdom Come. Trust me, there ain't enough napkins to stop the runny nose you're gonna have."

She winks again then makes sure I have all I need.

"I'll get another Guinness started for you," she says, noticing the sizeable dent I have put in my pint.

I don't realize the extent of my hunger, but after the first bite, my strength returns. My voracious mouth takes down one of the triangle quarters in three bites. The rest of my beer washes it down just as the bartender sets its replacement in front of me.

"Looks like someone had a late night," she says.

"Later than expected anyway."

"In a good way or bad?"

"I'm not sure. I got drunk."

"But did you make breakfast for the girl? That's the real question."

It's a forward question considering we don't know each other that well. I glance down to ruggers at the end of the bar to see if they had put her up to it. They seem more preoccupied with the soccer match on the television than my previous night.

"I tell you one thing, if I did, I'd have company right now."

"I'm Erin," she says. "I haven't seen you in here before."

"Mike. I don't come in much. Only during the quiet hours."

"You don't like Irish bars?" she asks, half playfully, half seriously.

EMILIO IASIELLO

"I like Irish bars just fine," I say. "I just don't like the people who go to Irish bars, and I don't mean the ones with the fetching accents."

Erin's eyes narrow for a moment to see if I'm making fun of her or am being earnest.

Back in the day, an ex broke-up with me because she was unable to tell the difference between my bone-dry humor and my serious side. Humor was an often-overlooked stumbling block when it came to relationships, and often not cited as the primary catalyst for love to end. Her type of humor was up front and obvious, two qualities that made comedy predictable. She had no patience for subtlety. To her, nuance was a perfume name. What made her laugh were stupid drink names like Sex on the Beach or Blow Job shots, which she always said were her favorite beverages and things she liked to do on weekends. Then she laughed because if she didn't laugh at her own jokes, no one did.

I search Erin's face for a positive reaction, and thankfully, she softens a bit when she accepts my remark as a witticism and not an indictment on her heritage. I usually try to avoid hot button topics of discussion that alienate people at this hour of the day.

"Where you go then? Lickety Splits? The Crow Bar?"

I pull deeply from my pint and look her square in the eyes.

"SoBe."

"Never heard of it," she says. "Is it downtown?"

"More like down the block. In the courtyard in back of Days, and next to the government building that tries to be incognito but can't because of the 24/7 guard with the MP-5 machine gun checking IDs."

It takes her a second or two, but she understands the location to which I'm referring.

"That's a karaoke place, isn't it?" And before I can answer, she gets it. "Ah, you're one of those."

One of those. Her words, not mine.

I hold my arms out. "Ta da..."

Erin returns to her Irish compatriots. She whispers something to them, and they start to laugh. Karaoke gets a bad rap, but the thing is, most people when bombed flock to it like moths to an open flame. And if anyone should not rag on the merits of karaoke, it's an Irish bar

96

whose big attraction aside from promoting everything green is the weekly Paddy McGonigles who sing "The Wild Rover" over and over and over again.

In the stool next to me, the urn gets me thinking about the envelope in my pocket. I pull out the pages and skim through the writing, trying to remember where the story was going.

What most people don't get is you have to treat writing like wine. In fact, many of the same descriptions of wine can be applied to writing as well. It can be immature and need to breathe a bit. The sentence structure can be austere and dense, or complex and layered. You get the point. If you try to read something that isn't ready you run the risk of not getting a fair taste of what it's like or can be. Sometimes it seems too tight; others, too loose and fluid. The best approach is always to open it up and let it sit a while to get a sense of what it's really like. That's when you find out what its true character is. But you must give it that time.

I haven't read this in a while, but my initial impression is it's not bad. It's a bit clunky, but that's because two writers are tackling the job of telling one unified story. But the substance is there. The voice is singular even if the word usage and writing style is varied. There's a clear hero, or in this case, anti-hero, which gives the piece an important centralized point-of-view. The story unfolds through his eyes and perceptions, which makes it relatable on a human level. Even if the location may be foreign to the reader, the emotion of what he's feeling is universal: the absurd inescapability of life, the detachment from the set social norm, and the unwillingness to play or conform to its dictates.

"Hey there, stranger."

I look up from the pages to see Maggie slide next to me on a stool. Standing behind her is a fellow bartender I know as Sheila, although we have never formally met. I've ordered at least twenty drinks from her over the course of a month and she still refuses to acknowledge me by name.

My hand tucks the pages back in my pocket. Reading can wait.

"You're up early," she says.

I check the clock. It's now almost noon. I don't think that's early, but then again, I don't live an existence where your morning is dark, your night is light, and your midday is just plain confusing.

"Yeah, well, I did some laundry."

"Oh, good for you. I like to see my regulars enterprising."

Sheila makes a show out of yawning, so I lean over and extend my hand. I don't usually bust balls, but in her case, I make an exception

"How are you doing? I'm Mike."

She takes it and gives a limp-fish shake.

"Sheila. I work over at the Tavern."

"Really? I'm there pretty frequently. I don't think I've seen you there."

She waves a hand to end the conversation and looks around. Her eyes search for shiny bright things to distract her like the new Magners vintage cider mirror on the near wall.

Sheila is not a good conversationalist, and it's obvious she doesn't want to spend a moment longer here then she has to. I prolong her agony by staring at her face pretending to find a connection. I shake my head after an exaggerated effort.

"Nope, still can't place you. Must be one of those things." I turn my attention back to Maggie before Sheila can retort.

Maggie smirks at me; she gets what I just did, and she's amused by it.

"Mike's more of a singer," she says.

This commands Sheila's attention.

"Really? You're in a band? Which one?"

"Not exactly. I sing at her joint." I point a thumb in Maggie's direction.

"Oh." The disappointment is unmistakable. She turns to her phone for refuge from further conversation.

"Where were you last night? You cheating on us with someone else?" Maggie asks. She sounds almost sincere enough to pass as valid concern.

"Had to go to a lame work party," I tell her. Not too much of a lie, all things considered.

"Well, we're about to have lunch," Maggie says. "You want to join us?"

As much as I want to stoke the horror burning in Sheila's eyes, I do the honorable thing.

"Can't. Got to meet Bart at Days. He's going through Mike-withdrawal."

"You can say that again. All night long it's, where's Mike? Where's Mike? God, he was so wasted. Shots of Lagavulin at the end."

"You working tonight?"

"Nope, I'm a civilian. Maybe I'll see you around."

"Maybe." Although I doubt it. Bartenders in this area rarely patronize the establishments they work at. Not that it's against any local laws, it's just they have the opportunity of going to other places; places more infinitely fun, where they can score free drinks, and choose the people with whom they want to see.

"Is that what I think it is?" She points at the urn on the other side of me.

"Austin, meet Maggie. Maggie, this is Austin."

"Wait–are those ashes?" Sheila's revulsion is more than evident in her tone.

"I think so. I haven't really opened it. But I can check if you want a peek."

"Disgusting." Sheila walks away. "Coming?"

Maggie shrugs sheepishly at me, then follows her friend. I look at the urn and pound back my Guinness. When Erin walks by I order two more. She looks at me funny, so I gesture to the urn.

"My buddy," I tell her as if that's going to assuage the concern in her face. "You know, friends don't let friends drink alone."

Moments later, two of the male bartenders I recognize from the night shift at Days – Double-D, and Alex – walk in. They are popular bartenders; Double-D for the sheer fact he's been at Days going on eight or nine years and keeps on bartending despite increasing amounts of gray hair and depleted boyish charm; and Alex because he's everything that Double-D is not: young, good looking, and if rumor is correct, has fifteen inch biceps. Together, they get more ass than a toilet seat. They ignore me, move on down to the end of the bar when they see Maggie and Sheila.

I down the rest of my beer and leave a few bills on the bar.

"You need change?" Erin shouts.

It's an interesting question. I flip through a million possible responses in my mental rolodex. "Who doesn't?" "Change is good." "All things change."

But I just shake my head, and as much as I want to, force myself not to glance back at Maggie on my way out the door. The beer has taken the edge off and I'm in a manageable feel-good haze. The blinding light pierces inside briefly, and the vampire crowd behind me scoot their stools away from the brightness.

"What about your beers?" Erin calls out to me, but I'm too committed to moving forward to retreat back.

11

Days is nearly empty. There are four people at the bar staring glassily up at the panoply of televisions mounted on the walls. Throughout the summer, the best thing about going to a sports bar during the day is everyone is someplace else. Baseball and golf dominate televised events, and neither is interesting to watch on the tube. Most people in the area attend the Nationals downtown if they really have to watch the game. For those not so sports-minded, they flee to one of the beaches like Rehoboth or Dewey, taking their drunken games on the road in search of the strange.

One thing is clear: you don't patronize a sports bar on a Saturday afternoon to make a social impact. A social statement, maybe, but not an impact.

The bar forms a long "U" in the center of the room. Lots of wood. Lots of brass. It could be *Cheers* only that if you don't tip well or look hot, you can be assured no one will know your name.

Bart is already sitting in his customary position at the top of the "U", his back facing me as I enter, a customary Bud Lite in his right hand. He turns as I pull up a stool next to him setting the urn on the bar.

"Hey, Buddy," he says. "How are you feeling today?"

"Like shit."

He laughs his big Louisiana laugh.

"Let's get you something to remedy that. Michelle, how about a Miller Lite for my boy here?"

Michelle slides down the bar with an ice-cold long neck. Around five foot five with long straight blonde hair, blue eyes, large breasts, and well-toned legs, she's a centerfold model posing as a day bartender. Nights are more her domain when she can separate drooling fools from their money. This hour is beneath someone like Michelle, which makes me think she must be covering for someone or else needs the extra dough. Even though she is flat-out hot, her bright smile and infectious laughter complement a body built for bikini ads and calendars. She's the complete package and has received her share of generous tips from us. Like other elites in her profession, she does not and will not date customers, but that rule is about as sacred as the Mafia living up to its code of *Omerta*. What separates Michelle from most of her colleagues is a Business degree from the University of North Carolina. She was on the fast track at AT&T before giving it all up to become a bartender, an odd turn of events until you learn that her ultimate goal is to run her own place. She's been at Days three years, picking up shifts, always shadowing Billy when he's onsite. Some think she's trying to fuck him but anyone with half a brain can see she's trying to learn the intricacies of how to keep a place like this afloat. Her mind is like a chess player's, paying less attention to the board in front of her and more to what it could look like three or four moves ahead.

"Someone looks like they had a rough night," she says, and I wonder exactly how bad I look even after a long shower, shave, and a change of clothes. "What did you guys do?"

I sip my beer. "Don't ask. You wouldn't believe it."

Michelle sets up in front of me. She glances at the urn briefly. "Try me."

"Let's see. I went to a party. Hooked up with a trans woman. Came home and ate hot dogs."

Michelle laughs. Like I said, it's a nice sound, refreshing. A cool drink of water in a river of hot muck.

"Tell me you're not serious," Bart pleads.

"Fine. I didn't eat hot dogs."

He doesn't know how to respond to that. Fortunately, I'm saved when he sees me wipe a smudge off Austin.

He points a meaty finger at the gunmetal vase. "Why the fuck do you have an urn with you?"

I finish my Miller Lite and Michelle sets me up with another.

"Now that is a funny story," I say. "First some introductions. Bart, this is my friend Austin. Or was. Or still is. He's just ashes now, so is he still a friend or not? I'm not sure."

"How is that funny?"

"More irony-funny than 'ha-ha' funny. He used to be a para-slave with me. Then he moved out to La-La Land to become a journalist. Or writer. Or writer-journalist. And now he's just dead."

"You really know how to liven up things. How'd he die?"

"He offed himself."

Michelle flinches. "I'm so sorry," she says.

"Goddamn. The good times just keep coming. How'd he do it?"

"Drowned himself."

"What the fuck?" Bart says. He wipes the lip off the new Bud Lite bottle Michelle hands him.

"I'm still trying to wrap my head around it myself. He just showed up on my door this morning." I take a deep breath. "Suicide is such a big step. How bad does something have to be to drive someone to do that?"

Bart sips his beer and sets it down on the bar. "Hunger."

"Funny," I say.

"Hold on there, Trigger. Hear me out. Suicide is a self-destructive feeding thing. Like smoking, or drinking, or taking drugs. Why do we do these things? To eliminate the pain, or at least reduce it in some way. He was feeling pain. He fed that hunger."

I mull this over a bit, then shake my head.

"I don't buy it. Some people, yeah, sure. I can see it. But not Austin. His biggest vice was watching too much news."

"Have you seen the news lately? Doesn't get much more depressing than that," Michelle offers up.

"Still, you don't kill yourself on a whim. It's a commitment. And commitments need a catalyst. Action-reaction, type of thing. I've been mulling it over all morning, and for the life of me, I can't come up with an answer."

"It's not hard to connect the dots, Mikey," Bart says. "Writer goes to L.A. Doesn't make it. Puts two in his head, so to speak. It's a ridiculous cliché. I hope to hell you write better than he did."

It's kind of a dig but I can't argue against it.

Thing is, since I started the law firm, I've been working on a novel that has gained no traction. For whatever reason, I can't get past the fifth chapter; every attempt to write through the obstacle has met an unconquerable resistance. I don't know if it's because I ran out of things to say or maybe just had nothing to say. The pages are entombed on my laptop tucked neatly away in a file that reminds me that I lack the courage to salvage it or kill it. And so, it remains trapped in creative purgatory, a stagnant mess borne from a mediocre idea or talent or both.

Now, don't get me wrong. It's not like I'm under any impression my first work will rival the first books of some of my favorite authors. I'm more grounded than that. But to be fair, the writing in the first few chapters is good and clean and honest. It's the type of writing I know I can write. And while I accept the fact that all writers will eventually hit a wall, in my case, the wall has been winning for more than a year now.

The novel is an important data point because the day I was going to ask him to read it was the day he told me he was leaving for California. We were eating lunch in one of the conference rooms being used to store documents responsive to an official legal inquiry. All week the itch to write had resurfaced and I was willing to give the novel another shot and thought fresh eyes might be the ticket to get out of the hole. But before I had the chance to ask him, he broke the news the way he always shared information: without emotion and without consequence.

The West Coast was where he was going to make it. Not in the film business but in journalism. The East Coast papers were a racket too difficult to break into. In his estimation, D.C. papers lived and breathed biased partisanship. Their stories were filled with adjectives that pushed a narrative, but rarely informed. The days of Bernstein and Woodward were long gone.

But the West Coast was full of opportunity. They needed true journalists because all of their writers worked for either the large or small screens. Even their news focused on the "biz."

Here was the chance to be a part of something that was still developing, he said. It wasn't the ground floor, per se, but it was still raw enough to make his mark.

A couple of months ago he wrote a news piece for the city paper in D.C. about a Louis Farrakhan rally he managed to attend, a hard feat given that he was white and not a member of the Nation of Islam. The piece was one of the city paper's best, and he was nominated for an award. He sent the piece to some papers out there and they loved it, he said. Unlike the suckers that chased the celluloid dream, he'd have a job in a week, two max.

I didn't really take him seriously at first. Austin had plans of leaving D.C. for a while now. First it was New York, then Chicago. Kansas City was a brief destination for about a week. This just became talk, you know, something to keep your mind active during a boring day of collating hundreds of pages of exhibits. Like pretending what you'd do if you hit the lottery. Austin and I talked about big dreams all the time. That's what writers did. We shaped the world into the realities that we wanted to see and experience. It was fun, but it didn't necessarily make them so.

I didn't really think he'd do it. So, when I told him I'd come out after he got settled, it was more my way of contributing to a story he was creating than being honest with my intentions. Ever since I read Bukowski, I envisioned walking down his streets and drinking at his bars, a romantic vision softened by steady pay and a full belly. Struggling never seemed so bad as long as you were doing it in a favorable climate.

We left it like that, a bookmark for a future discussion to be held at a later date that never transpired.

Fast forward to today, and my novel has never progressed. It's something people ask me about, something I talk about, particularly in social settings where the conversation has gotten stale and people are looking to fill the void. I talk about writing and what makes good writing. But the novel has been dead in the water for some time.

Sure, I boot up the laptop every now and then but end up surfing porn on the Internet. It can take a long time to put substantive words on a page; it takes less than five minutes to give myself an orgasm.

Now I consider re-reading and re-editing old pages of works-in-progress as a form of creative expression.

It isn't, but it makes me feel better.

"How'd you get stuck with this shift, Miss Michelle?" Bart imparts all the female bartenders with a "Miss" before their names. He says they do it all the time back home in Baton Rouge. I've never been there so I don't know if that's true or not. It does give him a Southern sensibility, a trait that is accentuated when he extends his drawl out longer as the day progresses, and beer is substituted for liquor in his glass.

"Covering for Diane," she says. "I owed her for Teddy's wedding. So you guys feel like a shot? I've been experimenting with some ingredients."

I want to say, thank you, but no. My liver wants a break. But the freshly-washed shot glasses are already on top of the bar before I can even open my mouth. Protesting at this point is a moot point, and Bart speaks for us both.

"Hit us up, Miss Michelle."

Michelle makes the drinks. Bart looks at me.

"So, what are you going to do with that thing now that you got it?"

I shrug. "It didn't come with directions."

"Someone sends you ashes, you're supposed to take care of them. Spread them somewhere he liked."

"Yeah, I know, but Austin didn't have a favorite spot in D.C. Hell, he obviously didn't like D.C. enough not to move in the first place."

"Then fuck him. Throw them in the trash." Bart is pragmatic in the purest sense.

Michelle sets two doubles of a brown liquid tinged with scarlet.

"What's this?" I pick up the glass and sniff it.

"Something to get you up on your feet," she says.

"Drink up, brother." Bart raises his glass. "We got a long row to hoe before SoBe opens up."

"I have to hear you guys sing sometime," Michelle says.

"Not really," I say. "We sing loud, not good."

Michelle laughs. "Cheers, guys."

I toast my friend, touching the glass once down on the bar for good luck before raising it to my lips. It starts sweet but has a tinged burn to it. I look at Michelle who smiles.

"That's the Cayenne. Native Americans have been using it as medicine for the past 9,000 years."

I shut my eyes tightly as I listen to the dark chug of liquor empty down my throat.

It feels good to be medicated.

IT'S five-thirty in the afternoon. By the number of black stir straws littering the space in front of me, I've had five drinks and two beers since I came in here at one. I don't even try to count what Bart has anymore. Beer to him is like water; I've seen him down thirteen beers in a span of a few hours. It's when he mixes beer with his booze that he gets in trouble. Usually he likes to have a buffet of liquor to choose from at one time. Sometimes he'll have wine and scotch, other times a Mai Tai and a shot of bourbon, but always with a bottle of Bud Lite to wash it all down.

More people arrive to watch the Nationals ballgame on TV. They fill up the tables in the center of the room. Large plates of bar snacks come out of the kitchen one after another. I scan the room and smile when I see Jennifer at a table with three girls and three guys. She cleans up well and has a casual elegance about her. When we make eye contact, she waves enthusiastically.

I wave back.

Bart sets his beer a little too hard on the bar. Foam rises just over the lip and glides down the side of the bottle. He folds his hands on the bar and leans in close. "Who's that?"

"Just a girl in my building."

"She's cute. You should tap that."

"Too close to home, if you know what I mean."

He grunts and I take it as acknowledgement that no one should ever shit where they eat, or in this case, fuck where you live. There's more bad that can come out of such an arrangement than anything positive.

"You see Georgie?" Georgie is a friend of ours, another outcast who latched onto our group a little over a year ago and has been a fixture ever since. At first glance, he gives off the impression that he's a fully patched-in member of a motorcycle club. A former military reservist with a perpetual buzz cut, Georgie has let his hair and beard grow long and he tends to wear faded denim. Like Bart, he's from the South, meaning a thick accent. Only difference is he's Alabama born and bred, and if you're talking college football, a mortal enemy of Bart's LSU Tigers.

I shake my head. "No, where's he been?"

"The hell if I know. He wasn't out last night. Neither was Wendy or Jessica."

"Judging from that crazy texts on that chain, they were both out on Wednesday night at the Tavern. But that was almost forty-eight hours ago."

"Shit, you can't have a hangover that long!"

I shrug. Wendy and Jessica are the group's only female members. Wendy worked with Bart at a tax law firm, only as the head librarian and not an attorney. Bart has since hopped firms while Wendy remains content overseeing legal research and managing the day-to-day operations. Truth to tell, I always thought being a librarian would be a cool profession if it only paid decently enough. Jessica, on the other hand, is another fairly new acquisition. She started off like many of us, a frequent patron and familiar face at the same bars, a hanger on with personality and connections of her own. We often joke about it now – between her and Bart, we must know about 85 percent of the bartenders in the area. How we got that exact percentage, no one knows, but it seems about accurate. In a town where politics drives the flow of business, knowing bartenders is about as advantageous as knowing lobbyists. They are the eyes and ears of a neighborhood, a town, a city. They are in a perpetual state of six degrees of separation, often having access to people without even knowing it. Whether you're looking to cozy up next to power, or the waitress downtown, knowing your local bartenders, and by extension, whom they may know, is a step in the right direction.

Bart nudges my shoulder with his elbow. "Look what the cat dragged in."

I turn and see Jaxon and his posse standing by the door. Jaxon is part of a clique that believes the louder they talk and the more aggressive they are with girls, the more irresistible they are. We call them the "beautiful people," not because they are more attractive than the rest of us, but that they "think" they are. He's our age though, not a Philistine, proof every generation has their fair share of assholes.

Sad thing is, as much as I hate his personality and style, it works more often than it doesn't, which is a damning testament to the fact girls, at one time or another, will always like "bad boys" even if they aren't bad in the original sense of the word. Thankfully, he doesn't do karaoke, at least as of yet. He has one sole purpose driving him: immersing himself into all situations trying to separate the gullible from the herd one pair of Capri pants at a time.

They shuffle over to the opposite side of the bar. Jaxon nods when he sees us. He drums his hands on the bar top and fires finger guns at us. "What's up, boys?"

"Drinking the afternoon away," I say. Bart doesn't hear him or isn't going to bother with a reply.

"Shots?" he offers. The posse nods eagerly. There are three of them – two wear their ball caps turned around, and the other wears a SHOW ME THE HONEY t-shirt. They're basically cut from the same bolt of cloth: guys who were probably big deals once in college but have since found a level playing field among the professional crowd. These are the type who still pine for the days of lying around in a hovel with other boys playing video games and recounting sexual conquests or the amount of drinks consumed the previous night.

Jaxon doles out cocktail napkins like playing cards for each shot. He pauses before tossing two in our direction. "You guys in?"

"I'm good," I say. Bart just keeps his eyes fixed to the jumbo screen. The Big Guy doesn't like Jaxon or his crew for the same reasons I don't. What I admire most about Bart is he doesn't fake it; you know where you stand with him one way or another. That's not to say that his opinion can't be swayed or changed over time, but he never straddles a fence with his opinions, wherever they may lie.

Me, I lean more toward diplomacy, never quite sure where a person may fit into an arrangement later on down the line. Enemies don't necessarily have to become friends. Sometimes allies works just as well.

"Come on, Bart. You sure? Patron Silver?" Jaxon prods. He knows Bart doesn't like him, but he pushes the envelope anyway. Jaxon's greatest strength is the ability to wear people down, a tactic that has worked to his advantage with the lithe bodied but dim-witted twenty-somethings who frequent Days. He's like the bright light, blinding you with sharp brilliance until you're forced to close your eyes. Making people feel uncomfortable is an asset that keeps Jaxon one step ahead of the competition. It puts them on the defensive and gives him that necessary edge.

We end up giving in. So much for being principled outcasts.

Michelle delivers shots to everyone and after we drink, sets down to talking with Jaxon. By the flirty lilt in her voice it's obvious she "like-likes" him and is on the course to breaking one of her bartending rules. We watch as she plays the coquette; a laugh, a flip of the hair, lots of eye contact.

When she leaves, Jaxon feels the need to include us in conversation.

"You guys been down to 18th Street Lounge?"

"No," I say. "It's too near where I work. The last thing I want to see is pretentious lawyer jerk-offs when I'm on my time."

I say that too cavalierly not knowing exactly what Jaxon or the rest of his posse actually do for a living. The more experienced barflies are like that; we generally know each other only during drinking hours, and rarely see each other during our professional day-to-day duties. In this way we are like debauched superheroes, maintaining two distinct identities, preferring not to merge these two worlds if possible, content in showing a specific face to whichever world we are entering.

Besides, I try to live up to my own standards of never asking a person what he does as much as possible, largely because, I just don't care and don't want to appear that I do.

"Dude, you got to go. Friday nights they do all the old-fashioned drinks. Tom Collins, Whiskey Sours, shit like that. You're a whiskey drinker, right?"

"Bourbon," I correct him.

"Same shit. They do drinks with that too. The tail that occupies space on those stools is unbelievably prime," he says, conscious to lower his voice enough so that Michelle, who's nearby but far enough away, can't hear him. "Check out Leah if you go. Huge fake titties. She used to be a Hooters girl out in Fairfax. She was on last year's calendar. Miss October or something."

His posse chuckles, making not so subtle innuendos about breasts, flotation devices, scoops of ice cream for some reason, and jugs.

"Sweet," I say, keeping my voice at a noncommittal monotone that doesn't betray my antipathy but doesn't sound too welcoming of the prospect of joining him one night.

Jaxon sees where Michelle is before he liberally takes in Jennifer and her friends. "We're going to go there tonight. You guys should come with."

"Not me," Bart says, finally finding his voice.

"He doesn't cross the Potomac," I say.

"What about you, Mikey? You cross the Potomac?"

"Only for chicks with dicks," Bart says. It comes out so matter of fact I can't help but laugh.

"Yeah, well you know… it WAS big, so…"

Bart cracks up. Never to be one on the wrong side of a private joke, Jaxon smiles broadly, although it's clear he's not sure why.

"That's cool," he says. "Text me. You got my number, right?"

"Michelle has your number," I say.

"You want to bolt?" Bart checks the time on his Rolex.

"Definitely."

"I got this." He lays two one-hundred-dollar bills on the bar, which gives Michelle about a $65 tip. The benefits of having rich friends is they never mind picking up the tab when you're a little light on funds. Sometimes this generosity embarrasses me because I don't want to always seem to be a charity case and like to pay my fair share. On the other hand, since I make a fraction of what he does, I am usually a charity case and try to make it up by being a reliable drinking partner and karaoke demigod.

I kick back the rest of my beer.

"What's in the vase?" Jaxon calls on my out.

"The heart of a small boy," I answer back before stepping out into the late Saturday afternoon air.

12

The Byline is a newspaper-themed bar in Arlington. It's a satellite location; the flagship being smack dab in downtown D.C., it used to be the main watering hole for many of the newspaper men before Watergate was a thing. Since then, the younger set moved in as they are so apt to do, pushing the grizzled reporters out. The bar lost its nostalgic appeal but made so much fucking money it launched a second place across the river. The Arlington branch is similar in layout and design, trying to capture an era long since passed where wrinkled-shirt-wearing, chain-smoking insomniacs belted down three fingers of scotch before they had to meet their evening deadlines.

I don't know who even buys newspapers anymore, paper copy being on a dangerous one-way trajectory that sunk the Dodo bird, travel agencies, and disco.

Like Days, the Byline is sparsely populated at this hour except for a few Arlington born and bred locals perched around the bar. I don't know their names but recognize some of their faces. They are the people who run the locksmiths, unclog drains, work the hardware stores, and do the general contracting. The very blue-collar jobs everyone needs, but few ever want to pursue as a career. They frequented this spot when it used to be an Uno's Pizza, not because they liked bad pizza, but because it was on the way either to or from their jobs.

That's how you know they're locals. A change of aesthetics doesn't mean these people alter how they drank or where. This place could be a gay nightclub for all they care. As long as it's open when they want a drink, then by hell or high water, they are going to sit at the bar ordering pitchers of Bud drafts. Location, location, location.

We find space at the far end of the bar, a nook that has the video trivia game. The ball games and a NASCAR event are on the televisions, but no one's really watching them. Stella's working behind the bar. She's a tall strawberry blonde who used to work at Days, then quit, then worked at SoBe, then quit. Now she works here. The funny thing about Arlington is most of the bartenders we know have worked at one or more of the bars we patronize, which gives us name recognition and an established relationship that continually develops. As long as you don't piss off the owners and get blacklisted from working in the area, being a bartender means you sling drinks; it doesn't matter what color the shirt or the logo that is on it. Personally, I've always wondered if there's a deal among the owners to keep their profit margins roughly in tandem with one another – and in doing so, they periodically rotate bartenders to keep the flow of regulars going to all of their places consistent so every bar and every owner makes a fair buck.

"Hey you two," Stella says. She pulls a Bud Lite out of a nearby ice chest then holds a Miller Lite just in case I want something else. I take the beer.

Bart slides a few dollars into the trivia game. "You seen Georgie?".

"No," she says. "He hasn't been here in a few days."

Bart nods. With his first drink, he nearly knocks back half of his beer. The first one is always quick, like a shot of medicine. Afterwards, he usually slows the pace down, but that initial taste it's like he has a burning thirst he needs to extinguish.

"You know, I took Katie out on Wednesday," he says suddenly. He peruses through the trivia categories, his fingering hovering over "Movies" for a second before he selects the "Music."

I nearly drop my bottle on the bar.

"Katie? The bartender at Capital Grille, Katie?"

"How many Katies you know? We went to that Italian joint at the harbor. How many original Supremes were there?"

"Four," I say. "Wait. Back it up a bit. You took Katie on a date. A date-date. Nice clothes and all that? Corsage?"

He rolls his eyes at me. "You think I go to the Capital Grille for Steak Thursdays just because I like their prime cuts? Their ribeye is fine, but the scenery is so much finer."

I don't know what to say. Being a barfly means more than just knowing your way around a dynamic bar scene. You know owners. You know serving staff. And most importantly, you know bartenders. You know all types of bartenders. Those that give generous pours. Those who'll give you buy-backs even though it's a generally frowned upon practice. You know bartenders you want to avoid. And yes, you know HOT bartenders. Katie fits into the latter classification. Working at a high-end steak house requires impeccable serving credentials or a non-slutty attractiveness that appeals to both the lobbyist and Congressional staffer crowds. She has both, a consummate professional with Swedish blonde hair and high Nordic cheek bones and eyes as crisp and blue as a glacier's waters.

"Wait a minute. How did you... I mean, when?"

"I kept asking, buddy. She kept saying 'no.' Fifth time was the charm."

Maybe there is something to Jaxon's wear-down and tear-down approach.

"But, she's so... so..."

I can't wrap my head around this. The whole thing literally doesn't compute, causing me to trip over my tongue in disbelief.

"Hot?" he says. "Yeah, unbelievably fucking hot. I put on my best suit. Got a car service to pick us up and drop us off. Had a great dinner. Ended up having drinks at the Gibson. It was nice. I'm seeing her on Sunday."

"Holy shit," I say. And I mean it. Katie is quintessentially out of everyone's league, save for maybe a handful of people who are clearly a cut above everyone else. People like George Clooney or Beckham or Bradley Cooper. I know plenty of people who would donate a kidney to take her on a date, or to be anywhere one-on-one with her. She's arguably one of the most beautiful women in the DMV. Don't get me wrong. Maggie is still number one in my book, but Katie is the type of person that makes you rethink the choices you've made. Hitting the progressive jackpot on Caribbean poker is more likely than being able to call Katie your girlfriend.

Bart laughs at my reaction. He inserts another dollar into the trivia game. "You ask out your squeeze yet?"

"Maggie? Yeah, no."

"Well why the fuck not?"

"Let's start with the five-hundred-pound elephant in the room. I'm not rich."

"Bullshit! It ain't about that. She's not in the most luxurious job either you know."

"Bartender ranks above paralegal last time I checked this year's *U.S. News and World Report* employment rankings. So does cleaning up the bathrooms at Union Station at the end of the day."

"You know what your problem is? Confidence. Women like confidence, Mikey. They want to know the man they go out with will be strong and self-assured. They like that. You don't have confidence."

"I don't have a cigarette."

The conversation is put on hold as I pull out my Rothman's and a lighter. Bart's right about the confidence issue, but confidence isn't something you can pick up on a whim, or despite popular belief, after a few drinks. I'm about to leave Austin sitting on the bar, but think better of it, and take him with me.

—

OUTSIDE TWO LOCALS smoke their Mavericks. One is a potbellied man in his fifties with long white hair and white goatee. He sports a faded black Jack Daniels t-shirt with the sleeves cut off. The other is a skinny woman who is pushing the other side of forty. She's got denim cut-offs and a hot pink tube top she has no business wearing out in public or any other place for that matter.

They halt their conversation a moment when they see me carrying the urn and setting it on an old *Washington Post* on the table. It seems out of place, even in an establishment that seeks to commemorate a bygone era. The paper twitches in the wind like the pulled-off legs of a Daddy Long Legs.

Austin used to buy the papers. He had subscriptions to both Washington, as well as the *New York Times,* and the *Philadelphia Inquirer.* I used to stop by his apartment in DuPont Circle and it would be a fire hazard of old newspapers stacked in neat piles according to topics splashed across the front pages.

The one thing that my friend always said was there were never more than ten or twelve subjects that ran on the front page of newspapers. One day he spent hours showing me the method of his organizational madness, his own version of a *Beautiful Mind,* teetering on that thin line separating genius from full-fledged crazy. He proceeded to "prove" how news moved in a geographic pattern not unlike the rising and setting of the sun and how headlines were just wave cusps riding out a long exaggerated current.

There were stacks of paper, articles that he had spent hundreds of dollars translating from Japanese, Turkish, and French newspapers so he could track the flow of information in its most comprehensive and natural state. His normally sallow sleepless eyes caught fire when he explained the process, advocating how it was the journalist's job to capture its movements exactly as they were and not influence its essence through extraneous adjectives or preconceived judgment. This was the guy who had his TVs permanently running on FOX News and CNN in order to follow both biases across the news spectrum because he lived in the space right in between. He wanted to live there. He needed to.

Despite his love for the Fifth Estate, Austin rarely if ever logged hours at the Byline. But the fact is he rarely drank at all. Not that he was a teetotaler, or allergic to alcohol, or was morally or religiously opposed to it. No, Austin was energized by other things, like the promise of what the news could bring. He got his highs and lows off the headlines, and the secret gems that were buried in the later pages of the later sections.

In this way we differed; I found an immediate companion in liquor;

he found a trickster hell bent on stopping him from doing what he loved: reading to his heart's content.

"Who died?" the woman in a southern Virginia accent says. Her boyfriend, husband, brother, God-knows-who, has since gone inside. When I look at her strangely, she gestures to the urn with the burnt end of her Maverick.

"Friend of mine." I take out another smoke. I see she's almost done and offer one of mine.

"Thank you," she says. Then looking at the box, "Ohhhhh, you got the fancy smokes."

"I like the way they go down."

She giggles at my unintentional innuendo. I lean over and light hers.

"A gentleman. Your momma taught you right. Three things a gentleman always does-hold open a door for a woman, pull her chair out for her, and always, and I mean always, light her cigarette."

I smile and politely nod.

She talks with her cigarette in her mouth. "So, how'd he die, if you don't mind me asking?"

"He killed himself."

"Shit. How?" Her cheeks redden when she realizes she's walked into business she doesn't need to know and quickly apologizes. "I don't mean to pry, just curious is all. I read once that how a person chooses to commit suicide tells you a lot about how they thought their life was going. I mean, it's more than just taking your life, if you think about it. It can mean something as well. Like, maybe he wanted to just give up. Or maybe he was doing something reckless just to see what happened." She inhales thoughtfully. "Maybe he just felt he was worthless."

The last one sends a chill down my spine. I touch the urn, letting my fingers run down the side.

"What do you mean by worthless?"

"Well, I don't know exactly. Self-esteem, I guess. I think people sometimes find themselves in positions they never quite expected for themselves. That can be a scary revelation, especially if you don't have a fucking clue how to get yourself out of it. Toughest judgment you can receive is from yourself."

"He drowned," I tell her.

"What? Like in a pool or something?"

"The ocean. He walked out into the ocean without trying to come back. Can you believe that?"

She regards her cigarette, mulling this over.

"Any idea what that's supposed to mean?" I ask.

"Well, it's like this. You figure shooting yourself is pretty much a one-way ticket. So is hanging. But other ways don't seem so definite, you know? Like pills or poisons. There seems to be a way back from them. Maybe he wanted to have the option of walking back."

I shake my head. "He couldn't swim, and he chose to walk right out into the biggest ocean on earth. That seems pretty definite to me."

"I'm just saying that what a person intends can be a pretty complicated thing. You can look at suicide in two different ways, sweetheart. An escape from something bad or an entrance into something new."

She takes a last drag and stubs out the butt with her the heel of her sandal.

"Thanks for the smoke," she says.

"What's your name?" I ask her before she heads inside.

"Why? You looking to ask me out?" Before I can respond, she says, "I'm kidding. Bonnie. My name is Bonnie."

"Mikey," I say.

"Nice to meet you, Mikey. Take care of your friend."

***

BACK INSIDE I find Georgie sitting next to Bart. Georgie's a little tipsy as he and Bart talk in decibels not required for the current occupancy. Having the two southern boys laugh at the same time is the equivalent of what I imagine a hiccupping rhinoceros sounds like.

I slide next to Georgie with Austin in my arms. "What's so funny?"

"You'll get a kick out of this, Mikey," he says with his deep Alabama twang. "A man and a woman started to have sex in the middle of a dark forest. After about fifteen minutes of it, the man finally gets up and says, 'Damn, I wish I had a flashlight!' The woman says, 'Me too, you've been eating grass for the past ten minutes!'."

Both crack up again. It's a pretty good joke, but not that good. Must sound better with a more robust buzz. I laugh anyway.

Georgie strokes out the hair on his chin. "Y'all headed to SoBe?"

I check the clock above the wall. "Yeah, in about an hour."

"What happened to you the other night?" Bart orders a round of shots.

"My dog had issues. He hadn't been feeling well. Didn't eat anything the night before. I figured he was fine, just moping around because I've been working so late. Next morning I'm getting ready to leave. I give him his favorite chow, a clean water bowl. A couple of treats. Still nothing. Fuck it. I got to go, right? Well, I come home to a house full of shit. I mean the dog just let it rip everywhere."

I cringe. His dog is a St. Bernard named Hercules. A shit on a good day is like picking up a bucketful of sand. That dog with the runs, you're looking at a California-sized mudslide.

"Took him to the vet. Turns out, he ate one of my socks. Messed up his G.I. Spent most of Thursday night cleaning and disinfecting, if you know what I mean."

Stella sets the drinks in front of us. She looks at me with a quick wink. I can tell it's my favorite.

"Makers neat, boys. Drink up. Happy Saturday," she says.

I pick up the glass. The bouquet of the wild honey-colored liquor hits my nostrils hard.

"Let's get fucked up," Bart says, as if there was any doubt to the night's objective.

Georgie raises his glass. "Why not?"

I knock the shot back and feel the burn on the way down and its slow climb back up against my throat. Some call it rotgut. Others call it whiskey. I call it the sweet that burns.

Getting fucked up.

Why not indeed.

WE DECIDE to walk to SoBe from the Byline instead of calling a cab much to Bart's chagrin. Based on the mass he has to move, and the fact he has two bad knees dinged up from playing college football, Bart's not a fan of walking long distances.

The evening settles into place nicely. The humidity of our summers hasn't quite taken root yet. We have about two weeks before the entire D.C. area becomes a thick wet blanket on your chest. But now it's comfortable, and we get to see pretty joggers go by in their running tank-tops and nylon shorts. Besides, Georgie and I get to smoke as we go.

"You going to tell me, or do I have to guess?" he asks me finally.

I offer up the urn. "You mean this?"

"No, your choice of dildoes. Of course, that, Mike. What the fuck's that about?"

"It's a friend of mine."

"No shit, Sherlock. Bart let me in on that. Is there a reason why you're schlepping him bar to bar?"

"You know, Georgie, beats the shit out of me. I got it today in the mail. My friend offed himself and he gave the remains to me."

Georgie gives me one of his bug-eyed looks he gets when he's on his way to being shit-faced. "Interesting friends you have," he says.

I laugh. "Present company excepted or included?"

Georgie slaps my back. "Fuck, included, man! Who was this guy anyway?"

That's the first time someone has asked me to describe Austin since I've been hauling him around with me today. Who was this guy? It's a good question. How do we describe anyone we know? Do we accentuate specific characteristics he had? Do we use a word? A phrase? What defines us as individuals, no less, as friends?

I'm stumped because the question raises the possibility that I didn't know Austin as well as I thought. Then I think, how would Georgie or Bart or anyone for that matter answer that question if asked about me?

"I don't know. He was short. He was misanthropic. We worked together at the law firm. He split like a year ago."

It's an incomplete answer but I don't really know how to make it better. Maybe I didn't really know Austin.

"He was B-U," Bart says, his breath a little labored from the jaunt.

Georgie waits until Bart catches up. "B-U?"

"Before Us," Bart says.

"He was just a guy from work," I say.

"So, what of this dude? Why the fanfare? You giving him a last night out or something?" Georgie blows smoke out his nostrils.

"Yeah. Maybe that's it."

Truth to tell, I'm still trying to figure out why I brought him out. Georgie's question sounds as good a reason as any. He mulls my answer over.

"That's the way I want to go too," Georgie says. "Someone taking me out bar to bar. You know, I may just put that in my will."

Wills. That reminds me of the time Austin found out that his mother had died. It was an uncharacteristically slow time at the firm. Since it specialized in corporate litigation, there were always at least four or five cases in some process of preparing to go to trial. Downtime was rare for paralegals since if a case was idle, you were invariably indentured out to one that needed the extra hands. But we were slow, nonetheless. I tossed a Nerf ball through a shaky hoop and he just sat at his desk, an uneaten sandwich in front of him. His mother had passed away a couple of days earlier and he was still reflecting on it. He wasn't necessarily sad about her death; he wasn't especially close to her any more than he was close to the rest of his family. Austin's silence was his way of showing respect for a woman that bore him, even if she did ignore him later on in childhood.

"She had lived her life in fear," he told me. "She was scared of marriage, scared of her husband, scared of being a mother. She was scared of just living."

Austin rarely shared details from his family life. I never knew what to say when someone shared intimate details like that. Everything came across as insincere. Expressing too much interest seemed too much a force platitude; too little interest made you seem distracted and unfeeling. People didn't share in a vortex; it was a piece of them that they casted out there to see if and how it would be received. You had to say something. My contribution was just lame.

"Sucks to live in fear," I said. It was the best I could offer.

"I'm not going that way," he said. "Not like that. Not afraid. I'd kill myself first."

"I'll tell you one thing," I said. "I'm going to be cremated. No box for me. I'm going to set up a death fund, and whoever wants to spread my ashes gets an all-expense-paid trip to Cape Cod. Cast my remains into the wind at Falmouth Heights."

He looked at me and barked out a laugh. "You thought about this," he said. "Why Cape Cod?"

"After college," I replied. "Best summer I have ever had. No school cares. No job cares. I just existed for myself and myself alone."

"You were free," he said. "I don't want to die without ever knowing I had lived."

"So, don't," I said.

"California," he said.

"When did you fall into all that movie bullshit?"

"Not movies. Writing. You can write serious news shit out there. D.C. is all politicized. So is New York. L.A. is starving for real news from real newsmen, he said."

"California is real news?" I asked.

"Real news is untainted. We should go. Me and you. Think about it. A fresh start for both of us. I'll write the news and you just write. It'd be good for you, Mike."

That was the last time we ever discussed going to California. After not seeing him for a few days at work, I went to his first-floor apartment. The door was locked, and no one opened it when I knocked. I went to the stoop and peered into the window. Not much could be seen mostly because there was nothing there. The prints of Billie Holiday and Tom Waits had been taken down. Only the nail holes were evidence of them having once hung proudly in display of anyone who walked by and peeked inside. The room itself had been cleaned; no longer were Austin's books and newspapers stacked on the floor. Those limited odds and ends that gave the space its limited personality had been stripped away, and in the process, so had any indication of my friend, or anyone for that matter, having lived there. When a girl who lived in the building came up the steps, I asked her if she knew Austin. She just shook her head. I wasn't surprised.

Two weeks later, I received a letter from Austin telling me he was in Los Angeles. He sold what little he had, bought a shitty car, packed up, and drove cross country. I'd have a place to stay once he got settled. Once I was ready to commit to the West Coast, we'd live together. Then I wouldn't be so scared.

I couldn't help but think that was deliberate on his part. Saying I was scared to move to something new.

He was right, though. Austin always instinctively knew how to reach the essence of people, pushing aside the bullshit to find the core.

About two weeks after he got there, he sent the beginning of the story.

I PULL the folded-up pages from my inside jacket pocket and flip through them now as we walk.

Re-reading the first line of the story reminds me how strong it is. The girl behind the glass. Very imagistic.

I scan the first few paragraphs. Judging from my limited handwriting, I added to it sparingly at first. After a page and a half, it's evident I'm not sure about this character. I don't know him. His motivations are uncertain, his inner drive, undefined. Even how I picture him is as unclear as viewing a face through frosted glass.

At first the anti-hero is almost comical. This outsider stumbling into a scene clearly not his own, trapped in the eddy of expensively clothed bodies swirling him around from group to group like a solitary glove dropped from a ship and forgotten. He comments on the loud music and the trendy elite that press themselves close together to be heard. Their lips hover so close to their partners' ears that they leave the faintest sheen of saliva glistening off the rims and lobes. I can picture the scene even though I've never been to L.A. myself. Crowds are the same wherever you go and you either fit in or you don't.

It becomes abundantly clear our anti-hero doesn't.

I don't remember how much time elapsed between the rabid scribbling on the pages, but Austin had increasingly taken the story to a dark place.

The hero/anti-hero strikes out with every girl he talks to at the hotel's clubby bar. It's not like he's invisible; people see him. It's just that no one cares he is there. That he even exists. Being shunned is one thing; it's a purposeful act. You have to recognize the person you're shunning, acknowledge he's there, and invest time and energy into putting up barriers. In many ways, indifference is a worse death for people looking to make some connection, if even a momentary one. A fleeting gesture that removes all doubt you are in fact a person. You are not alone. If shunning is a quick blow to the head, indifference is slow and terminal like a poison designed to amplify the suffering before everything goes dark.

Our anti-hero is at this point. Another faceless body in a room full of more interesting and flamboyant characters. He is the embellishment of the unsaid. That spot of gray in a field full of brightly colored poppies. Like a below-average batter behind in the count, he knows his time in the box is coming to an anticlimactic end.

Save for one.

The girl behind the glass reading Henry Miller.

I throw my cigarette on the ground. Skimming through the remaining pages, the bulk of what's there is in Austin's handwriting. My efforts are not as extensive as what he's written. They are also less frenzied and chaotic.

One thing's clear: it doesn't look like I did my fair share. The business of living catches up with everyone, and while that may be true, I know it's no excuse. Not really.

I think back over the past six months of my life. During this period, I went through a revolving door of dating and heartbreak.

I drank.

I found karaoke.

I sunk into work-induced depression.

I drank more.

I fell in love with Maggie.

I moped around.

I drank more.

And then this morning I woke up to find a mailman handing me over a box with an urn and my friend's ashes.

And the unfinished story.

His unfinished story.

Our unfinished story.

He had a plan for it. Would it end the way he set it up?

In death, Austin claims the last laugh. In passing, he sidesteps the responsibility of finishing what he had started, giving me responsibility to validate his words, and by extension, his choice, or provide an alternative ending?

I smile. Son-of-a-bitch.

13

W̲e hit SoBe just as the sky transitions from dark blue to charcoal gray. In the courtyard out front, a young drunk couple smokes clove cigarettes. Georgie and I exchange a look. Cloves are for the hipster set. I may smoke an English brand, but when it burns, it smells like tobacco, not some herb better used for flavoring soups or sauces.

"Dayyyum," he says. "Somebody's smoking air freshener."

The two don't hear him, or if they do, don't bother to acknowledge him. They are content in their closed-off world, staring into each other's eyes, laughing at whatever nonsense dribbles from their mouths.

The Philistines have been making their presence felt more and more. I pinpoint their emergence on the scene the very moment SoBe started offering Pabst Blue Ribbon, another hipster revivalist effort. This has been a disconcerting trend among bars in Arlington; providing cheap domestic beer as an enticement for these 20-somethings to "slum it" in their establishments as a way to generate foot traffic, and by extension, profits. It pisses me off because they usurp real estate with their frat boy airs, crowding the bar with their Irish car bombs and Jaeger shots, all the while drinking the blue-collar beer of my grandfather's generation. These hipsters know nothing about those times or working jobs where grease under your fingernails is a common day occurrence. I don't get my fingernails dirty like that either, but I have a strong appreciation for those who still do.

These are the types of people who attend private social gatherings and buy membership into places like *The Leadership Institute*, an elitist non-profit specializing in teaching campaigns, fundraising, grassroots organizing, youth politics, and communications to those barely out of college. For the life of me, I can't imagine what type of leadership qualities someone who has barely stepped foot in the professional work force has. They are all too pretty and too coiffed to understand their very imbibing of PBR is an insult to those who did something with their lives. They epitomize the soft hands of bankers used to counting money instead of earning it.

We find reprieve inside SoBe. The short bar is empty save for Benny, an older gentleman who's a transplant from Connecticut. He sits with his glass of white wine, arms folded, watching the game on the television on the wall. Benny is a good guy. He can talk to anyone and is always genuine. He's a rare breed, a throwback to times when good manners were perpetual, and you bought a round or two because it was the right thing to do. Benny comes in early to avoid the Philistines as well. I've tried to get him to sing karaoke, but he refuses. To him, karaoke is a young man's game. I'm not sure what he means by that, but that's just the type of guy he is. He knows how to throw out a statement that always makes you think.

We take seats by him. I look around for the Captain, but he's got about a half hour before he shows up. A bourbon is set in front of me. Angela smiles wide. She's a looker, much as any of the bartenders are here. She reminds me of Cleopatra: long straight black hair and black eyes and a fetching smile that reveals her bright, white teeth.

She leans on the bar with both arms. "Where're you guys coming from?"

"The Byline," Bart says a little bit too loud. He's getting drunk, but so what? It's Saturday. Who isn't?

"He's got his boy with him," Georgie says, referring to me and the urn I've set up on the bar. "That's Austin. Give him a drink too."

Angela looks at the urn and then at me.

"That's not…"

"It's just a decorative artifact," I say, picking up the glass.

"And you named it Austin." Angela says, understanding my verbal side-step. "How sweet."

"It's got a nice ring to it, no?" I say. "The last of the romantics, that's me."

Angela smiles again and shakes her head.

Georgie and I clink shot glasses and drink.

THE CAPTAIN SHOWS up at eight on the nose. SoBe has filled in some, but we own the bar. All six seats are occupied, and I can already feel that excitement of the promise of a good night. I nurse a Miller Lite trying to edge back to being drunk.

There's a table of seven sitting in front of the small stage. You can tell from the way they're dressed they are part of the Captain's contingent. He's a bit of a Pied Piper in his own way, and I don't mean just because he's been known to play a flute before he starts his karaoke set. These are people he's lived with, or taken drugs with, or slept with, or jammed with. They all have that look about them, sort of like a cross between people at a Phish concert and the Maryland Renaissance festival.

The Captain finishes setting up and bolts for a smoke outside. I follow him out.

He lights both of our cigarettes. "Where were you last night?"

"Don't ask," I say.

"When you get an answer like that you know you asked the right question." He smiles broadly.

"Went to a party, then went and passed out. I didn't get laid, if that's what you are wondering."

"Never crossed my mind, but speaking of which. This August you're coming to Fenwick, and I'm not taking 'no' for an answer. Consider this ample notification to get your affairs in order."

The past two summers the Captain has tried to get me to go to this week-long, retreat/escape/commune/fuck-fest deep in the woods of Pennsylvania. He describes it as a no-holds barred delve into the primal urges of human nature – food, sex, fun, and music. He also says it's very family friendly as well. Evolved savages, he says, trying to paint a broad brushstroke of the characters who take this quasi-religious sabbatical annually. Even retro-hedonists have a sense of responsibility to the young. I see them more as the people who woke up from their acid trips at Woodstock only to discover that the party had long since moved on. Instead of following, they remained, too unmotivated to venture forth in fear of finding out that the fun was only momentary and their lives, long.

"Fifty bucks' registration. Bring whatever food you want. If not, no biggie. People always bring more than what's needed. Eat, drink, smoke, drop acid as much as you want as long as you want. One of the Fenwick elites is a heart surgeon, and he always comes with his black bag. Working latrines, a nearby lake. It's got something for everybody." He smiles having finished his sales pitch.

"Definitely," I say. "I'm in this year. Pinky promise." I figure I have two months to come up with an excuse of why I cannot attend. Last year it was a wedding. The year before, a vacation. This year, who knows? My mind starts to rolodex file through excuses, already knowing it's on the clock.

"You're up first," he says, grinding out his smoke.

"I didn't put anything in yet," I say.

"Dealer's choice."

THE STAGE IS SMALL. Maybe ten feet wide, one foot high. Just enough to raise you above the din of the chatter of the bored and beleaguered. People like karaoke for different reasons. Some are wannabe singers, pretending for at least the duration of a hit or popular song that they are where they should be. Others like the attention, demanding all eyes to be on them. It's their voice people are hearing whether they want to or not. Me, I like it because it's my personal "fuck you" to everyone else. I don't cater to the crowd looking for yet another round of *Sweet*

Caroline or *Don't Stop Believing*. I cater to the music. To the bands that I love. Springsteen. The Pixies. The Replacements. Blur. The Clash.

And then it starts. I recognize it right away and jump right into the song. You don't limp into the Sex Pistols; you jump in with both feet and both guns blazing.

The frenzied music catches people off guard, especially as an opening number. It's a good choice because I don't have a good voice to begin with and I can't sing any worse than Johnny Rotten. The beat is jagged. Pulsing. I glance at the crowd. Most in the bar are completely turned off. They look away from the spittle flying from my mouth. I love it. What do you expect, people? It's the fucking Sex Pistols, for crying out loud. Subtleness was never part of their charm.

The Captain's table appreciates what I'm doing or else they're just too high to know better. One of the girls is kind of cute and I catch her eye. And then it hits me. Austin was the one who got me into the Sex Pistols. I'd heard them before, but he loaned me the first tape I listened to start to finish. It wasn't everyday music; but under the right circumstances, in the right emotional context, it was unbeatable.

I pick up the urn as the song comes to its climax and wave it at the audience like a belligerent middle finger. Rotten would so approve.

So would Austin.

No feelings.

The name of the song, and my general disposition to the start of my night.

AT THE BAR, Angela hands me another bourbon that I down in two gulps.

"So, who was he?" She points to the urn.

"A friend that's no longer with us," I tell her.

"Like, no duh. I figured he was your friend, but why is he with you?"

"He sort of fell in my lap today."

"I'm sorry. I hate when people our own age die. It throws our mortality into our faces."

She's right, but I don't feel like heading down a discussion about life and death and the sweet thereafter. I shrug.

"What are you going to do?"

Georgie's on stage singing some David Allen Coe. His husky southern rasp is perfect for the song. Bart talks with the night manager, Jimmy, who just started his shift. Jimmy manages Days and SoBe. He started off as a bartender at Days, working his way up to night manager until he got mixed up in cocaine and illegal gambling and ended up serving four years in a state prison in Maryland. After he paid his societal debt, the owner welcomed him back with open arms, which started a rumor that maybe he was fronting for Billy and did the time for compensation on the back end. Either way, he says he's been clean ever since, although there have been times when his eyes looked a bit too glossy to be the result of one too many if you know what I mean.

"Buy you a drink?" A voice calls out behind me.

I turn to see the cute girl from the Captain's table.

"No, but I'll buy you one." I signal to Angela for two more without even asking her what she wants to drink. If she is with the Captain's crew, brown liquor isn't the worst thing she's ever put into her mouth.

"Sex Pistols. Nice choice. I'm Chandra."

"Mike."

She smirks and rolls her eyes. "I know. We've met before."

"We have? I have to apologize. I must have been drunk."

"You were. So was I. It's no biggie. It's not like we fucked and you forgot."

"Did we? Fuck, I mean."

"I just said we didn't."

"Okay, I wasn't sure if that was a passive aggressive attack or not."

She laughs. "You get that a lot? Passive aggressive attacks from women?"

"Only my mother."

"You sleep with your mother a lot?"

"Only on Sundays. It's our special time."

She laughs again. We take a break from the parlay to sip our drinks, readying ourselves for round two.

"Don't take it so hard. Didn't you know only women understand women?" she asks.

"Yeah. It's called lesbianism. You sing?"

"Sometimes. I mostly listen. I support Donny."

I forget the Captain's crew doesn't call him the Captain. That's reserved for just us.

"Great guy," I say. She catches me looking at her legs. I immediately blush.

"The best," she says with a slight smile forming. "Why are you blushing?"

"That happens sometimes."

"What was it? When I said we had met before or when we had fucked or is it just my legs?"

"You are definitely someone not afraid to speak her mind."

"Why shouldn't I? Does sex embarrass you often?"

"Not usually. Sometimes. Mostly because I don't get enough. That was probably too much information."

"It's no big thing. It's what people do. You finally going to come out to Fenwick this year?"

"Not sure yet."

"It's a fun time. There's a lot of fucking there. Anything goes." She smiles when my ears flush red before adding, "Within reason of course."

"Of course."

I want to ask her what the exact parameters are but don't want to look like a complete sexual deviant. Besides, from what the Captain has told me about what happens there, I can't imagine what falls out of "reason" in that group.

"It's mostly a good way to just remove yourself from one world and immerse yourself into another," she says.

She tells me about an incident from last summer. They have this tent dedicated to S&M but nothing hardcore. Just some feather whips, fuzzy cuffs, a paddle board for spanking. They do a version of trivia where two teams, composed of just men or just women, compete. When a team gets a question wrong, the winning group gets to instill a "punishment" on the loser. She tells me she hasn't been spanked like that since she was a kid.

I realize how foolish my "too much information" comment to her must have seemed.

"Seriously," she says. "It was amazing. I mean, being spanked in front of a group like that. It was so liberating and so... I don't know – thrilling? People watching you bent over, Guccis down around your knees, your ass exposed for all to see... and then the paddle. Slap! Slap! It was exhilarating."

She never loses eye contact with me, watching my lip twitch and my face flush red for the umpteenth time. I wonder if the Captain put her up to this in order to guarantee my participation this year.

As she continues to talk about Fenwick, I see Catherine enter the bar with another paralegal whose name I don't remember. Anita... Jolene... something like that. Catherine glances around the room and sees me. She's cautious to approach, unsure if I'm on the make or not. When I give her a subtle nod, she comes right on over.

"Mike, is that you?"

"Yeah," I say, not sure what she's doing but trying to play off her anyway. "Catherine, right?"

"Jesus, what's it been? Three years? Four? I haven't seen you since grad school. What are you up to now?"

"You know, living the dream. I'm sorry, Chandra, this is Catherine. Catherine, Chandra."

"Hiya," Catherine says. "This guy saved me an entire semester. If he didn't let me copy his notes, I would have been screwed. I have to buy you a drink."

"I'll let you two catch up," Chandra says. "Talk to you later, Mike. Promise me you'll think about it. Fenwick is the place to be."

Chandra finds her way back to the front table.

Catherine leans in close "You looked in need of rescuing. Did I do good or bad?"

"Good. How about that drink?"

"I thought you'd never ask."

Catherine orders a vodka soda; I stick to bourbon. Anita/Jolene finds a group of friends she knows and goes over to them.

"That's new." I gesture at Anita/Jolene.

"She called me up and asked if I wanted to go out. What's the count?" She motions to the bourbon.

"Three and two. It can go either way. Where's your better half?"

Catherine stirs her drink with the swizzle stick. "In hell, I hope."

"Ah, lover's quarrel?"

"Nothing so passionate. I tried to make him a romantic dinner for his birthday, and he wanted to go out with the boys. He said he told me last week, but I know he never did. He doesn't have the imagination to fabricate an excuse or even a good lie for that matter. He makes up his mind to do things he wants when he wants."

"So, you found yourself across the Potomac."

"You talk enough about this place at work. When Anita said she was meeting some people here, I decided to come with her. I hoped to run into you and see you in your natural habitat."

"Very *Wild Kingdom* of you. Impressed?"

"Jury's still out."

She glances at some of the first arriving Philistines. The girls are young, pretty, with striking bodies. Catherine frowns.

"Oh, Mike, tsk, tsk. Are we going to be seeing you on *To Catch a Predator*?"

"Very funny. They're invaders. Believe me, if I could cut out this cancer I would."

"There's my curmudgeon," she says. "Cheers."

We stand a moment in awkward silence. For someone who knows a lot about me and me her, this seems too much of a forced pairing than a happy circumstance.

"So, you want to meet Austin?"

"He's here?" She looks around.

"More or less."

I grab the urn from the bar and hand it to her. Catherine's face remains expressionless trying to ascertain if I'm joking or being serious.

"Shut up. You're fucking with me."

"Nope. This is him. Or what's left of him."

Her eyes go wide and she shoves the urn back into my hands.

EMILIO IASIELLO

"What the hell's wrong with you?"

"What do you mean?"

"You're an eccentric guy, Mike. But this is a little too Dean Koontz, don't you think?"

I shrug. She's probably right.

Catherine sips her drink. "Two questions. Why do you have that? And why do you have that out with you?"

"Believe it or not, it was a gift. His last gift to me. Or his last prank. I'm not really sure. I'm still working that out. Want to smoke?"

She downs her drink with impressive speed and orders another.

"Yeah," she says.

WE STAND to the side of the front door and smoke. Catherine is a social smoker, which means she bums cigarettes from full-time smokers when she's out drinking. Good-looking women get away with shit like that all the time. Even when the cost for a pack of smokes is pushing the ten-dollar mark.

"So, he died and left you his ashes." She blows a row of perfect little smoke rings.

"No. He *killed himself* and left me his ashes," I correct her.

Her face registers the suicide. "That's some heavy shit," she says. "We were just talking about him the other night. I mean, what are the odds?"

"Beats the shit out of me. But he's deader than a doorknob and I'm lugging around an urn."

"You know what you're going to do with it?"

"No. What should I do with it?"

"How the hell should I know? That's your call. Obviously, he trusted you with doing what's right."

"What's that mean anyway? Doing the right thing with someone's ashes. It's not like there's a *For Dummies* book that helps with this."

"You'll figure it out. You were close, right?"

"We were best friends. He knew I couldn't be trusted with a friend's girlfriend, no less someone's final resting place. So, the more I

136

think about it, the more I'm convinced this is his way of fucking with me."

"I think it's kind of cool he did that."

"Why is that exactly?"

"You have his life in your hands, so to speak. You have the control to put him in a dumpster or a final resting place. I don't think that's a joke."

Her sincerity cuts through my cynicism.

She grinds out her cigarette. "Are we going to sing or not?"

CATHERINE PICKS out a typical girlie song. Brittany Spears or some shit. I let it pass because, well, she's a friend and she's a girl, a combination of which I don't have too many in this world. After she turns in her slip, I pass the Captain a sawbuck to get her into the rotation earlier than the other newbies that periodically show up and think they can monopolize karaoke by inundating him with slips. I think the Captain would do it for free largely because his antipathy for the Philistines runs bone-deep, but a few extra green backs doesn't hurt. He lives in a house with five other people to cut rent costs. So, slipping him a ten or twenty is the least I can do. If I promise to go to Fenwick this year, I could probably sing all night for free.

I make sure Catherine has a fresh drink before I excuse myself and cut my way to the bathrooms in the back. It's eleven o'clock and SoBe is reaching maximum capacity. The old familiar faces slowly give way to the kids who can't be bothered going downtown for fun. This is yet another indictment on the Philistines: they can't even invest effort to go into the city to spend money in the very places that want their business. When I was fresh-faced and optimistic, we were in D.C. all the time. That's what it was for; a better, more happening place. True, there were limited options in the Clarendon area at the time, but we still made the trek because that's what was done.

The Philistines are so lazy they expect fun to find them. I hate them for it because it usually does, just at the next generation's expense.

I stand at the farthest urinal along the wall when the door opens and Curt wobbles in. He's a server at the Tavern and a complete jackass, the type of guy who was born an asshole and just grew bigger. Curt's around my age, a person born into the service industry. In addition to working in most of the bars in Arlington, he claims his mother gave birth to him on the floor of a Big Boy restaurant. While I would normally call bullshit on a statement like that, if you met Curt you could see how such could be true. Much to my disappointment, when he's a civilian he usually ends up here. I do my best to ignore him, but sometimes you can't ignore annoying people. Like gnats, they find a way to buzz into your face no matter how hard you try to swat them away.

"Hey," he grunts, pin-balling his way to the commode next to me, a deviation of bathroom protocol when there's three available urinals. He's two sheets to the wind. Like most people, SoBe is where he ends up and not where he begins his nights out.

"What's going on?" I hope the neutral tone will end any further discourse.

"Was downtown at the Bijou. Carla works there now."

I have no idea who Carla is, nor have any desire to go to the Bijou, a modern-day equivalent to the speakeasy of yore. The Bijou is D.C.'s version of Dave and Busters but for drinks. People think it's fun largely because that's how it's marketed to them. Large full-page colorful print ads project the Bijou as a throwback to a time when people dressed in tuxes and gowns to imbibe illegal liquor. Where else can you get a Sloe Gin Fizz? It's the rage right now but it will suffer a quick death once the owners realize there's a reason why no one drinks Sidecars, Bees Knees, or any other ridiculous cocktail. The flocks of the easily-bored and disenchanted will move along to the next big thing (lumberjack bars anyone?), and what is prime real estate will become yet another Chipotle.

Curt barely manages a cigarette into his mouth, forgetting Virginia bars went smoke-free a while ago.

"Got a light?"

"Can't smoke in here." I finish my business and move over to the sink.

"Yeah, that's right. I always forget that. Never thought Virginia would fall."

"We all fall one time or another," I say.

"You got my lighter?" he suddenly asks.

Ugh. This again. About two weeks ago, I ran into Curt at SoBe. I was drunk, he was drunk. We were smoking outside. I bummed his lighter and handed it back to him. Since then, he thinks I took it for whatever reason. Even though I don't like him, I'd never keep his lighter, largely because it would prolong our talks. Either way, it was a shitty Bic lighter to begin with. It wasn't like it was a Zippo or one of those expensive butane lighters.

"No, man. I gave that back to you. You gotta ease up on the booze, Curt. Fucks with the brain cells."

He turns, staring at me hard with glassy, blood-shot eyes. I can almost hear the squeak of the wheel on which that hamster runs inside his head. When someone looks at you like that you can be assured of two things: he's thinking about something bad and he's thinking about doing it to you.

"Later, man." I head back out to the bar.

———

BACK AT THE TABLE, Catherine thumbs through the song menu. She glances up briefly as I take my place across from her.

"It's about time. I was about to send in help," she jokes.

"I ran into someone."

"In the john? How charming. What an interesting life you lead, Mike."

I see Curt exit the bathroom and use the wall as balance to walk down the hallway into the bar area. "It's not even worth the breath speaking about."

Catherine plays with the ice in her glass. It's a squat tumbler instead of the slender highball she had before I went to the bathroom.

"Vodka, rocks," she says when she sees the confusion on my face. "I'm playing catch-up."

I lift my glass in a toast. "Godspeed."

We drink.

"So, Austin," she says, looking at the urn between us. But whatever she's going to say is put on hold when the Captain announces Catherine is up.

"My public awaits," she says slides from the seat and walks on stage. She's up again pretty quickly for someone who just sang a few songs ago. I wonder if the short tight skirt that hugs the right curves and a blue silk blouse buttoned just so might have had something to do it. The way the Captain grins when he hands her the mic when she gets on stage tells me I'm on the right path.

And it starts. *Rolling in the Deep* by Adele.

I'm not quite sold on Adele right now. I always preferred Amy Winehouse, rest in peace.

But the song starts. And Catherine is right in the moment.

The throatiness comes through. I don't know if Catherine's practiced this song or just has sung it so many times that it flows out unforced and natural. The bar picks up; they immediately respond to not only good singers, but those who either perfectly mimic the original or somehow – and this is rare – make it their own. Catherine lands somewhere in the middle of the two. She moves around on stage as much as the microphone cord allows her. It works. People like her. I like her.

She plays to the crowd, but catches my eyes every so often, the faint corners of her mouth betraying the slightest of smiles. She plays up the Adele persona and ends strongly.

There is a lot of applause. *A lot.* All smiles, Catherine takes compliments on the way back to the table. She kicks back a good amount of her drink.

"Whoa, that was fun!" she says.

"You nailed it," I tell her.

"I just like the song," she says. "But I have to say. It's pretty energizing up there especially when everyone gets into what you're singing."

"Am I sensing a convert?"

"I just might be," she says. "I mean, I don't know if I could make a meal out of this like you, but I definitely see the attraction."

One of the servers brings two drinks over to us and points to Bart at the bar who raises his glass in a toast. We lift our drinks to him. When he's in a good mood, everyone benefits.

"Don't tell me. That's Bart," she says. "I can tell. He's just as you described him."

"One of the last southern gentlemen in the Yankee north."

She gestures to Austin. "So, you figure out where you're going to dump this guy?"

"Nope."

"Well, if you don't figure something out, people are going to talk. You'll be like the proverbial cat lady only it will be more macabre. Before you know it, people are going to start including you in their wills to take care of their remains. *Sixty Minutes* will do a story on you. The crazy urn guy."

"How much do you think I could charge for that?"

"Not as much as you think."

"You have to admit, it's definitely a conversation piece. It might attract the ladies."

"Yeah, if you want Emos and Goths." She makes a face. Emos and Goths are two subcultures Catherine hates.

"Thing is, Catherine, I don't know what I'm going to do with him. It's not like he had a place or a favorite thing to do. We just sat in his office or my office at the firm and made fun of everyone. Hell, we didn't even really go out. He'd never come to a place like this."

She nods thoughtfully. At the bar, Bart waves his hand to get my attention.

"Hold that thought." I remove myself and head to the bar.

"What's up?"

"She's here," Bart slurs out.

At first I don't know what he means, and then I see her talking with Jimmy near the swinging doors leading to the kitchen. Maggie's here with her bitchy friend, Sheila. They've changed since I last saw them. Both are in much tighter, revealing clothes, and their hair is done up just so.

The problem with Sheila I've figured is her energy is all wrong. She is pretty as long as she doesn't open that cruel mouth of hers. But once

Rubicon is crossed, her looks fade quickly without hope of ever getting back to that first impression. She needs a come-to-Jesus epiphany or at least a visit from three of the most horrifying bitch slapping ghosts.

"Talk don't stalk, buddy," Bart says.

"What am I going to say? 'Hey, Maggie, long time no see. Want to talk to me?'"

"You're a writer. Make something up."

He gives me a shove. I make my way not so subtly over to her, almost clipping one of the servers who carries a tray of Jell-O shots.

"Hey," I say to Maggie, and can immediately kick myself for not finding something wittier to open with.

"Hey Mike, you sing yet?"

"This guy?" Jimmy offers. "He sings so much he's going to cut a live album." Jimmy's a bit red in the face so I know he's had a nip or two behind the "Employees Only" door.

I go immediately blank and struggle to say something that doesn't make me trip over my tongue. "You made it out."

"We're just stopping by. We're headed to McFagin's," she says.

"Which we are late for," Sheila interjects.

"Oh, hey, Sally, didn't see you there," I say, purposefully screwing up her name.

"It's Sheila."

"I don't know why I keep forgetting your name."

"You should come," Maggie says. "A bunch of people are going to be there. You know Kenny and Melissa, right?"

I do, but there's knowing people and running in their social circles, which I do not. Showing up without previously having been invited is a major protocol gaffe that is apt to have bad repercussions like public embarrassment or a private beating. Sheila looks at me with those cold eyes as if to say, *don't you dare...*

It's so tempting to bust her balls, but I just don't have the heart. Besides, it's not like I can leave Catherine alone with the Captain.

"We'll see."

"Come on, Mags." Sheila tugs her friend's arm and heads out the door.

I go back to the table with two fresh drinks.

"You do drink a lot," Catherine says. "I know you've always said that you did, but I wasn't sure if that was just an act or not."

"Well, it's not like I'm trying to set records. It's just what we do."

"We?"

"My friends and me. We were all castoffs from our original groups and found each other in the welcoming embrace of Clarendon watering holes."

"That's so touching it should be on the Hallmark Channel."

"I told you I was a teddy bear."

"So why don't you have a girlfriend?" Catherine asks seriously.

"How'd we go from the virtues of alcohol to that?"

"Call it stream of consciousness. Isn't that what Kerouac did? Stream of consciousness writing. Well, this is a stream of consciousness conversation. Besides, we don't get to talk like this in the office."

"Like what?"

"Regular people."

"First, kudos for knowing that's how Kerouac wrote. I've said it once, I'll say it again, you're wasting your talent in law. Second, I don't have a girlfriend largely because," and I lean in close to whisper conspiratorially, "girls don't like me in that way."

She waves me off. "Oh, please. I saw the way you looked at that girl. You like her."

"That doesn't make it reciprocal. Besides, I don't know her. Not really."

"She seems nice."

"She's nice to everyone. That's her job. She's in the hospitality industry. Don't get me wrong, I think she's pretty. And yes, she is nice. But I don't know. Dating bartenders seems like a better idea than actually doing it. You know what I mean?"

"It's like rubbing scar on scar," Catherine says matter-of-factly.

"What?"

"It's too close to what you love. You love bars, that's obvious. You love pretty girls. But to date a pretty girl that's in your area of refuge may be too much. Like, what happens if it doesn't work out? Will she tell everyone your little secrets? That you're a lousy kisser or a bad lay?

Maybe you fart too much? That may be what's stopping you. Fear of failure, or maybe, just maybe, fear itself."

She makes a point.

"Cigarette break. Let's continue this outside."

I SET Austin down on an outside table as I light our cigarettes.

"My two cents?" Catherine says. "If you want to window shop, you need to window shop. See what's out there. Have a few one-night stands. Love 'em and leave 'em fast. But that's not what you really want, Mike. Maybe for a run in the sack or two, but not over the long haul. And with bartenders, you'd have to live a nocturnal lifestyle. Start your nights at two in the morning, having Mondays off, things like that. That's fine if you're in the life, but you're not. That wouldn't work for you in the end, even if you didn't work at the firm."

"So, who should I date?"

"Now there's a million-dollar question. Let's see... Someone smart. You like looks but that's just an appetizer. It won't sustain you. You also need humor. You're someone who needs funny in your life, Mike. You're a pretty serious guy. Humor balances you out. And, of course, you need a sense of perversion."

The honesty of her remark catches me off-guard.

"Excuse me?"

"What? We haven't talked? You like things that may be off the menu, so to speak. You like your kinks and therefore you need someone who has similar tastes or at least understands them. You're not a full-fledged kink machine. You don't want to wear masks and get enemas. But you want to share your vulnerability with someone without feeling... I don't know. What's the word? Inadequate? No. Embarrassed? That's not it either..."

"Different," I offer.

She looks at me. "Yeah. You want to know it's okay to like those things and she won't think of you as strange because of them. Acceptance. That's what you ultimately want, Mike. Someone to accept you. The whole you."

Acceptance. I read somewhere the first step toward change is awareness, and the second step is acceptance. Is that what's tearing me apart inside? The idea that I have to change or I'm afraid of it?

"You got anyone in mind?"

She looks at me, smiles, and shakes her head.

She laughs. "Not right now and not like this."

"Bum a light?"

Curt wobbles by me. I hand him my lighter and try to get back to Catherine.

"I knew it," he says. "Blue. This lighter's fucking mine."

"For Christ's sakes, it's not your lighter," I say. "It's a blue lighter, just not your blue lighter. But if you want it, take it. Call it a gift but just stop hounding me about—"

I don't see his fist. And when I do it's too late. It catches me right across the mouth. The punch isn't on target, but there's enough weight behind it to make a point. I wish I can say that I take the sucker punch like a man and just stand there, wiping the blood off my lip nonchalantly the way John Wayne would have.

I wish I can say that.

But what really happens is I go careening into the four-seat metallic table. My arms try to stop me from falling, but the table is already on its side and I can't grab anything to slow my inevitable hard landing. When I hit the ground, it's hard enough to knock the wind out of me.

If trying to catch my breath isn't difficult enough, Curt kicks me a couple of times in my stomach and ribs. Thankfully he's too blotto to focus, so his aim is off as well as his balance. This causes him to deliver weak blows that my forearms can mostly absorb.

Catherine yells at him to back off. I'm not sure what happens next, but after the fifth kick Catherine helps me to my feet. Jimmy tosses Curt to the side. The thing about Jimmy is he used to be a big-time amateur bodybuilder back in the day. Although that time has long since passed, his body still retains the power lifting frame that made him a summer champion in Virginia Beach. He grabs Curt by the shoulder and drags him across the outdoor patio space with ease.

"Cool off!" he orders Curt.

Curt slaps Jimmy's hand away. "He stole my lighter!"

"Get out or I'll call the cops!"

Curt flips him the bird but takes off when he thinks Jimmy is coming after him. He shouts out that I got what I deserved or some shit like that.

Jimmy looks over at me, a big shit-eating grin on his face

"What'd you do to him?"

"He thinks I stole his lighter."

"What?" Jimmy just laughs and shakes his head.

"You okay?" Catherine asks.

"Fine," I say, trying to act a little tougher than I actually am.

"Shit. You're bleeding."

"What? Where?"

She licks her finger and dabs along my lip. I cringe from the sting.

"Let's get you cleaned up."

Inside the bar, Jimmy gives Catherine some damp napkins and she takes care of my face. I ignore the curious looks from the Philistines. Some look on, confused, wondering what happened. Most don't care about a fight between two dinosaurs that didn't end up with both being hauled away in cuffs.

"Have to say, this is one of the more interesting nights I've had," Catherine says, inspecting her work between the dabbing. "Are you always this much fun to be around?"

"Don't make me laugh, I think he cracked a rib. Where's Austin?"

"Right here," she says. "He was about to tip over after you collided into the bar, but I rescued him before his ashes got muddled with the beer puddles on the ground."

"Thanks."

"Sure. Oh, and you also dropped these, when he knocked you into next week."

She smirks as she hands me the pages of the story.

"Shit." I quickly ascertain if all the pages are there. They are.

"What's that?"

"This is a story me and Austin were writing. It came with the ashes."

"My, oh my, you are full of surprises, aren't you? What kind of story are we talking about?"

I tuck them safely into my pocket. "I'll let you know when I figure it out. We had this thing. He wrote a part, then I wrote a part, then he wrote a part, and... you get the picture. I never knew how to end it and was always hoping he was going to. Instead, he passed that responsibility off to me when he sent me his ashes."

Catherine narrows her eyes in thought. I'm not sure if she's freaked out by it or just tired from a night that is about as foreign as she's used to experiencing.

"Come on," she says. "Let's get a drink."

"I thought you'd never ask," I say, about to flag down Angela from down the bar. Catherine intercepts my hand and brings it down.

"Coffee," she stresses.

"Irish?"

"Coffee."

14

A t the diner I order bacon and eggs with a bottomless cup of Joe so thick I can almost chew it. Catherine parses through the pages of the story. She's quiet, reading the words closely. From time to time, she sips her own coffee without needing to look up; a talent she's picked up from cite checking pages upon pages of legal briefs. Her attention to detail, the fastidiousness with comes with that precision, will no doubt spurn her successful career as a corporate attorney. When she commits to something, she's all-in. That's the type of person she is.

"So..." I say

She raises a finger to cut me off.

Four Philistines at a table across the way give their waitress a hard time. Three guys and a girl, they all look to be in their early or mid-twenties. Two of the guys have baseball hats turned around on the backs of their heads, solidifying the typecasting. They are loud and crass, making very audible comments about the customers around them. The waitress sighs, her patience running at an all-time low. The one hatless guy keeps asking her about things on the menu, an obvious ploy to be funny for his crew. They try to stifle their laughter but are pathetically unsuccessful.

My desire to punch them right in the face makes me think of this scene at the end of *Death Wish*, a Charles Bronson movie about an architect turned vigilante after his wife is killed and daughter raped. He dedicates his life to tracking down criminals and killing them in a way to avenge the tragedy he was unable to prevent. Bronson's character ultimately rids the city of some vermin but not before he's seriously wounded and picked up by the cops. The detective on the case gives him a pass because he understands the man's motives even though he doesn't condone his actions. The end scene shows a group of miscreants running into a woman and knocking the purse out of her hands. They don't stop but make jokes as they scurry away. Charles helps the woman, kneeling to retrieve the item but not before making a gun with his fingers and pointing it at the thugs.

I imitate art and take aim at the table and squeezing off some imaginary rounds.

Catherine slaps my arm. "What are you doing?"

"Punishing wrongdoers."

"One bloody lip isn't enough tonight?"

"Don't let that one altercation define my abilities to scrap."

"To scrap? I don't think that word means what you think it means. Scrapping is what young girls and old women do to preserve their memories."

"Mix it up, then. You know, rumble? I got to protect what's mine."

"Whatever, Ponyboy." She goes back to flipping pages.

I fork scrambled eggs into my mouth, wincing as I chew. My jaw is starting to throb where Curt snuck in a kick. The clock on the wall says one-thirty, although I know for a fact it's about twenty minutes fast. Some post-bar people are here. You can tell by their frenzied laughter and just overall loud conversations. Their buzz is still riding the high crest of the wave, looking for a quick repast of breakfast food to either soak up the alcohol or provide a shot of sustenance before the next sojourn to the after-hours establishments.

Catherine sits back and finishes her coffee.

"Wow," she says.

I study her face for some indication if she likes it or not. "What do you think?"

"It's pretty intense. It needs a general comb-over to even out the obvious places where you can tell two distinct authors are meshing their narratives together, but I have to say, it's pretty dark. I wasn't expecting that, especially after the opening. I didn't know you write like that, Mike."

"Austin started it, but yeah, I guess my stuff can be dark too."

"Don't get me wrong. It really sets the stage. And the character is just so interesting. He has such a lost quality about him. I totally get his displacement. Feeling so alone amidst a crowded room. That's a strong sentiment that many people can relate to. How are you going to end it?"

"Beats the shit out of me," I say. "I've only skimmed it a few times. The whole bury-my-ashes thing has kind of taken precedence."

"Maybe it shouldn't."

"How so?"

"Maybe they're not two separate things at all. Ever think that's why he didn't finish it himself? He wanted you to find a final resting place for him because you're the one that would know how to finish the story?"

Catherine gives me a satisfied smirk. She makes a good point. But my head hurts too much to work it all the way through. I keep thinking of Austin walking toward the ocean. The emptiness weighing on him when he took that first step, flinching as the cold water collected around his ankles, a painful reminder of the danger he was putting himself in the deeper he waded into the surf.

"I keep asking myself, what drives a person to those steps? It's not like Austin had a terminal disease or was trying to give the insurance money to a destitute family member."

"Hmmm..." Catherine muses.

"What's hmmm?"

"Well, maybe, it's not what made him do it, but what was stopping him from doing it in the first place, or in this case, what failed to? What makes you not kill yourself, Mike?"

"You're morbid, you know that?"

"I'm taking an alternative approach to getting the answer you're looking for."

She stares at me intently waiting for a response. She raises her eyebrows as if to say, *well?*

"I wouldn't kill myself," I say. "I like things. I'm attached to living for the most part. Drinking is swell. So is sex."

"What about purpose? You like purpose?"

"I like to have a purpose. I don't think I have one now, but I'm hopeful that I'm going to find one sometime soon."

"You think you can pick up purpose like you pick up a six-pack and condoms?"

"I wish I was like some people that know what they want to do and what they want to be when they're young. I'm not and I don't. I know more about what I don't want to do than what I do."

"And what about Austin. What was his purpose?"

I shake my head. "To be something better. To be a newsman."

"So maybe he was still searching for one."

"Maybe. I guess."

"Let me ask you something and don't get mad. How well did you know him? I mean, really know him? It sounds like you were barely acquaintances."

I shift in my seat. "I was his friend. Maybe his only friend."

"And yet you can't tell me if he had a purpose?"

I don't answer because I can't.

She leans across the table. "Ask yourself this question and answer it quickly. Don't think too much. Go with your gut. What did he really want and not get?"

These tactics are straight out of Psych 101 – get the patient to be instinctual and not think so much. She refuses to look away, hungry for information. I shake my head. She sits back on her side of the booth.

"When you find that out, you may have something." She glances at her watch. "Come on. Finish your eggs. We have someplace to be."

"Where're we going?"

"You want another drink, don't you?"

"Right now I'm good with coffee."

"Half-time is over. Alcohol," she says, smiling brightly.

"Aw, Catherine. You always know the right thing to say."

THAT SOMEPLACE IS A HOUSE. Not the same house that almost had me hooking up with a trans woman. This is another place, somewhere off the U Street Corridor in the District. Inside is an after-hours gathering of beautiful people, and I don't mean Philistines. This is entirely another class up in appearance, in attitude, in just about everything. It looks like an art collector's residence – large, perfectly framed paintings adorn the walls. Some of the frames probably cost as much as the paintings they enshrine. Several of the rooms are arranged to feature bronze and ceramic. I don't know if that's Feng Shui or not, but there's a distinct impression the furniture is placed around the sculptures and not the other way around.

Catherine steers me to one of the side rooms where three young stunning professionals make boredom look like a virtue. One platinum-haired Swedish blonde, one amber redhead, and one Asian – the coven is a poster board for affluent social diversity. They text on their phones while simultaneously carrying on a conversation I can't help but overhear.

"Did he text you back?" the Swedish blonde asks.

"Not yet," the Asian says, frowning.

"He will. When he does, turn off your phone. When he texts again and you don't answer, he'll actually try and call, and it will go straight to voice mail. That will drive him crazy."

"You're such a bitch-" the Asian says in delicious approval.

I turn to Catherine, not understanding why we are here.

She nods in their direction. "Talk to them."

"I don't think we speak the same language," I reply.

"Just do it and don't be such a pussy."

I hand her Austin and walk over to the group. My mind flips through the rolodex of good ice breakers. Usually the best are the ones most immediate. Like my cut lip or the bruise that's beginning to show on my cheek. The story pieces itself together. A thief taking a GW student's book bag and my intervention. Something believable but not too heroic. You can only push a lie so far regardless of what Goebbels believed.

But these aren't women impressed by feats of drunken bravado. You only see these types in the bars of high-end hotels or else at charity events and fundraisers showcased in *The Washingtonian*. These three are money brokers, associating only with the true power elite in the city. I wonder how Catherine got us here since this doesn't appear to be her normal scene either. But I'm learning more and more about my office mate as the night drags on. She loses no time in conversing with a guy with an unmistakable French accent.

Sidling my way over, I take a tactical approach behind the women waiting for a pause in the conversation to make my introduction. Positioning is very important when making an introduction. You want to be close enough to be noticed but not so close that it encroaches on personal space.

It doesn't really matter. They don't acknowledge my presence. I can blow a trumpet right next to their faces, and these women aren't going to flinch in the slightest. This doesn't dissuade me as much as reaffirm that Washington, D.C., can be as fake and one dimensional as Los Angeles, a point Austin brought up on more than one occasion. The only difference is that the adored are unknown lobbyists and Congressmen instead of A-list actors. The suck-up is still the same though, and asses are best kissed with soft lips. At least there's consistency in that.

Here goes nothing.

My hand sweeps around the overly luxurious room. "Looks like someone went to Restoration Hardware, am I right?"

No reaction. Crickets.

The joke falls flat faster than the Hindenburg post-explosion. It isn't my best, but as I pretty much expected, these girls don't even blink an eye as they press on in their conversation. So much for relying on plucky humor to break the ice. I look at Catherine who is still chatting with Frenchie. She gives me the hard look to press on.

"I'm Mike," I say, a little louder this time on the chance they may "not" have heard me speak the first time.

"Oh, Anika, you know who I met the other night at Morton's?" the redhead with the freckled nose says, turning to the Swedish blonde.

"The Cultural Affairs Officer for the British Embassy. They're having an event next Saturday at the Ambassador's House."

"I heard. Kieron over at Pearce and Stovell on K Street told me about it," Anika interjects, "I'm his arm candy. The Brits love their caviar, and so do I."

"Funny you should mention that. I was thinking of popping a handful of laxatives, stripping down, and shitting all over this rug while singing 'God Saves the Queen'," I say.

The Asian looks over at me with disgust

"I'm sorry, this is a private conversation, so if you don't mind…"

"Great. One of you speaks English. I was just saying 'hello.' I heard it was the thing to do at social gatherings where strangers congregate. I also heard you say your name as a way of introduction but was less clear on that one. So, I'm Mike, and you are…?"

Nothing. The Asian doesn't even do me the courtesy of rolling her eyes. She shows me her back and their conversation just keeps going. She talks about who may be at the Ambassador's house, who they think they can meet.

It's a lonely walk-of-shame back to Catherine, who has graciously accepted the French man's business card. She hands it to me. Gérard La Chaussée, an officer at the World Bank. *Oh, la la.* I hand her the card back. She sets it on a nearby perfectly lacquered mahogany end table.

"Well, that didn't go well," she says.

"You think? Any other bright ideas?"

"Have a drink." She hands me a drink of brown liquor. Then she hands me back Austin.

"Maybe I should have introduced you," I say to the urn, clinking my glass of the metal before taking a large sip. "You're dead, their personalities are dead…"

"Come on, we're not done yet," she says.

WE MAKE it to a well adorned hallway, cutting our way between groups of couples that are oblivious to the people trying to pass by. It's amazing. Even physically brushing by these people yields limited reaction from them, as if they can feel whether you belong to their clique or not by the lightest of touches. I even inadvertently goose a short girl in a black dress on the way and she doesn't even move a muscle. Whomever she's talking to is in for a real treat if he can seal this deal. The brush by was clean meaning she wasn't wearing anything obstructive underneath the silk.

Catherine's cell phone rings. She checks the number. I don't have to see the number to know it's Julius. She excuses herself.

"Let me take this," she says.

Catherine finds a quiet corner as I look around. Three bourbons later and my buzz is back at the level of the great Rumble in the Jungle at SoBe. I hear music playing in a nearby room and follow it. It's Billie Holiday whose soulful cracked voice is literally music to my ears at this tender hour. I find an old record player media console that has to be at least forty years old. The scratchy vinyl pops, a very reassuring sound.

"Oh lover man where can you be..."

I remember reading an interview with Billie Holiday and she said she never sang the same song the same way. And the times when I've heard recordings of her music, I think that's an accurate description. Billie sings with such depth and sadness. It's not a cut-your-wrist sadness some of today's singers convey. There's always an uptick in the way she sings. Her songs can be both melancholic and hopeful. A sorrow whose ending fosters a new beginning; an optimism that intimates things can come around no matter how bleak they seem.

It's moving to have a voice able to touch the deep recesses of a person's soul. If you feel, then she can reach you. That's Billie's power – her ability to extend beyond herself and into you. Her life was tragic; that's true. But that's an irrelevant byproduct of who she was. Billie was royalty in those few moments when her voice made a room stop talking and everyone was compelled to just listen and feel.

Billie's someone who would understand a line like, *"The girl behind the glass reads Henry Miller."*

So is Catherine.

Weird.

I watch her talk to her boyfriend of three years on the phone. I met the guy only once, at the firm Christmas party last year. He seemed decent enough. Almost six foot two, he had a linebacker's body with long neatly cropped dreadlocks that fell just past his shoulders. Julius might have looked like a thug, but he was well-spoken and comfortable in an inter-racial relationship. Rum and coke was his beverage of choice and although he didn't contribute to the conversation voluntarily, he politely answered questions directed to him. As is my habit, I tend to side with all things men when it comes to disputes with the opposite sex. I always seem to see their side better and that may be because of the pair hanging between my legs.

But Julius is different. I only hear how he mistreats Catherine, and I don't mean physically. He's never raised a hand to her as far as I know, and I think Catherine would tell me if he did. But he's not there for her emotionally. That much is clear. The things she does for him, to him, warrants more than he's giving in my opinion. Why she's with him, one can only guess, though I can't help but think it may have something to do with size and girth. That seems crass, I know, but when you haven't had a girlfriend in a long time, the only reason women are with men comes down to size: size of their cocks, their wallets, their houses. It's a jaded view, but when you have nothing, the most convenient answers are the easiest to grasp onto.

Her voice gets louder, and I know he's said and/or done something to set her off. For someone with usually an even keel, getting Catherine to that level of anger is extremely difficult. It also means you've incurred the ire of someone whose wrath is best avoided.

She hangs up and is so mad, I think she's going to toss the phone through the window. Catherine is passionate that way. It's hard not to be, especially when you invest yourself 100 percent into everything you do. Whether it's copying legal briefs or trying to keep a relationship together, she's always all-in until there's nothing left in the till to give.

"Come on." She grabs my hand and pulls me toward the hallway. "I need a drink. I need a shot. You want to do a shot with me?"

My liver protests, but she needs it and what the hell? Maybe I do too.

We head over to the makeshift bar in what appears to be the third living room and she pours two fingers worth of Tequila into short glass tumblers. No plastic here.

"I prefer darker…" I stop myself when I see that she's on a quest and know nothing that I say is going to stop her from her chosen destination. She hands me a glass.

"You know where that shit-head is? He's at FOAM. He told me he was just going over to Jamal's and hang out with the boys. What a fucking liar."

She downs her shot and looks at me. I down mine but not without a little trouble. In my defense, it's difficult to cross hard liquors when you're drinking them neat.

"Why do boys lie?"

It's a good question. It could go for both sexes, but she's not in the state for an objective debate.

"We lie because we are afraid we won't like what would happen if we told the truth."

"I don't buy that."

"Well, I can only speak from personal experience. I don't know why Julius lies or would lie. I mean, maybe he did go out with the boys and they decided to take their game on the road? Or maybe he lied because he didn't want to hurt your feelings with the truth – that he wanted a boys' night out with his crew instead of hanging out with his girlfriend."

"On his birthday," she reminds me. "This was a makeup dinner for Friday, remember?"

Now I do. That's twice he's pushed her off. Such a douchebag move.

"I never bitch about him spending time with his friends. I've sacrificed things that I wanted so he could do that. He knows that. He can't give me one night?"

She pauses to pour a little extra in her glass.

"Do you lie to girls, Mike?"

She wants the truth, so I tell her the truth. "I have."

"What about?"

"God, lots of things. Let's see. I've lied about liking gifts or pretending to like their friends and families."

She waves me off. "Not that stuff. I'm talking about real things. More important things. 'Couple' things."

She's looking for honesty, not the right thing to say.

"I've lied when I've cheated on them," I say.

"You cheated on a girlfriend, Mike? You don't strike me as the type." She sounds disappointed, and I feel bad even though it's not like I cheated on her.

"It's the truth. I'm not proud of it, but I did it nonetheless."

"Why?"

"I don't know. The few times I did cheat, it wasn't like the girl was any prettier than the one I was dating. It was just there. It was convenient. She was different. New. I was new to her. It's not like it was an ongoing affair. Both times was just one night and then that was it."

"Hugh Grant Syndrome," she says suddenly.

"I'm not following you."

"Remember when Hugh Grant got arrested for soliciting that prostitute in the nineties? That woman was not more beautiful than Elizabeth Hurley. But he still had the need to get something on the side. Maybe Liz didn't give blowjobs or jiggle his balls the right way. Maybe he didn't think blow jobs were a big deal because it wasn't like he was sticking his dick into another vagina. But that's still no reason to cheat."

She finishes another Tequila and checks her watch. It's two-thirty in the morning.

WE HAVE a cigarette outside as we wait for the cab. I'm impressed with myself that I'm still lugging around Austin all this time and haven't once dropped him or left him someplace, especially with the mix of booze swimming in my system. Either I'm a better friend than I thought, or else I'm beginning to develop an idiosyncratic attachment to dead things.

"All kidding aside, Mike," she says, interrupting the silence. "I flirt with you all the time. I like you. You're a nice guy. But I would never be with you when I'm in a relationship. You know that, right?"

"I got that. I mean, to be honest, at first, I didn't. I figured you were just a progressive woman."

"You mean you thought I was a slut."

"At the time, yeah. But I know you aren't like that."

She looks a bit hurt when I tell her the truth, but bounces back quickly. Catherine can handle bluntness with maturity unlike the rest of us.

"I'm not someone who likes to spread extra heartbreak."

We stare at the empty road for a while. My mind goes back to the unfinished story. I take it out and turn to the final few pages. The last part of it was written by Austin. The sections he authored show a progression toward a dark climax. While I usually don't mind dark endings, this one is unnerving because I can't help but think I'm getting an inside glimpse of how he changed, and this may be part of the reason we ceased calling one another. Whatever he experienced had reached a boiling point and this was his final attempt at trying to make sense of it all.

THERE'S a part in the story where the anti-hero feels in his pocket for the pistol he bought earlier that day. The cold handle butt is reassuring to him. A comfort.

He's almost made the full rounds at the bar and has been shut out and shut down by pretty much everyone there, both male and female alike. Desperation starts to take over, blooming from within him and expanding out, eating up any hope that remains. There is this brief moment when he looks at the crowd in front of him and understands he is not part of this society, but an outsider, something he is always destined to be.

And in that moment of realization, he goes into the bathroom and locks himself behind a stall door. He takes out the gun and inspects it. A small .38 snub nosed revolver. He feels the weight in his hand, inspecting inspects its lines, its shapes. His fingertips trace the smoothness of the nickel plating.

The revolver seems almost like a novelty item, so small and almost feminine. In this period of frequent mass shootings, where heavy, multi-magazine and high caliber weapons are critical to achieve the maximum casualties possible, the .38 in comparison seems too much like a toy to be taken seriously.

The irony makes him smile.

What a truly wonderful thing I hold, he thinks to himself. How something so small can change so much with just a simple pull of the trigger. He imagines the crowd staring doe-eyed at it, disbelieving any weapon other than a Glock or Sig Sauer could do any real damage.

And there's this sense he's either going to go on a shooting rampage or he's going to kill himself. This social outcast, this miscast actor in a play, has made a decision. You don't know what it is at that moment, but you sense a course of action has been decided.

EVEN THOUGH I know I didn't write it, I realize I could have easily done so.

The character's at a turning point in his life.

He's lonely.

He doesn't fit in.

Something has to change

He has to change.

But he can't conform to the reality in front of him. That's not who he is.

And as he tries to seek validation from these vapid people, he comes to the realization there is no redemption to be had. His life is where it is and that's all there is. And as the drinks start to numb him, he starts to prepare himself for a moment of decision. The forked road is in front of him and he must choose a path, for better or worse, to head down. And neither one is well-lit nor inviting.

It's a sentiment we both shared for a long time. We never really discussed it once we became friends. There never seemed to be a need to self-explain. But we knew it instinctively because we both lived it on a daily basis. We saw it in each other, and in quiet recognition, it seemed to be enough.

Alone, it was difficult to face the day. To see people you hated in a job you couldn't stand going in a direction you never envisioned for yourself. It was an overwhelming existence that could ultimately devour you without a second thought.

But with a kindred spirit, the struggle became manageable. You don't need numbers to go against a majority; you just need similar sensibilities. You need someone to validate your thoughts, and beliefs, and feelings. You need to be able to validate someone else's.

Not being part of something greater than yourself can be a self-imposed burden as well as source of strength and individuality.

The headlights of the cab pull into the driveway.

"Come on," Catherine says. "Let's call it a night."

I walk over to the cab and open the door for her. Catherine smiles, touching her hand on my arm the way girls do sometimes.

The cabbie fiddles with the radio. "Where will it be?"

Before Catherine can answer, the words escape my lips without filter. Even she is surprised and looks at me with a genuine surprised expression on her face. I wager for the first time in her life, this strong, proud woman is speechless.

"FOAM," I blurt out. "We're going to Club FOAM."

15

FOAM is a nightclub scraped out of the recesses of an abandoned warehouse in Southeast D.C. Originally a gay dance club, the advent of a highly successful lady's night to spurn revenue has caused it to be overridden with heterosexuals, a rare occurrence in a very gay-friendly location. Now the club has a "gay night" on Wednesdays, but only between the hours of 7-12. After that, it reverts back to its loud music, roped-off VIP sections, and overpriced bottle service for the tables.

Regardless of the clamor raised by social issues advocates for all measures of equality, in the end, money makes the world go around.

Over the past two years, FOAM has been substantially remodeled and re-packaged. A new promoter invested 10 million dollars to refurbish it into its current condition. Inside is a spectacle worthy of a moveable feast for the senses. FOAM uses the same concept controller that runs the lighting effects at Epcot Center in Disney World. The warehouse has been artfully divided into a DJ sound stage complete with 300 separate light fixtures along the ceiling over the dance floor. A separate but adjoining room hosts a long bar with 15 mixologists that runs almost the full length of the wall. Drinks are not allowed out of this section. The 20/20 Room, or the VIP section of FOAM, offers the illusion of exclusivity for those willing to expense 20 bottles of Cristal or 20 bottles of Grey Goose for the evening. It doesn't matter if you drink them or not, the 20/20 charge is the price of admission to sit among the privileged. Unlike other private rooms at other trendy clubs, the owner doesn't cordon off the 20/20 Room with velvet rope; here the elite clientele sit high up on an elevated platform that separates them from their lesser-statured admirers and sycophant wannabes.

Oh, and there's also foam.

At certain periods of the night, but especially just before closing, foam shoots indiscriminately from nozzles and fills the dance floor in bright, neon blue, purple, red, yellow, and finally pink hues. Pink is how they always end the night at FOAM, a casual nod to its former gay days. From the pictures I've seen, it looks like a washing machine exploded. People in their thousand-dollar outfits laugh hysterically when this happens. Foam gets all over their silks, their leathers, their suede. Like the Jazz Generation plunging into fountains with their tuxedos and evening gowns to celebrate their rebellious spirits, these bored rich (and not so rich) glitterati show up weekly to indulge their in-the-moment carefree lifestyles by paying fifty-dollar cover charges and twenty-dollar drinks to get their trendiest outfits damaged by cheap Chinese-made suds.

The outside still looks like an old soda pop bottling plant. Only the long herd of aspirants chomping at the bit to get inside betrays the establishment's true hedonistic promise. The cab lets us off and I'm immediately depressed at seeing the snaking column waiting to be approved by the doormen. Even after-hours clubs close their doors at four a.m.

"We're screwed," I say.

"Hush up and follow me," Catherine orders.

She takes my hand and leads me past the smirks and quips of the people in line trying to figure out if we are people of importance or just ballsy interlopers about to get a rude awakening to the proper etiquette of D.C.'s hottest nightlife.

Catherine marches right up to the largest of the three doormen perched in front like Kerberos before the gates of hell. He's large, which goes without saying when it comes to bouncers and security personnel. It's just that he has a *quantifiable* size of largeness one expects of an individual whose former profession was offensive tackle for the Washington Redskins. Catherine informs me he was a third stringer that didn't see much if any playing time and lasted only three years in the big leagues. I wonder if he now realizes a parks and recreation degree and a 320-pound body don't lend themselves to a vocation outside of sports and carnival diversions.

"Hey Ray-Ray," she says, putting on her charm.

His impassive face breaks into a huge grin, exposing large white teeth.

"Snowflake," he says. "Where you been, girl?"

"The real question is: where haven't I been?" she offers. "And don't you even think about it. These lips are sealed."

Ray-Ray lets out a big laugh that I can only classify as a "guffaw."

"I want you to meet a good friend of mine. This is Mike. Mike, meet Ray-Ray."

"Hey." I offer my hand. It disappears into his as he gives a limp-fish shake. Apparently, he immediately reaches the conclusion I'm not a threat and skips trying to figure out who squeezes the hardest.

"Julius inside?" Catherine asks.

"Yeah, he in there," Ray-Ray says. Then he adds, "With people."

The subtle ambiguity is not so understated that the meaning is lost. Catherine's face gets very serious.

"I want to see for myself. Will you let me do that?"

He shifts his weight from foot to foot, debating if he should or not. Just when I'm certain he's going to send us away he nods his large head.

"Yeah, go on in."

He motions for one of the other guard dogs to unhook the maroon velvet rope to give us passage. Ray-Ray gives me a long once-over trying to assess if I'm really a friend along for the ride or the next boy looking to plant his flag.

"What's that?" He points to the urn.

"It's a present for my mother."

"You can't bring that in here."

I feign offense. "You don't allow presents in here?"

"I don't know what it is. It could be a bomb," he says.

"Oh, for God's sakes it's not a bomb," Catherine says. "Ray-Ray, it's me."

Ray-Ray finally relents and nods his approval. I hold Austin closer to me as I pass Ray-Ray and the rest of the Funky-Bunch. When I look back to say thanks, his heavy eyes are locked on me. They don't even blink. I guess when you play at the professional level, and you're physically more intimidating than most of the population, no one makes you bat an eye.

Inside is slamming. The bass is so heavy I feel it in my heart. Lights flash so quick and bright I think I'm going to have photo epilepsy. The problem with club music is it can only hold you for so long; the repetitive beat hammers until you feel flat and disengaged. On the other hand, most of the club rats, from what I can gather, are having a good time. I can't be sure because there are too many bodies pressed against one another. For a moment, I'm not sure if I'm on the dance floor or in the throng of people waiting to get overpriced drinks at the bar.

"I'll get us some drinks," Catherine says and disappears before I can tell her that I don't need one.

The real reason I don't want her to go is I don't want to be left alone. I'm not a frequenter of such establishments and feel as foreign standing here as Ray-Ray would standing in line to get into SoBe. Personally, I derive no satisfaction or pleasure being force-fed fun through a fire hose of lights and music, even if the girls are pretty. There's just too much going on. How people pick each other up in places like this is beyond my comprehension. I can't hear myself think no less try to be able to hear someone else talk.

Maybe this is what the future has in store for us. Instead of trying to meet people through conversation, you go to places like this, eye each other up, and copulate to perpetuate the human race listening to extended dance remixes of Nicki Minaj.

I look at Austin and can't help but think how funny this seems. We swore we'd die before we stepped foot into a place like this. In fairness to Austin, he's stood by that promise. Here I am just the same amidst the unorganized chaos convulsing to the rhythm of the night.

Catherine hands me a beer. I didn't expect to see her until closing with the line in front of the bartenders, but she knows people, and whether you're in a country club or in the hippest D.C. funk club, membership has and always will have its privileges.

"I think he's over in the VIP section," she says. "That's what Darnell the bartender told me."

"Is there anyone you don't know?" I ask her.

Her look is curt with just enough sharpness in her glare. Catherine's not in the playing mood right now, and I immediately shut up. Her eyes mechanically scan the faces in the VIP room with the precision of a biometrics scanner.

Julius is hardly the most well-off individual in Washington. He and Catherine live together, something he agreed to once Catherine insisted on paying the lion's share of the rent and expenses. I'm not quite sure what Julius does for a job. He dresses well largely from the fruits of Catherine's overtime hours on nights and weekends. Unsurprisingly, his tastes run along the lines of Bruno Magli shoes rather than penny loafers, and Hugo Boss shirts instead of what's off the rack at Target.

"Come on, I think I see him," she says, and I dutifully follow her through the crowd. We head up toward the entrance of the VIP section where we encounter yet another keeper of the velvet rope. Only this guy is bigger than Ray-Ray, if that's possible. He has a face that would make the heads on Easter Island look like comedy masks, with a clean-shaven head and a neck that sprouts out of his shoulders like a tree trunk. His forearms are massive and folded across his chest. At their base they are each about as wide as my waist. I have little doubt there are very few people that give this man pause.

"Heya Giggles," she says. "Julius in there?"

Calling this guy "Giggles" is like calling me "Tank."

"Ah, Snowflake," he says in a deep baritone voice. "What do you think?"

Catherine's eyes darken and she looks like she's ready to spit fire.

"Is it Tamika? Is he in there with Tamika?"

"I don't know who he's with."

"Fuck that, G. You know, now tell me. Is she there, yes or no? Don't bullshit me. I'll know if you're lying or not."

Catherine has a way of putting herself at the level of whomever she's with. In this case, the level is of someone pushing six foot eight inches tall with fists the size of two steam shovels.

Giggles looks sheepishly at her, the mannerisms of a boy caught in lie. The Catherine-affect.

"Yeah, 'flake,'" he says. "She's in there with him."

It's what she expected but never wanted confirmed. Catherine takes a deep breath and looks at me. What can I say? I just nod to show her support.

"Let's go." She pushes past Giggles and drags me behind her

Giggles doesn't try to stop me. He is well-versed in the adage of hell and fury and scorned women, and probably has been on the receiving end of that wrath at one time or another. Or he might have had a mother teach him the finer things about women. Either way, he isn't going to get in the way of that, especially since he is not the one who caused it. I wish I remembered to look around to see if I recognized anyone in the elite spaces of the best club in D.C., but I'm too worried about Catherine and hope she knows what the hell she's doing.

Julius sits at the far end of the VIP room at a semicircular sofa/table combo. He's with three of his friends and four women. Julius has his arms around this young woman I can only assume is Tamika. Her hair is in long tight cornrows with white beads. She wears designer glasses and simple but stylish clothes: designer jeans and what looks to be a black backless pleated blouse (don't ask why I know that, I just do). The group is immersed in their own discussions, locked away in the private enclave of a room full of the rich and glamorous. Maybe they are loaded too, I don't know. Maybe they just want to pretend for an evening. They are a small world unto themselves, unto their own needs and desires.

Julius doesn't see us at first, which I find hard to believe as Catherine makes an unfettered beeline to him. I mean, how do you miss the fact a shark is swimming straight at you? Catherine makes it in front of the table before he looks away from Tamika.

"You want to tell me what the hell's going on?" Her voice is firm but measured, not letting emotions get the best of her. She's controlled that way, able to think and act rationally even in situations where the opposite is warranted and probably expected.

It takes a second or two for Julius to register her. He stares blankly trying to put this face in context to his location. When he finally does, he immediately sits up, launching into desperate "spin" control.

"Baby, what are you doing here?"

"Never mind what I'm doing here, what are you doing here?"

"We were kicking it at Spider's crib, and, you know, decided to head out for a few drinks."

"With dates?"

"Them, not me, baby. Tamika's just keeping me company. I didn't want to be no third wheel. You understand that, right?"

Tamika rolls her eyes and picks something from her long pressed-on nails. She doesn't have a dog in this fight, and it shows on her face. Tamika's strictly along for the ride and from the bemused expression on her face, enjoys the fact Julius is squirming in the hot seat.

"Can we talk about this later?" Julius desperately tries to avoid a conflict from which he will not recover quickly. Not to mention being emasculated in front of his friends, and the rest of FOAM's VIPs.

"Now. Over there."

His boys climb out of their seats to make way for him. They watch as Catherine leads him to the back of the room. Taking this opportunity, one pays the check and they all bolt out before being unnecessarily dragged into this couple's spat. Only Tamika remains at the table. She doesn't glance over at Julius and Catherine. Instead, she helps herself to the champagne in the bucket.

"Why don't you cop a squat? This may take a while," she says to me.

I slide in next to her with Austin.

"Want some champagne? It's Cristal. It's on them so might as well drink up. Nearly a full bottle here."

"Sure. Thanks."

She pours me a healthy glass.

"To boys spending too much money." She takes half the glass down. "So, what's your deal?"

"Who me? I'm nobody. Just a friend."

"We're all friends of somebody, Mr. Nobody. I mean, who are you?"

"Oh, I'm Mike. I work with Catherine."

"Tamika."

"I figured."

She shrugs. Tamika looks over at the urn.

"Who died?"

"My friend."

"He a nobody too?"

"What?"

She rolls her eyes. "Relax, player. I'm just fuckin' with you. I know he's your friend unless you have a thing for carrying around a stranger's ashes. Which if that's your thing, that's cool. I don't judge or anything."

She finishes the glass and pours herself another.

"So why bring him here? Your friend liked clubs or something?"

"Austin? God no. He fucking hated them."

"And so, you're bringing him around here is to what – fuck with him in the afterlife or something? Mess up his karma?"

"Not exactly. But between us? I don't know what to do with him. If anything, I think this is his way of fucking with me."

Tamika narrows her eyes, skeptical.

"No, that shit's a serious responsibility. My aunt got herself cremated. My uncle keeps her in the kitchen. She used to make pies. All kinds of fruit pies. Cookies sometimes too. If she saw you lingering in her kitchen, she'd push you out with a broom. It was her favorite place and so that's where she sits. What was his favorite place?"

"I don't know."

"What do you mean you don't know? You're his friend, right?"

"If he liked the Lincoln Memorial or Mount Vernon or something, this wouldn't be an issue. I'd scatter him around, say something nice, and go back to my life. I've had him a full day now and I'm no closer to figuring any of this shit out."

She refills my glass.

"You just got him today? No wonder you're lugging him around. Thought that maybe some booze would get the ol' noggin juiced? Figure out a path through the woods and shit."

"Something like that."

"White people are crazy," she says.

"It's complicated." I try to gather my thoughts. "We were close when he was here. Then he moved away to California. Didn't really talk to him much then. We wrote letters, but that's about it."

"Wrote letters? You have heard of the phone, right?"

"He hated the phone. So do I."

"I see." Tamika takes a thoughtful look at her glass. "So, what I'm hearing is regret. Is that right? You sorry you didn't get to talk more?"

"Who, me?"

"You ain't dead, are you? Your friend is. What didn't you do for him in life that you're carrying around a fucking urn all over D.C. for then? Yeah, you're sorry for something."

I think hard. It's a direct question. Something I haven't considered before.

"Go with him," I say finally. "He wanted me to go with him to Los Angeles. I didn't."

"You didn't or you didn't want to?"

"I didn't want to."

"Ah, now we're getting someplace... what was your name again?"

"Mike," I say.

"That's right," she says. "Okay, now. You didn't pursue manifest destiny and all that shit. Why? You got a good job? You bleed D.C.?"

"I'm a paralegal."

She makes a face like I just farted in front of her mother. "And you like that shit?"

"I hate it."

"You got some sense at least. Paralegals are just one step above chicken sexer."

"What the hell's that?"

"Farm job. Tell if a chick is a boy or girl."

"People do that? That's awful."

She shrugs. "Paraslave is no better. You still deal with other people's messes, you know what I'm saying? So, the job didn't keep you rooted. Was it a girl? Your honey? Someone you didn't want to let go of?"

"I haven't dated anyone serious in a long time. Dates here and there, sure, but nothing over the long haul."

Tamika nods.

"Maybe it's a girl you want to be yours. You got someone like that in your life?"

I think of Maggie and start to flush.

Tamika laughs.

"Alright, alright. Who is she? Snowflake?"

"What? No. A bartender where I go."

"She know about it? Your feelings, I mean. She feeling the heat?"

"No. I haven't told her."

"Ever? Damn, you give up your boy's back to stay for this girl and you never even asked her out? That's some messed up shit right there."

"What if she says no? I couldn't go back there."

"So what? There ain't like a million places to score a drink in D.C.?"

"I really like that bar."

"Hold up. You one confusing boy, Mike. You like the bar, or you like the girl?"

"Well, both really…"

Tamika shakes her head. "My two cents? You like her, you make a play. You just like to look at her, that's a different game altogether. But I got to be honest. I don't think that's it, Mike. Nope, that doesn't sound like that's keeping you fixed to your spot."

"I'd be very appreciative if you told me what is."

"What do I look like to you? Sigmund Freud? Damn, player, I just met you. But I will offer you this. Keep pressing, Mike. The answer is somewhere in there–"

She taps my chest with her finger.

"You just have to find it," she says.

I sip the champagne. What am I looking for?

"Everyone dies," Tamika says matter-of-factly. "It's just that love dies faster. You don't believe me, just look at those two."

I glance over at Catherine and Julius. He has the desperation of one pleading a case without a lot of evidence to support his position. Catherine stands, looking him dead in the eye, unflinching. I wonder how she'd do in a stare-down with Ray-Ray. She's not budging. I can't tell if this is one of her tactics or not. I've heard about these blowouts in the office but have never seen it in person before. Usually, she makes him self-flagellate before taking him back. A week or two passes, gifts provided, sex ensues, and before they know it they're back to square one.

"Let me ask you something. You think they love each other or is this just a relationship of convenience?"

I turn back to Tamika. "She likes him a lot."

"Julius loves nobody but himself. He's not even a legit player. He likes to think he is but he's all pomp and bullshit. Flash without the substance."

"Then why are you with him?"

"Oh, honey, he wants in these panties, he's got to ante more into the kitty than just champagne. Julius is still a kid trying to fit into his big boy pants. He's good for laughs. So what? If you asking if I'm with him, the answer is a fucking 'no-way.' Would I get with him? Not even for a night. I don't wreck homes, Mike, I build them. The shit between them is a card house set on a pile of sand at the onset of a hurricane, feel me? It's not going to last because it never was set up to last. It was constructed as an experiment, see? Like a model. Look, an inter-racial couple can find compatibility. But that ain't the same as harmony. And it ain't about race. I'm not talking about black and white or red or any other fucking color of the rainbow. I'm talking about who you are on the inside. And how you act. And how you treat people. That shit's forever."

A long silence permeates. The urn has lost its shiny gunmetal newness since I opened the box this morning. It's been dinged and scraped along the way, battle scars from an evening that never seems to want to end. Austin was never much of a drinker; that was always my game. But he's been in it tonight, even if only in a posthumous manner. I can't help but think he'd find a blissful irony in the fact he's been to more drinking establishments in a single day then he probably had his entire time in the DMV.

What am I going to do with you?

And as that thought lingers, the whole room erupts.

Everywhere soapy bubbles shoot out of various nozzles tucked away in the ceiling. They rain down on the club in a thrash of pink foam. The crowd explodes in a fury of cheers and whistles; it's officially the end of the night, at least for the club-hopping crowd in Southeast D.C. I see one Latina girl who looks too young to even have made the cut at the door try to gather up in her arms as much of the pink foam as she can. A few drunk guys pretend to swim in it. The rest jump up and down as if this is the moment they have been waiting for all evening, not so much as an escape, but as true believers in a night without end, that would never end, as long as the pink foam keeps flowing.

These people are joined by this common experience of wanting something *more*, and in coming here, they achieve that end. It doesn't matter that they won't see each other during the week or back in the club next week for that matter. There will be someone else here, someone who mirrors their own selves, and their inner desires. They will laugh, drink, dance, and wait until the end of the night when the pink foam will fill their room and their expectations. And then they will find completeness.

Austin wanted to go to Los Angeles.

That was not my inner desire. Even Tamika recognized that, and she had just met me.

What is my inner desire?

What is it that I really want?

Catherine storms over to me, pushing the pink foam away from her face.

"Ugh, this is annoying." She doesn't look at Tamika, nor vice versa.

"Yeah," I say. "But I thought this was your scene."

"I didn't realize how stale it's gotten," she says. "You ready to bolt?"

I slide out and grab Austin.

Tamika sits back, sipping her champagne, watching the pink bubbles dance in the shuttering of the strobe lights.

"Thank you, Mike," Tamika says.

"Thank you? For what?"

"For an unexpected but delightful turn to my otherwise predictable evening."

I don't know how to answer and just give her a smile before Catherine tugs me along. She cuts a path though the beautiful and damned, and seeing these gyrating fools reminds me of that scene in *Independence Day* where the mindless idiots on top of the building ogle in wonder at the spaceship moments before it blows them to smithereens.

There is a logjam of people up front and I take the opportunity to wipe foam off Austin on the back of some guy's shirt before we exit. Austin would have appreciated the sexualized innuendo of the gesture if he was here with me.

WE DON'T TRY to fight with the crowd of people waiting for taxis. Catherine knows a good spot about a block away where cabs are more likely to drive by. I sometimes forget the trendiest places happen to be in locations that are not necessarily the safest. When we reach an intersection, I recognize the name of the cross street where there was a double homicide the week before. A half-block in any direction could find yourself at a drug corner or a gang's turf. Neither one takes kindly to strangers. When it comes to partying, clubbers don't mind risking their lives in pursuit of fun, whatever that definition entails.

"Are you going to tell me how it went, or do I have to guess?" I light up a cigarette as we walk.

She storms down the street.

"What's to say? He's a jerk. Story of my life. I find the lowest pieces of shit I can find and try to make them better people."

"There are worse things," I tell her. "More importantly, how are you doing?"

She tops walking. A long sigh expels from her mouth and her eyes look suddenly tired or sad, or more likely, the combination of them both.

"I don't know. Incensed. Miserable. Confused. I want to put him through a wall. I want to go home and throw out everything that's his and change the lock. But we'll probably get back together before the weekend is out. How's that for pathetic? I've been in this position with him a thousand times, and each time, we find ourselves together."

"Why?" I ask.

"Why what?"

"Why do you put yourself through that?"

"You can't be serious. You really aren't the one to be lending advice on love matters, Mike."

"I'm no pinnacle of virtue. I get that. But I also know that you deserve better than some freeloading asshole taking advantage of you."

"What do you care? It's my life."

"It is your life. That's why you should aspire for better."

"Is that what you've been doing? Tell me, Mike, when's the last time you were excited about something – anything? You hate your job, yet I don't see you do anything about it. You're not looking around, exploring options. You're not going to school. Hell, you aren't even writing. You used to write all the time in your office. Now, every time I come back to your desk, you're staring off into space. And girls, Mike. What about them? You look at girls, but don't want to talk to them. Shouldn't you aspire for better too, or are you content with your mediocrity?"

Each observation strikes with the precision of a dart and stings just as much.

"I deserve that."

"You bet your ass you do. Because it's not easy seeing someone you care about sabotage himself a little more every day. That becomes painful to watch. Am I in a great relationship? No. But it's the only one I've got and I'm trying to keep it from falling apart. What's your excuse?"

There's no response when someone confronts you with the truth. Any argument looks apologetic and weak. She's right of course. Where am I going? It's the same question that keeps popping up. It's rephrased but the intimation is the same and where I find myself failing to answer.

Austin had a plan. He was sick of the shit that was his life and did something about it. It took two suitcases and a crappy old car, but he drove clear across the country to make something new for himself. And when he discovered that the promise of L.A. was gilded in fool's gold, he did something about it. Yes, it was selfish and bat-shit crazy, but he changed his reality into something else even if the outcome was ultimate and extreme.

Maybe that's why I'm stuck in the rut I'm in. People say change is good. That the possibility of what could be outweighs the quantified known. But I don't buy that, because when I see change around me, it hasn't always been for the better. Sure, I could leave the law firm, but to go where? What if I end up in a more mindless place than the one I'm at now? And Maggie. Sure, I could ask her out and she could say yes. And what if we do go out and it turns out she's not the person I imagined her to be? That the dream was more alluring than the reality.

I think in some regards Catherine feels the same way with Julius. What's the alternative to a womanizing louse? Are you guaranteed the next guy is going to be a step up? What if he's worse? Julius cheats on Catherine but it's not like he hits her.

No one ever promised change would be for the better. I think that's what tears me up most. Just look at Austin. He changed his life twice and see where it got him.

We walk in silence until we get to another intersection. One farther away from where the Wildboyz or the Killamafia preside, street gangs known for body counts and dope. There are very few cars around, but Catherine seems confident we'll catch a cab here.

"I'm sorry," I tell her. "I didn't mean to poke my nose where it doesn't belong."

"Skip it," she says. "It doesn't matter. It's been a long night."

"Still doesn't make it right. It's your life. You make your own decisions. That's the way the game's played."

"Why does it have to be a game? Why can't people just be nice to one another? Why the deceit? The lies? You get together. You try to make it work. If it doesn't, then hey, you move on. You don't take advantage of the situation."

"That would be refreshing."

We let that thought settle between us. I'm thankful Catherine is such a forgiving person. That's the part people use and twist to suit their own needs. I hope she doesn't lose it. Forgiveness and empathy. Two endearing qualities so few of us have.

Then as an afterthought I ask her, "Snowflake?"

A hint of a smile on her mouth.

"What? It's a nickname. Don't your friends ever give each other nicknames?"

"You have a lot of friends."

"I'm nice. Nice people have friends."

I open a fresh pack of smokes and start to open it.

"That explains a lot of things with me," I say.

"Mike, you're a good guy. I think that's what scares you the most. Because by being nice, you're offering up a part of yourself to someone you don't know or don't know well enough. And in doing so you make yourself a little bit vulnerable. So rather than risking that, you immediately put them on the defensive with your sarcasm and biting comments. But I think that if you give them a chance, most people will surprise you."

"I have friends," I say. "We drink and sing together."

"Don't get me wrong. They seem like really great people. But they ever give you their ashes to bury?"

"They're not dead."

"Austin is. Don't you see? It's your chance to prove yourself to be the friend you always say you are. For whatever reason you let him in a lot closer than the others. And when he went away something inside you broke. You ever think that's part of the reason you never followed him out? You didn't want to be hurt by someone like that again?"

Another arrow strikes the bullseye.

"Jesus, you ever get tired not hitting your mark?"

"You fell out of touch and in doing so you were looking to break any bond that was left between you. Only the story was left. The girl behind the glass. You think it's a coincidence that the last thing you ever wrote is in that story? You tried to pawn it off on him to finish. You wanted him to end it because in your own way you were hoping that would be the final resolution between you two. But Austin had his own hurt he was dealing with, whatever that was. You didn't follow him like you said you would. That was part of it, no doubt. But something didn't materialize for him when he got to L.A. like he thought it would. Maybe the combination was too much for him to bear. So, he removed all options off the table by walking out into that ocean and never coming back. Don't you see, Mike? He left you the clue to finding his final resting place. Finish the story, you'll find the answer."

A shrill whistle and a waved hand hails down a pair of headlights and a Capitol Cab pulls over to the curb. Catherine opens the door and looks back at me. It's four o'clock in the morning.

"You coming?"

I toss my freshly lit cigarette to the ground. As we pull away from the curb, I see the orange ember fighting to stay lit in the dark. I know it won't, but seeing the cigarette roll in the breeze gives me hope.

16

SUNDAY

Neither of us speaks. Catherine looks out the window, no doubt replaying the confrontation with Julius over and over in her mind. I feel bad for her; she's invested a lot of time in this relationship, but I also know there is no such thing as tenure when it comes to being together. Or at least, there shouldn't be.

People can really suck sometimes.

I keep a quote tacked up on my wall at work from Charles Bukowski:

"I don't really hate people; I just feel better when they're not around."

Me and Austin in general kept people at arm's length as a general rule and then let them earn our respect or prove our initial reservations wrong. Very few did and even fewer tried. Yes, it was a backward approach, but it suited us fine. It's what sustained us through the grind of being grunts in the trenches fighting for an army of which we didn't want a part. We believed ourselves better, smarter than the jobs we did, and certainly the people we worked for. We refused to accept it was all part of the system, that you did your time and worked your way slowly out of the shithole in which you started. There were first- and second-year associates younger than us that felt it their divine right to piss all over everyone beneath them because that was the process the firm had in place. And if I hated their condescending remarks and bullshit, I can only imagine what the reprographics folk in the basement felt. Those poor bastards. They had to literally photocopy all day every day – eight, ten, sometimes twelve hours at a clip. Thousands and thousands of documents copied thousands and thousands of times – some saddle stapled, some in ring binders. Sometimes it was the same document over and over again. You worry about people going postal in work, my money's on a guy whose sole job is to consistently produce pristine copies of original documentation in the decaying basement of some hot shot firm.

One of the shift leads, Tyrone, took it all in stride. Tyrone didn't let anything get to him. Stress? Not this guy. I used to think he was Cool Hand Luke-tough, the way I romantically imagined myself to be. Get knocked down? Big deal, I can still stand. Break me? Forget about it.

Everyone needed this type of champion, the one who tilted at windmills because they were there and needed to be challenged. These people gave us hope. Tyrone impressed me with this until he let me in on his secret for maintaining his counterinsurgency of indifference – marijuana. He lit up blunts in one of the stairwells two to three times a day. It kept him numb, the required state-of-mind for anyone standing in front of an industrial-sized copy machine for eight hours a day.

Somehow, self-medicating to get yourself through the day seemed a lot less Cool Hand Luke and more like Bill and Ted.

I still try to hold on tightly to this existence: the lone guerrilla combatting the entrenched forces of the oppressor. The thing is I know my grip is lessening no matter how tightly I try to cling to that philosophy.

People like Catherine can muster the shred of optimism in a dismal cesspool. And while the Pollyanna act can really grind your gears, it also has the habit of rubbing off. It's true. Hating cheerfully optimistic people only lasts for so long. In the end, its uninterrupted flow often erodes the roughest of edges until what you have left is a casual acceptance and those infrequent moments give way to something bordering on contentment.

The real test for her is if she can maintain that composure when she starts drawing those fat checks after law school. Everyone can keep it real when they're poor and hungry; it's when you see how long the numbers are on the remittance line that the planted seeds of change start to slowly sprout. Money is not so much a destination as a state of mind, an existence that centers on branding and price tags, a truth that attorneys know better than most professions except for maybe the medical field. You don't buy a car; you purchase a driving experience. Why tell time with a Seiko watch when a Rolex says so much more? Money puts you in the position to buy things. Not necessarily what you like, but what you can afford.

You think Julius knows if Bruno Magli shoes are more comfortable than any other expensive brands based on his personal experience? He just knows he wants the brand, and if he has the money, buys it. To be fair, the money's not his, but you get the picture. First thing most junior associates do with their paychecks and signing bonuses is to buy a BMW or Lexus simply because they can. Law school loans are put on the backburner. How can a lawyer at a big corporate firm settle for a Mazda 6?

Money buys the things that fit the image you want for yourself.

That's one of the things I don't understand about Austin's move. Los Angeles didn't fit the image of who he was, or who I thought he was. Los Angeles is not "newspaper" real the way Detroit or Chicago or New York is newspaper real. It's a city without scars, too modified and too well exfoliated to ever bear a blemish. It's a mall store of perfectly manicured candy; bright and colorful; a panoply of intoxicating patterns and swirls. But you don't eat this candy. You can't. You can only look at it because the reality of its taste will ultimately betray its appearance. And once that's on your tongue the illusion of perfection is gone.

So, if L.A. didn't fit the image of who he was, what was the image he was looking to be?

Austin was no star-fucker. He rarely if ever watched movies, and he wasn't looking to break it into either the film or music industries.

But for whatever reason, L.A. held something special to him.

I hold up the urn. What illusion were you chasing, Austin? What were you after so badly you risked your life in the hopes of attaining it, if even for a moment?

"The girl behind the glass reads Henry Miller…"

The story is the clue, only my head isn't ready to tackle subtext and nuance at this hour.

The sun just breaks the horizon when the cab pulls up in front of my apartment building. I hand the driver some money and turn back to Catherine.

"You going to be alright?"

"I'll be fine," she says, unconvincingly. "I'll go back home, and Julius will be passed out on the couch. There will probably be a pizza box on the floor, and crusts strewn God knows where. I'll take a shower and sit on the chair across from him. Maybe I'll make myself a cup of tea and wait until he wakes up. We'll spend the next four hours yelling at each other, dredging up shit from the past. I may throw something at him, I have before. I don't know, in the end, we'll retreat to the bedroom where I'll suck him off while he tells me how sorry he is."

She's not making this up. No one can make that up. It flows from her naturally, without any sense of self-editing. These are the facts and they are indisputable. They are also downright depressing and… sad. This isn't someone who's excited for the future. I should know. In this instant, she sounds a lot like me.

"No, you're not." I take her hand and get her out of the cab. She doesn't protest.

I lead her and Austin up the steps to the front door of my building. She looks around at the worn-down exterior as if looking at something for the first time. And then I realize she is.

"You know, I've never been to your place, Mike."

"It's not much to look at. One room efficiency. World War II-era kitchen and bathroom. And roaches pop around every so often just to remind you they can never ever be eradicated."

"Sounds perfect," she says.

We enter and turn to my apartment on the left. Jennifer walks up the steps from the basement where a door leads to the back parking lot. Despite the hour she doesn't look drunk or even tipsy from her night's activities. Jennifer startles when she sees me coming in at this hour and with a girl in tow to boot.

She glances at Catherine and arches an eyebrow. "A good night?"

"Long night. Jennifer, this is Catherine. We work together. Catherine, Jennifer."

"Hiya," Jennifer says, giving Catherine a once-over as if trying to determine if she is a friend or foe.

"Hey," Catherine says, reciprocating with her own assessment in kind. A stalemate settles between the two.

"You look exhausted. Get some sleep," Jennifer says.

"On the way," I say.

I take out my keys and open the door.

"Oh, Mike," Jennifer says. "Our mysterious pervert struck again yesterday. My black pair. I swear, I find out who's doing this, I'm going to hang his photo on every telephone pole in Arlington."

"I'll keep an eye out and let you know if I hear anything."

"Thanks. You look exhausted."

She eyes Catherine one more time briefly before heading down the hallway to her apartment.

Catherine steps through the door and takes in the limited ambience. Her eyes take in the prints of James Dean, Charles Bukowski, Chet Baker, and Nina Simone on the walls. Anytime someone new enters your place it's like you get to see it for the first time again. You pause at things you typically ignore any other day. Catherine walks up to each of the prints, taking her time as if she's at the National Gallery of Art consuming the directness and honesty of a Toulouse Lautrec or Mary Cassatt.

"I love black and white prints," she says.

"Me too. Color just doesn't have the same depth or coolness."

"These are good portraits. They neither moralize nor romanticize their subjects. They are just people, capable of joy and sadness like the rest of us."

"Let me get you some clean clothes and a towel. You can take a shower and I'll fix us something to eat."

"I'm too tired to eat," she says. "I'm too tired to do anything."

I come out of the closet/bathroom nook with sweatpants, sweatshirt, and a big fluffy towel I stole from my lone stay at the Ritz

Carlton in Montreal, Canada. Catherine sits on my bed holding Jennifer's pair of black panties by a finger.

"You'll keep an eye out, huh?" she says, a lone eyebrow raised.

"It's not what you..." I stop myself. It's exactly what she thinks. "Here." I take the panties from her and hand her the clothes. "The shower runs hot. You like pasta?"

"You making me something to eat?"

"Shower, eat, and sleep. Everything a body that has consumed too much alcohol on too little rest needs."

She climbs off the bed and heads to the closet/bathroom nook.

"One more thing," she says, but her voice is muffled when the bathroom door closes.

I SPOON the spaghetti into bowls as Catherine comes out of the bathroom wearing my old college soccer sweatshirt and pants. It's been a long time since a girl stayed over and worn my things to sleep when she didn't have any.

"I didn't know you played soccer, Mike." She sits down in a chair.

"My former life." I hand her a fork. "Dig in."

She takes a bite, chews thoughtfully, and swallows. Then she twirls a bigger amount. Her appetite awakens.

"This is really good. You make the meatballs and sauce yourself?"

"Yeah, one of the things I take pride in. Momma taught me how to make a good red gravy and that meatballs need equal parts of chopped pork, lamb, and beef."

"Gravy," she says. "Such a New England term." She cuts up a meatball and attacks with the same relish.

"You cook for your dates?"

"No."

"You should. They'd be taking off their panties for you. You wouldn't have to steal them." She suddenly stops. "I'm sorry. I didn't mean that. Here you are being very generous to me and I'm acting like a shit."

"It's okay. I sort of deserve it. I mean, you know..."

"You're a good guy, Mike. In your heart. That's all that matters."

We eat a little while. The exhaustion of the previous night quickly catches up to both of us.

"I need to shut my eyes." She heads over to my bed and lies down. I grab a pillow from a chair and toss it on the ground.

"No," she says and scoots on over. "We both need some Zs."

I'm too tired to argue and slide in next to her. I already hear her heavy breathing before my head hits the pillow. I don't remember my eyes closing before I'm asleep as well.

CATHERINE SITS at the table reading the short story when I wake up. It's almost 1 pm. All evidence of the early morning feast has been cleared away. Catherine glances at me, and pours a glass of wine, and slides it over next to three aspirin.

"Drink this and take those," she says. "I hope you don't mind. I needed something to get me up on my feet. For someone who drinks an awful lot of bourbon, I expected to see some in the cabinet."

"I drank it all."

"That makes sense."

I shove the aspirin in my mouth, take a sip, and grimace. After a long bender, the first drink is always tough to get down. The third sip puts you back on pace. Catherine spots my eyeglasses on the nearby windowsill. Contacts are more my thing, but sometimes you need old reliable. She holds them up.

"I'm blind as a bat."

She sets them down and returns to the pages.

"You know, this is pretty good. Your styles seem similar on the surface, but you can tell that they're pretty different when you get down to the granular level. Like take this for instance. Austin is very character driven. You can tell right from the beginning when he starts with the girl behind the glass reading Henry Miller. I mean, I don't read a lot of this... what kind of writing is this called?"

"Literary fiction."

"Right. Literary fiction. But like, check it out. The woman that captivates the speaker most is not obtainable. I mean, look at her. She's behind a glass wall. But he wants her anyway. I get that. But what separates his wanting her from the other women at the club is not that she's more beautiful or has tattoos or something equally superficial. It's that she's reading. And not just pop fiction, or whatever you call Hollywood's industry trades, but Henry Miller. So, while she is physically unobtainable, she may be emotionally obtainable. If that makes sense."

She takes a deep pull from her wine.

"Your writing is more centered in the motivations of the character. What he thinks. What he feels. It's more internal, like when you know what the character is thinking. I think this is one of the reasons you two got along so well. You were two writing halves of the same whole."

"I like the stuff that makes people tick."

"I can definitely see that. A lot of what you do in the office makes more sense now."

"Motivation is everything. I want to know why people do what they do."

"And it shows. You can articulate what he can't. He understands the situations and how they are and how they break down. But you provide the in-between. He's laying brick and you're supplying the mortar."

I help myself to the bottle of wine and top off both of our glasses.

"Now admittedly, I had to search your bookshelf over there to see who Henry Miller was and what he wrote. And by the way, did you really read all of those books?"

"I was an English major."

"That's a shit ton of reading, Mike. Anyway, I wasn't really sure if and how that played into the story. To say that guy liked his sex is an understatement."

"*Tropic of Cancer* was initially banned in the U.S.," I tell her. "It took the Supreme Court to overrule that it was obscene."

"Interesting…" she says.

"Miller was bold," I say. "People loved him or hated him. There was no real in between. His writing has been described as bawdy and licentious but also honest and accessible."

"So, I have to tell you. I've read these pages four times since I woke up. They need some fine tuning but there's a story here alright."

"Four ti- How long have I been asleep?"

"The answer is in the story."

"What answer?"

"Get dressed, Mike."

"Where're we going?"

"To find where Austin wants his ashes spread."

AFTER A QUICK SHOWER and a change of clothes, I light a cigarette near the open window. Catherine exits the bathroom after a long shower. She wears her skirt from the previous night and one of my black t-shirts with "The Replacements" – one of the best 80s bands ever.

"Nice choice," I say, referencing the shirt.

"It matches my skirt," she says. "You ready?"

Catherine slings her small purse strap over her shoulder and takes the story and *Tropic of Cancer* with us as we walk out the front door. I tuck Austin under my arm.

"Where do we start?" I ask.

"I know where we don't start," she says. "No bars. Austin wasn't a bar guy you said. So, bars are out. Literary D.C.? Again, I'd say, no. It's not like you hung out in bookshops and did the poetry slam circuit. No, Mike, for this expedition we have to think outside the box, so to speak."

I nod. She's right, of course. Those aren't the things that made Austin, well, Austin. I stand on the front stoop of the building thinking about my friend. At my feet is a plastic wrapped Sunday edition of the *Washington Post* still unclaimed on one of the steps.

And then it hits me. I know a good first place to start.

"Come on," I say walking down the steps to the sidewalk. I raise my hand to flag down a Red Top passing down the street. He pulls over to the curb. I open the door for Catherine, but not before I ask her an important question.

"Why are you doing this?"

"Because maybe by helping you do this, I'm helping myself get back on track as well," she says.

It's a good enough answer.

She climbs into the cab and slides over. "Where are we going?"

"Where the underground news and the mainstream collide."

THE WASHINGTON CIVIC Paper is D.C.'s alternative newspaper, which is a nice change from the politically-biased Washington Post and Washington Times. Distributed on Thursdays, it commands a circulation of about or around 100,000 focusing mainly on local news and arts events. It is the closest thing D.C. has to the photocopied, saddle-stapled rags found littering coffee houses and independent bookstores in L.A. and New York.

The Paper, to its credit, is very freelance driven, which makes it an attractive medium for writers who believe they have something to say and are looking to cut their teeth in journalism. The headquarters is in the heart of D.C., an odd place one would imagine for a free news periodical. The cab lets us off and we walk into the lobby where we are met by a large bored security guard sitting at a desk.

"We're closed," he says, barely looking up from his Sunday sports page.

"I was hoping to go to the research room," I say. "I'm working on a deadline for Thursday's edition. I just need an hour or two."

He looks up at me with sallow eyes that appear to be measuring the veracity of my statement.

"Nah," he says, returning to the paper.

Catherine quickly assesses the situation and makes her move.

"Look, this is extremely important," she says. "I shouldn't be saying this but for the sake of transparency…"

She digs into her purse, pulls out a card, and hands it to him. She leans in conspiratorially close to him.

"I'm from the *Post*. We're working on a story about the school busing issue in upper North East."

The guard becomes more animated, shaken from his slumber. He glances at the card and at Catherine skeptically.

"You really from the Post?"

"The card doesn't lie," she says.

"You look young for a reporter."

"If by that you mean hungry, yeah. I'm looking to get my first solo story in the *Metro* section," she says.

He looks at the card once more before handing it back to her.

"Is this about the Ron Brown Middle School thing?" he asks.

"Do you know of any others? Only it's not just that school. Three others have the same issue and they're ready to speak up. My paper thinks this story has legs but doesn't want to commit until Mike here brought certain facts to light."

The guard looks over at me.

"Those facts are in the research room," I say.

"Dayyyum. My nephew goes to Ron Brown Middle. Buses don't cross the new re-districting he's gonna have to go to the next ward."

"We just want to make sure the word gets out. Put some pressure on those Councilmen."

A heavy sigh from the guard.

"Alright. 2nd floor. Elevators over there."

"Thanks," Catherine says. "Mr–"

"Duane. You can call me Duane, honey."

"Duane. You can call me 'honey' but no one's sweeter than you."

She winks at him and we go to the elevator bank. Inside, I hit the second-floor button and turn to Catherine.

I gesture to the card in her hand. "The card doesn't lie? Where'd you get that one?"

"The card didn't lie. I did."

She hands it to me and smiles.

THE RESEARCH ROOM is not as glamorous as it sounds. It has some sorely outdated computer equipment, lots of microfiche, and even an antiquated card catalogue to haphazardly capture the entire archives of the *Civic Paper's* works. Apparently, the lack of budget has prohibited the *Civic Paper* from fully automating its records keeping. Three other reporters/researchers are in the room. No one gives anyone else a second glance. Reporters generally have no interest in anything but the issue they are working on. Austin said that's what made them focused; I said that's just what differentiated their asshole behavior from anyone else's.

"Where did you get this?" I say, handing back the *Washington Post* reporter's business card.

"Leslie? I met him at the Hawk and Dove."

"Him?"

Another bright smile. "I just love gender neutral names. So, what are we doing here?"

I go over to the computer and check the records that have been accumulated.

"Looking for an article."

She rolls her eyes. "I gathered that, Woodward. Whose and why?"

"Austin's."

"Austin wrote for the *Civic Paper*?"

"No. Well, he got a story published. It's what ignited his interest in news and reporting. That's when he made the shift from writing fiction, to writing the news. The real news, he would always say."

After looking in a variety of places, I finally find his piece on microfiche. I take the box and sit at a nearby microfiche machine, scrolling until I find his byline.

"There," I say, sitting back.

Catherine leans in. She reads a bit.

"He went to a Farrakhan rally?"

"Yeah. He was the only white guy there. At first they wouldn't allow him to go in on account of his…"

I stop when another researcher, an African American, at the other terminal looks up from his screen. Catherine rescues my social faux pas.

"Hue?"

"Right. But that didn't stop him. He argued, he threatened, he pleaded. The more he pressed, the more they pushed back. They had four large security men in bow ties, the Fruits of Islam is what he called them, shoving him away from the entrance."

"No way."

"It gets better. So, these guys are pretty much the security detail for Farrakhan. They're all trained in martial arts and carry guns. But Austin wasn't going to be intimidated. He invoked his amendments, his right to sue, saying anything and everything he could. When they finally had enough of his shit, he thought they were going to beat the ever-living crap out of him."

"What happened?"

"Thankfully they were interrupted by Farrakhan himself."

"Shut up!"

"Farrakhan asked Austin why he would want to attend the rally since he really didn't fit the demographic of the target audience. What exactly was Austin hoping to do or to find? That's got to be pretty intimidating, right? I mean, the wrong answer was going to get him tossed out on his ass if not seriously hurt. So, Austin thought for a moment. And he said something to the effect of 'people say a lot about you. People say you're a racist. That you hate white people. That you preach a mixed message. But I don't want to listen to what people have to say. I wanted to come here and see for myself.'"

"Holy shit," Catherine says.

"And Farrakhan looked at Austin. I wish you could have heard him tell it. He looked good and hard at Austin. Then he turned to the security staff. 'What are you waiting for?' he said. 'Let the young brother in.'"

"Jesus," Catherine says. "That took some serious balls."

"He was like that. If he believed in something, he took the chance. He didn't let anything back him down. I remember asking him if he was scared. He said of course he was. He could have easily disappeared that night. So, why did he do it? I mean, he could have gone after another story, another human-interest piece."

"What did he say?"

"He said to get what you want you have to be willing to risk whatever you have. No one succeeded without putting their balls on the edge of a razor at one time or another. He had a story to tell, and he was willing to accept a few broken bones to be able to tell it. He got the story. He was the only white person at the rally, and he wrote one of the best nearly objective pieces on Farrakhan that I ever read."

Catherine mulls this over.

"He liked alienation. Maybe not alienation in and of itself but what it represented. He was a person that liked being on the fringe, that needed to be there. He was eccentric, idealistic, creative."

I hit the print button and grab the copies off the printer.

WE SIT outside the Skipjack having a beer and a smoke. It's almost four o'clock. I usually hate Sundays because they remind me where I must go and what I have to do the next day. But I'm not thinking about that right now. For the first time in a long time, I'm not dreading the hours as they click down to Monday. I'm having a good time, or as good a time as one can trying to figure out where to dispose of the last bits of his friend.

Catherine has her head in *Tropic of Cancer*, reading batches of pages at a clip. She puts down the book and drinks some beer.

"What is it about this book that he liked so much," she muses. "Henry Miller wrote a bunch of books, didn't he? So, what was it about this one that scratched Austin's itch?"

"Well, it was Miller's most popular."

"Yeah, but Austin was too smart to just pick the popular book. So are you. No, there's meaning behind it."

"Miller describes living in Paris with the rest of the downtrodden. He's there almost at the end of his rope, but not quite. He's a starving artist living by his own rules. He lived in crappy apartments. He was alone or else surrounded by the forgotten of society. It was pretty rough but pretty good too. I mean, it gave him the experience by which to write."

"So, it tracks Miller's life in France when he was a struggling writer.

"Yeah."

"Such an interesting title. You know why Miller picked it?

"I read somewhere he chose the title because in his estimation, cancer symbolized the disease of civilization. It was an endpoint. The necessity to change course radically and start completely over from scratch."

She stares at me with a knowing smile.

"Sound like someone you know?"

The realization hits me like a ton of bricks. I gulp my beer, spilling some in the process. Of course the book has meaning. How did I miss that?

"Austin, you clever son-of-a-bitch," I say, shaking my head.

"So, what made Los Angeles the place to be? Like you said, L.A. isn't the news capital of the world. There had to be something about it that was attractive."

"I never asked him, to be honest. He wasn't from there. No friends. No family. No immediate job offer. There was nothing really."

"Right. He went cross country to a place where he didn't know a damn soul, without a place to live or a way to earn money."

"Pretty much."

"Sounds pretty Miller to me."

Yeah, it does.

I never thought about that before. He was essentially living a Miller-esque life. He let slip one time during one of our earlier phone conversations that he had slept in his car for the first two weeks. When the public beaches opened up their public restrooms, he'd give himself a quick sink-bath like a homeless person. When I told him that I'd send him some money, he quickly retracted what he said, saying it was a momentary thing and that all would be worked out. I didn't think much of it at the time, but the way he told it, the embarrassment of the truth was a flash of light too bright to fully ignore.

We gradually lost touch after that, even when things turned around for him. That's the business of living for you – always imposing itself on all you do. Time gradually lapsed until all we truly had left between us was this story, which now in retrospect, speaks to why he fired off his sections as quickly as he received mine. To keep the connection alive.

And why he expected me to finish it.

I look at our empty pint glasses. "How are you doing?"

"Better," she says. "I'm glad I didn't go back last night. Nothing would have changed. Time and clarity, Mike. That's what everyone needs to make a decision."

"So, you've made one?"

"No, but I'm getting closer. The funny things about decisions like this? You work through them in your head, look at every detail, every moment that's been good, bad, or indifferent. You try to forecast into the future. Try to picture yourself with them and without them. You collect and aggregate all of this information in the hopes of making the best choice you can. And in the end, you go with what your heart says."

She steals a drag off my cigarette, making those small smoke rings.

"You know, Mike, I have to say. The last forty-eight hours have been a whirlwind, to say the least. And aside from the circumstances behind them, I'm having a pretty good time."

"Yeah, well, you should actually go on a date with me sometime and then you'll really experience a roller coaster ride you won't forget."

"I think I'd like that," she says sincerely. "You're someone who definitely keeps this world a little more interesting. Others would probably think so too if you give them a chance. Why won't you ask that girl in the bar out?"

"Maggie? I just don't think there's a reason to."

"Um, so she can give you panties instead of you stealing them. Teasing!"

She gives me a big smile, and I give her one back to let her know there's no harm done.

"I think maybe, just maybe, I don't ask her out because, I don't ever want her to say 'yes' if I did."

She sits up, not expecting that answer. "And why is that?"

"Because what's worse than not getting your dream? Getting it and finding that it's not what you had hoped it would be in the first place."

"And then realizing that's not what you wanted at all," Catherine adds.

"And then having to start from scratch to find what you do want."

"That's not always a hard thing, Mike. I think sometimes, that's probably the easiest thing of all. You need to remember to give people a chance. Not just girls. Everyone."

She kicks back the rest of her beer.

"We have another stop, or shall we drink some more?"

"One more stop." I leave money on the table for the waitress.

17

National Harbor is nestled along the banks of the Potomac River in Prince George's, Maryland. Even though we're technically in Maryland, the D.C. border is only a stone's throw away. That's one of the benefits of having the nation's capital consist of just 60 square miles of land. It only takes you so long to cut through the city before you find yourself in either of the states that bookend it.

The Harbor was a longtime pet project for developers in the area aspiring to turn an inconvenient-to-get-to location into an oasis of commercialism. These visionaries pumped in billions of dollars to transform nature into this opulent mixed-use eyesore it is now. Back in the late 90s, they met initial pushback from environmentalists concerned with the potential consequences to the 350-acre agricultural ecosystem that featured 30 species of fish. But like anything threatening to hinder progress, these protests succumbed to a larger power, and any complaints were filed away left to suffocate under governmental bureaucratic shuffling and reshuffling.

Nothing is ever truly shot down in D.C. as much as it is left to wither and die on the vine, a fate that can be secured or from which it can be rescued by the right million-dollar donation to the right cause.

The very heart of this community is the 2,000-guest room Gaylord

National Resort and Convention Center, the largest non-gaming hotel and convention center on the East Coast. Like everything else in this hamlet, it serves to be all things to all people billing itself as the perfect destination for a weekend retreat, corporate meeting, wedding, or any special event of your choosing. There are plenty of shops and boutiques at National Harbor. Restaurants cater to every major ethnic food you want and everything from cozy coffee shops to decadent steakhouses are found here. For those not intimidated by D.C. traffic during their commutes, you can even purchase the privilege of living in one of the luxury condominiums offering premium views of the Potomac River, the monuments, and depending where your windows face, the Capitol Building. In the summer months, festivals crowd the boardwalk filling the air with their music and grilled food. Wedding brides find hosting their receptions on the pier along the river to be scenic and memorable. Rumors have it a casino may even be built in the next few years.

We're not headed to any of these spots. Instead, I lead Catherine past the overpriced shops, past the lavish and overly sweet cupcake bakery, and the hipster Irish sports pub. I lead her straight to a large patch of sand near the water where my favorite statue has been relocated. It's the statue of the man struggling to get out of the earth that brings us here. "The Awakening." The purpose of this visit.

The statue is the product of J. Seward Johnson's genius. I don't know much about him or much about his other work but when people say art speaks to them, this is my understanding of what that means. I've always believed sculpture must exist in harmony with its environment. It must function in and with its surroundings. At 70 feet across and a good 17 feet at its peak, "The Awakening" is proof how sculpture relates to landscape, and how it creates a quality of spectacle.

The work is composed of five separate aluminum pieces buried in the ground. The left hand and right foot barely breach the surface whereas the left knee bursts into the air. The right arm and hand reach farther out of the ground, as if grasping for something just out of reach. But it's the face that hits the mark. It's the face that keeps people coming back. The face is bearded; the mouth open in mid-scream. The eyes are frantic, like the tortured look of a saint in a Renaissance painting.

The piece evokes much thought and emotion. Some believe it depicts man struggling to emerge from the earth. A man reborn, pushing forward. Others believe that he's receding, being buried, fighting against the inevitable darkness to which we all eventually succumb.

It's haunting because while we may not have all been buried alive, we're all intimate with the experience of being held down or back, unable to move, fighting desperately to preserve some semblance of control, some dignity. Sometimes we succeed in the effort, but most times we fail. Through it all we fight, and in that process, we find relevance.

Catherine inspects each piece, running her fingers along smooth lines.

"I've always been meaning to see this. It's amazing how little I take advantage of this town. All those museums, and for free."

"Last summer a cousin of mine from Italy came over. We spent two whole days in the Museum of Natural History. He couldn't believe they didn't charge admission. In Italy, every museum charges. He said we were very lucky."

Catherine climbs on top of the man's head. She smooths her skirt and sits facing the water.

"It really is something," she says. "So peaceful right now. I imagine this place gets packed, but it seems so quiet now, like we're the only ones here."

I climb up and sit next to her, setting the urn in a groove in the man's hair.

"This was the last time I saw him," I tell her. "I should have known something was up. He stopped by my apartment unexpected one Sunday morning and told me he wanted to get a beer. It was so strange to see him at my place. As close as we were at work, we really didn't hang out as much as you'd think outside of work. So, I said sure, and was going to take him to SoBe but he wanted to come here. We bought a six pack from a store and sat like we're doing now drinking beer and looking out on the water."

"What'd you talk about?"

"The usual things. Work. Writing. Things. That's when he said we should write a story together sometime. Take turns going back and forth and see where it took us. Funny thing is I didn't think it would work. But he said we should try it. I didn't think much about it then. It was another idea in a long list of ideas we'd bring up from time to time but never really act upon."

"Then he left?"

"It must have been that night or the next day. I got lost in work that week. They had just moved me to the steel case."

"The one we're on now?" Catherine asks.

"Yeah. It's been going that long... Damn...They sent me on a document production jaunt for two weeks. I was back another week before I found out he no longer worked at the firm. That he had picked up and left without telling anyone. The firm had trouble sending him his last check."

"Sounds like he had already made up his mind."

"That day I think he was trying to tell me something in his own way. Austin was a straight talker in everything but the way he felt. That was never for public consumption, the one part of him he kept to himself. That he would always keep to himself."

Catherine nods. "He finally drank a beer, eh?"

"Barely. Didn't even finish the one. I drank four. That was Austin for you. He got you to a place where he wanted to take you without you ever being the wiser."

Catherine picks up the urn and looks around.

"Is this it?" she asks. "Is this the place?"

Dusk settles in. The sun hangs low in the sky. It's a brilliant sunset if you're into those kinds of things. You really have to appreciate the palette of orange and red and every possible mix in-between. There's a peace and a beauty in moments like this when all you have is silence and a spectacle to see. There are no words for it, only a contentment that can never be commented on or described.

"No," I say.

"Are you sure? It sounds perfect. The last place you saw each other seems like a perfect final resting spot. Ashes caught in the wind and spread along the river shore."

"If it were my ashes, it would work. But not Austin's. What you just described is exactly the reason why he wouldn't want to go like that. Because it wasn't a true reflection of how he lived or who he was. His life wasn't a perfect scene on which to end the credits. So, his final resting place shouldn't be either. Bringing you here was more for me than him."

"This is your closure."

"Part of it anyway. The other half is the story."

"You got an ending yet?"

I shake my head and put my arm around Catherine's shoulders and draw her close to me. She doesn't resist, and for a brief moment this feels like the most natural thing in the world.

She leans her head against my shoulder. "The character in the story is similar. He is an outcast. Maybe not like a vagrant or transient but very much a social pariah. He comes into this place looking for a last chance. The people are all in their own worlds. They bump into him. They spill drinks on him. But otherwise, they ignore him. They ignore he's even there. This is the microcosm of his greater existence. He just isn't seen, he isn't recognized. He isn't acknowledged. The only thing that has made an impression on him is the girl behind the glass reading Henry Miller. So, there we have him in the last scene. This anti-hero is in the bathroom. He's got a gun. And he's at the end of his rope. He's not in a good place and everything is catching up to him. When he leaves that bathroom, he has certainly made up his mind about something."

"Am I the woman?" I ask.

Catherine sits up and looks directly into my eyes. "You're so close to the answer you can't see it. She's his hope, Mike. And his hope is a woman who doesn't ever look up. That's how frail it is. She doesn't want to acknowledge the faces on the other side of the glass leering at her, hoping she forgets to cinch up her robe when she steps from behind the privacy curtain. She is cut off from the world as well but hers is a self-imposed exile. The glass barrier separates her from the rest of the room. And in this separation, she's pure.

"He wants so bad to touch that glass, to hit it, to smash it and get inside. He wants to hold her and be held back in turn. That's the only way he will know she's real.

"But he doesn't. He knows he can't. He can't initiate the validation. She has to look up and see him. The real him.

"Because she is the only person who can save him. He's got a loaded gun in his pocket and all he's looking for is someone to look at him and say he exists."

It's a heavy epiphany, a burden I don't want on my shoulders but there it is anyway.

"I didn't read between the lines. I never picked up the phone. I rarely checked in with him. I'm a shitty friend."

Catherine shrugs and offers the slightest of smiles. "You were his only friend. I think that counts for something."

"And what have you decided? Your situation is as complicated as mine. You really going to go back to Julius?"

"No. I don't think I can."

"I don't think you should."

"I always knew we were over. It's just something you don't want to ever admit to yourself. Even if it's not working you don't want to be involved in something failing. You don't want to admit that you were a part of that collapse."

"Austin always said things fall apart because that's what they are ultimately designed to do. We keep pushing forward despite the collapse because that's what we are designed to do."

"It's funny. I mean, I never knew Austin, but he's taught me a hell of a lot about myself in the short time you've been carrying him around."

"That was part of his charm. He always had a knack for making people look inward. They didn't always like it, but they did it anyway."

"I'll get my things tomorrow. I can stay with my cousin in Bethesda in the meantime. Julius works at Footlocker in the mornings. I'll call in sick and get my shit out of there."

"I'll give you a hand," I say. "I feel myself coming down with something."

"You need to write the ending first. I'll be fine."

"I think you will be," I say.

I help her down and we walk to the taxicab stands. Along the way, music plays piped in from the speakers embedded along the walkway. It's Bob Mould, a local legend. The song is my favorite and I take this as a good sign. That I'm moving in the right direction.

The song's about trust. Trusting in yourself. Having others trust in you. Because in the end we all have confusions about who we are and what we are supposed to be doing with our lives. But when we find a person that we can connect with, there's salvation in that.

There's... what did Catherine call it?

Hope.

Yeah, this is a pretty good end to a pretty good day.

IN MY DREAM, I stand with Austin in the ocean–the Pacific Ocean. The water is at waist-level, lapping up against us as the tide lolls into shore. Above, gulls screech in the air, hovering in the wind, looking for something to eat. For what seems like forever, no one says anything.

Finally, he says, "You know, it's not so bad."

"What isn't?"

"The water. I always thought the ocean was frightening. Not because I can't swim but because it never changed. Its power comes from the fact it is essentially the same mass doing the same thing since the polar caps melted. On the other hand, the world is a completely different place than it was when dinosaurs roamed the earth. But not the ocean."

"That's not true," I tell him. "How do you explain tidal waves and storms?"

"That's not change. Those are temporarily altered states. It's not like a tsunami is a constant condition. When they run their courses the ocean returns exactly to the way it was before. Not bigger and not smaller. It's not the same thing as change."

As if to prove his point, the waves kick up a bit. They come in sets of threes. The first two sets are large ripples that pass through us. They are easily bobbed through. But the third one is the rogue. It builds on the first two's momentum, foaming at the lip, curling and rising up before collapsing down in front of us in what can only be ascertained as a threat or a challenge. If force of impact isn't enough, the undercurrent provides a strong, constant reminder of what could happen if you're caught unaware.

"Why are you out here if you can't swim?"

"Isn't it obvious? To see if I can change."

"If you can't swim, standing in the ocean isn't going to change that," I remind him.

"Change isn't always about the physical, Mike. You know that."

He takes a step deeper into the ocean. His face is remarkably calm for someone in rough water. Each step seems to put him in a more tranquil state than the previous one.

"I don't understand why you're doing this."

But he doesn't hear me now. He's up to his chest now. The waves ripple by his neck. The third splashes over his face. He coughs and shakes the wet hair from his eyes.

"Austin!" I scream, but it's drowned out by the susurrus that is the Pacific Ocean. When I wipe the saltwater from my eyes Austin is nowhere to be seen.

CATHERINE SHAKES ME AWAKE.

"We're here," she says. "I paid the cab. Let's go inside."

It takes me a few seconds to gain my bearings and recognize that I'm in the backseat of a cab idling outside my apartment building. It's dark now. Catherine takes my hand and leads me out of the cab and up the front steps.

"Austin," I say. "I left him–"

"Relax. He's right here," she says, showing me the urn. "I have him. He's safe."

Catherine digs in my front pocket for my keys and opens the door.

"This time I'm going to fix us something to eat," she says. "You have work to do."

I sit down in one of the chairs and re-read the story again.

The anti-hero stares at his reflection in the bathroom mirror. It's like he's looking at his face for the first time, or through new eyes. It's a moment of self-examination as if he's trying to peer into the deep recesses of his soul. The gun is in his pocket, its weight comforting against his thigh.

He's got a decision to make.

He's going to do something.

He has to act.

But the book.

The woman behind the glass.

The woman...

And then I pick up the pen and start to write:

"He exits the bathroom with a renewed sense of purpose. His gait is steady, his look fixed. He derives strength from his commitment. The weight of the gun is a reassuring reminder against his leg. He wonders if this is how the others felt before they embarked down their own dark roads, if the Rubicon had been crossed, if the dice had been irrevocably cast.

If they felt any fear at all.

The entrance to the patio area is where they congregate in packs. Even the privileged have their own hierarchy, he thinks to himself. The beautiful and rich know the fetid scent of an inferior. He watches the packs as they shift and move around the landscape, oblivious to those around them, their eyes in a constant flickering search of someone they need to talk to, someone better than the ones they're with.

There is so much to hate in this city. He hates this city because of the fakeness that permeates. He hates this city because it exists solely for itself and unto itself. He hates this city because the people don't connect, and if they do, it's for self-preservation and validation. It's because it's a part-time job ready to be discarded or abused for any reason.

It's in this moment that he starts to make his way, zombie-like through the throng of the entitled. They brush up against him, spill their drinks. No one says a word. No apology is offered.

Manners and decorum are a distraction at this point. He's committed. His shirt is wet with vodka and grapefruit juice. So what? It doesn't matter.

There is only the mission.

204

The targets congregate around the pool. The irony is too delicious not to savor. They don't see themselves as pack beasts but that's what they are, no different than the animals on the Serengeti seeking refuge at a watering hole. Theirs is a hive mentality. They need to be there.

And yet, the fact they must socialize where they can be seen exposes themselves to predators. He knows from watching nature channels that when a predator attacks, even members of the pack will readily give up their own weaker members in order to escape that fate.

He casually browses groupings before settling on a mixed group closest to him by the pool. Two men and three women. The men are young and have remarkably similar hair styles, well-coiffed and styled. One sports eyeglasses that look more for show than purpose. He wears black skinny jeans, a white shirt, and plaid vest. The other wears blue jeans, a gray t-shirt, and a caramel colored leather jacket. The women are all pretty, making personal statements with bright-colored neon eyeshadow or Frog Prince lip stain. What they don't understand is that a collection of beauty products doesn't accentuate the positive as much as mute and muddle it. The dirty blonde with bright yellow half-moons over her eyes sports a red silk blouse over a too-short white skirt and black knee-high socks. The Latina is decked out in all black. She wears a black leather jacket over a lavender shirt, and tight-fitting black leather pants with boots. The bottle blonde wears a black see-through V-neck shirt that reveals her bra over a black and white skirt, and black open work shoes. When she pouts, her lips form a sad, emerald "O."

They are caricatures of themselves and they don't even realize it.

Or worse, they don't care.

They flitter about not so much talking to each other as past each other, their eyes focused on other groups, other people. Even they don't connect.

Yes. This is the group.

He surmises the situation and makes his way to his position near the bar where the Woman Behind the Glass is. He doesn't look to escape. There is no escape for him. There never has been. No matter where he's been he's always been confined, suffocating, alone.

If there was another solution, perhaps. But there is no other solution.

He takes a final look at the Woman.

She still sits there, focused on the book. How he envies her. There is so much pleasure in discovery. To find an unknown treasure. To be exposed to the words and thoughts and realities of someone and be receptive to them.

How he wishes he could tell her other books she should read from unheralded but equally important voices. Fante. Celine. O'Toole.

His hand slips into his pocket and grasps the .38 by the butt.

He stares at her one more time and in that moment, she glances up from her book. Her eyes are dark, brown maybe, or hazel. They rest on him for a split-second then return to Miller as she turns the page.

She saw him, he thinks. But he's not sure. She could have been seeing an interior reflection of the glass. It's bright inside the transparent cube. It could have been her own expression she was looking at.

There can be no confusion. No mistake. Could-be won't suffice. Not now. Not at this juncture.

It's an all-or-nothing moment.

He reaches out to touch the glass but stops himself. If there's going to be a reaction from her, it must be genuine. Unforced. Willing. He couldn't be the catalyst, the finger-tap against an aquarium that sends the fish into activity. Glare or grimace, it didn't matter as long as it was the result of her own volition.

She looks up. And this time, smiles at him. Not a broad ear-to-ear grin but a smirk, an embarrassed acknowledgement that occurs when two people connect if only for a moment in time.

There's no mistaking it now.

And then he realizes something important.

She's both ogled and ignored by everyone. They see her but don't see her. They have that in common. She's beautiful and he's not, but they both share a similar existence in that people choose to see them or not. Here she is lit up for the world to see and aside from the sexual leers of the men, she is largely ignored.

And this makes him sad.

This makes him sad because until this instant, the rejection and isolation he's known and experienced has largely been his and his alone.

He's been selfish with his hurt. He's hoarded it. He's used it to strengthen his ability to face down the daily daggers of relentless steel and keep existing. Never once during the months he lived in his car, or the cheap motel, or any of the dense urban areas he sought refuge in when the money ran scarce, did he think of someone else's state.

She turns to face the social packs on the patio.

In this way he was very much like the people he hated. And it's this understanding that breaks something inside him.

When he turns back, the Woman Behind the Glass looks at him again, a puzzled expression etched on her face. She raises a hand up to her eye and runs a fingertip down her cheek.

It's then he realizes he's crying.

Palm extended, she presses her long fine fingers against the translucent wall between them.

An offering.

He raises his hand and matches hers.

An acceptance.

They keep that way for what seems like minutes, but in truth, he knows it's only a few seconds. But it's enough for now.

It makes a difference.

He walks out of the club and into the streets that make up so much of Los Angeles' character. The air is the same, and so are the smells, but they seem less offensive now, less demeaning. He understands the city is what it has always been, and for now, that suffices. A direction chosen, heads down it, following the streetlights strung up one after another like penny candy.

Once his salvation, the gun is now an unnecessary impediment. Down a sewer drain it goes, rattling off a wall before it plops into water.

The ocean. That's what he wants to see now. The one constant in a world that is anything but. Since he's been in Los Angeles, he's only been to the Pacific a handful of times. He wonders how often locals forget that it's even there. The problem with always being available is that it becomes an afterthought, pushed to the background, forgotten.

He doesn't know how to get there from where he is but he's going to find a way in the morning under the helpful comfort of the new light.

With each step, a sensation takes root and slowly spreads within him. It's a warmth he doesn't immediately recognize, but it feels good.

He keeps working it over and over in his head until he can put a finger on it. And then it hits him. He knows what it is.

Contentment.

As he turns down a side street, he understands the city is what it has always been, and not unlike any other city where the hungry and the damned struggle for relevance. That fight is always there and rarely won. The victory is in the battles, not the war. Taking something and carrying it with you.

Like a simple smile that reminds you that you are there.

That you've always been there."

18

MONDAY

I smoke on the front stoop with the urn by my feet. Coming off a writing high is never easy. You go over the words in your head, question narrative choices, sentence structures. In the end you are just left with how you feel. And I'm good. I really am. The writing is good and honest and imparts to me a quiet acknowledgement that something was accomplished.

Catherine sits next to me. She shuffles through the last of the pages, her face impassive and unreadable. I think she has read this story about thirty times in the last two days. Her poker face is tournament-worthy, and I'm not sure if she's purposefully trying to obfuscate what she thinks to spare my feelings or not.

Judging from the orange strip peering over the horizon and the occasional car that drives by, it must be close to dawn. I take a hit off my cigarette and hold the smoke before letting it sift out through my pursed lips. It's Monday. This is the first time in a long time when I haven't dreaded this day rearing its ugly head.

The urn has seen a lifetime of activity the past 36 hours. There are nicks and scrapes along the pewter, stains where drinks and God knows what else have been spilled on it. I'm proud that I haven't lost it in all the confusion. That must count for something. I have been a pretty unreliable friend, but even I have redeemable qualities. Or at the very least, a shot at redemption. And I think I've made good on that shot.

Catherine puts down the papers. She stands and grabs the cigarette out of my hand, taking a few puffs as she gathers her thoughts.

"I can't think of a better ending," she says finally.

"Did I do it justice?"

"I can't answer that for you, only you can. For me, I'm just the consumer of the story. I follow the character's thoughts and feelings and I go where he takes me. And you took me on a very powerful journey. You both did. But you, Mike. You took me to the end. A very satisfying conclusion. I never knew Austin, but I think I do now."

I smile and nod. It's what I wanted to hear.

"So, my question for you is – what are you going to do with him now?"

I pick up the urn and shake it. Inside the ashes swish around. Austin was never a big guy, but his stature is monolithic now.

The intersection near my building provides an unencumbered view of the Iwo Jima and Lincoln Memorials. It's a unique perspective because if you stand just right, the Washington Monument obelisk emerges from up between the two. If you catch the sun just right, it's an awesome spectacle.

I walk down the steps to reach that perspective, prying open the top of the urn in the process.

It takes a bit more effort than I anticipate but with some elbow grease it pops off. The wind ebbs and flows and I offer up Austin's remains from the confines of the gunmetal urn into a soft gust. Most of the soot-colored ash falls soundlessly to the street below, but the trailing amounts catch some of the current and are carried quickly down toward the Potomac River. We mistakenly refer to human remains as ashes; they are really pulverized bone fragments. The cremation process destroys all traces of organic, carbon-based matter and all bodily fluids evaporate and escape through the cremator's exhaust leaving a fine, soft powder. We are truly gentler in death than we are in living.

Catherine says nothing. Like me, she watches the next big gust of wind pick up the ashes in front of us and disperse them further and further down the street. The agitated current spreads them unevenly about; some ends up on the nearby grass along the side of the road; some never makes it past a sewer grate; some just gets lost in the surroundings.

Like many before him as well as many after him, Austin left for Los Angeles with a vision of what could be, for himself, for his future. He put so much hope in the process of starting new, remaking himself, only to find the same truths he tried to escape from facing him down from a sunnier, warmer coast. I can't blame him for his romantic vision, as even the most cynical of us have instances where the possibility of hope outshines the darkness.

He actually had modest success, landing a staff reporter job at the *Orange County Register*, a steppingstone to *The Los Angeles Times*, or other larger city brands in places like Chicago, New York, and even Washington, D.C. But the time it took to reach that destination was just too long, the struggle to get there too arduous to endure. As an obstacle, work is a manageable task for a person. But when the expanse of life is your opponent, the blows hurt deeper and last much longer. We may continue to press on, but our strength and determination ultimately wane.

In retrospect, dreaming of Austin committing suicide wasn't a projection of what was going to happen as much as the realization a close friendship had taken a bad turn, and the guilt I felt was not wishing a friend dead as much as assuming the guilt for not preserving the friendship in the way I should have done. Therefore, in looking at the dreams I see now they were the symptoms of my self-realization that I was not the good friend as I always imagined myself to be, and in having them, was punishing myself for it.

I don't know if I'll dream of Austin tonight or ever again. But if I do, I know it will be different. He won't be talking cryptically while walking straight into the ocean. In fact, he probably won't be in any precarious situation at all. He was never the type that wanted to bask in the spotlight as much as stand at its periphery, within enough proximity of letting its light touch a part of him without compromising his whole self. For me, he'll be there as he's always been there; a figure in the background waiting for his moment to step to the forefront. Because that was him in a nutshell; he didn't want to command attention as much as to be heard by the right person.

"What do you want to do?" Catherine asks. She puts an arm around my waist as we stare at the sun rising in the distance, the honey-yellow sky back dropping the Iwo Jima Monument down the hill.

The wind disperses the last bit of ashes from the ground. I try to follow them until I can't see them anymore. The street bears only the faint reminder that he was there at all, and I know he would like that.

"I want to go home," I say.

Catherine lays her head on my shoulder like it's the most natural thing in the world.

"Silly boy," she says. "Don't you see you already are?"

And for the first time in my life, I believe I really am.

ABOUT THE AUTHOR

 Emilio Iasiello is the author of a middle grade fiction book The Web Paige Chronicles, a short story collection entitled Why People Do What They Do, and the nonfiction book, Chasing the Green. He recently published a full-length book of poetry Smoke in the Afterlife and a chapbook, Postcards from L.A. He wrote the screenplays for five independent films and short films and has had stage plays produced in the United States and United Kingdom. A cyber security expert, he has published several articles on cyber security in peer reviewed journals. He lives in Virginia.